ARTFUL

ALSO BY PETER DAVID

Published by Crazy 8 Books
Darkness of the Light
Height of the Depths
The Camelot Papers
Pulling Up Stakes
Fearless

Published by Random House
Tigerheart

Published by Pocket Books
Sir Apropos of Nothing
Woad to Wuin
Tong Lashing
Star Trek: New Frontier series
Imzadi

Published by Ace Books
Knight Life
One Knight Only
Fall of Knight
Howling Mad

ARTFUL

Being the Heretofore Secret History
of That Unique Individual
the Artful Dodger,
Hunter of Vampyres

(Amongst Other Things)

BY

Peter David

47N⬡RTH

Published by 47North, Seattle

www.apub.com

Amazon, the Amazon logo, and 47North are trademarks of Amazon.com, Inc., or its affiliates.

ISBN-13: 9781477823163
ISBN-10: 1477823166

Library of Congress Control Number: 2013958006

Cover design by becker & mayer!
Illustrated by Douglas Smith

Printed in the United States of America

To Charles

ARTFUL

AUTHOR'S PREFACE

Which Reintroduces Us to the Acclaimed Mr. Jack Dawkins, Known to Sundry as the Artful Dodger, and Laments the Inattention Paid Him as Compared to More Simpering Examples of the Day

I t has been an inordinate amount of time since Jack Dawkins was left in the dire straits as described by his previous biographer, the acclaimed Mr. Dickens, who, for all the right and proper praise heaped on him, nevertheless seemed to have his priorities ever so slightly out of whack in his previous visitation with Mr. Dawkins, described and referred to by various and sundry as the Artful Dodger, or Dodger, or the Artful, depending upon your familiarity with, and respect for, the personage in question.

This is a rather shocking lapse in an otherwise laudable writing career that spanned two score of years in the first half of the nineteenth century. Mr. Dickens, a.k.a. Boz, received an understandable amount of acclaim for a career that included a variety of tomes of uplifting tales typically detailing the lives of people facing overwhelming odds in a society that seemed bound and determined to destroy them. More often than not, they ended up having their spirits crushed right before their lives were ruthlessly snatched from whatever was left of their battered and broken bodies. They were the sort of tales, in short, that could only prompt readers to rejoice in whatever minor travails afflicted their own meager existences, as whatever it was they were facing paled to insignificance in comparison to the relentless onslaught of misery and mayhem visited upon many of Mr. Dickens's cast of orphans, thieves, hapless fools, and misanthropes.

Standing upon the shoulders of many of these, however, remains Dodger, the renowned snatcher of handkerchiefs, purses, snuffboxes, and the like.

Why Mr. Dickens, in his biography of that particular moment, preferred to focus on the adventures of the orphan parish child, Oliver Twist, remains a matter of speculation and mystery to all subsequent scribes of those long-departed times: of a London nearly two centuries gone, back when it was a pox-infested, grimy, depressing, fog-bound, class-favoring, sprawling, noxious, odorous, and overall distasteful place in which to live and breathe and sicken and die—as opposed to modern times, wherein the pox has been largely attended to; so that's progress of a sort.

This is not to be uncharitable to Master Twist, who knew little enough charity in the first decade or so of his young life. Nor do we wish to detract from the eventual happy turn that his fortunes took. Nevertheless, the more unkind observer (which we would like to think that we are not . . . but which our actions would lead us to believe we are) would have to make note of the fact that Master Twist spent an ungodly amount of his time on the page weeping for some reason or other. Whatever circumstance confronted him, his default reaction was to burst into tears, which makes him seem to us—not with the intention of disparaging the fairer sex, but still—a bit womanish. This famed orphan of the storm tended to bob about as helplessly as a cork (embracing the cliché in order to maintain the metaphor) until matters happened to, through no effort of his own, land him upon safe and welcoming shores.

Contrast him to the Artful, who, when last Mr. Dickens graced us with his presence, was seen standing in a London courthouse, having been accused of snatching a silver snuffbox out of the pocket of some individual who no doubt needed it far less than the Artful. Indeed, it should be noted that so formidable an individual was Dodger that the circumstances of his being apprehended by the authorities was not even witnessed by the reader of Master Twist's "adventures." Instead, they were described in tragic detail by Master Charley Bates, or, as he was frequently referred to with equal tragedy, Master Bates (that is to say, Master Bates recounted it after the fact, and Mr. Dickens dutifully reported it). Faced with a pompous judge, the Artful Dodger disdained to defend himself or his actions, loudly declaring that this was not the shop for justice and that his lawyer would certainly attend to the scoundrels inconveniencing the Artful directly if he were not currently breakfasting with the vice president of the House of Commons. It was a performance of sheerest bravado that would have made lesser men leap to their feet and applaud—as opposed to the greater men, who merely scowled and declared that the formidable Artful was to be transported forthwith to the untamed and thoroughly criminal continent of Australia. Imagine, if you will, Oliver Twist in the same predicament. There is little doubt that his defense would have been to fall to his knees, sobbing and lamenting his lot in life, a performance that would unquestionably have united lesser and greater men to shunt the little whiner off the English Isles and into the Atlantic as expeditiously as possible, conceivably without benefit of boat.

Indeed, if pictures are worth a thousand words (and admittedly we have already consumed nearly nine hundred words) then one not need think beyond the classic renderings of the two gentlemen in question. Conjure Oliver Twist in your mind, and you will doubtless envision him looking upward in a pathetic, supplicating manner, holding up his empty bowl of gruel and uttering the immortal words, "Please, sir, I want some more." Hardly a defiant, brazen challenge to authority.

And while Master Twist's defenders will point to this moment as a transformative one in which the young hero asks for more because he can stomach no further dismissive treatment, I will simply say this:

Untrue.

He asked for seconds because he drew the short straw, taken as a consequence of a bully in the workhouse demanding that someone bring him a second helping lest the starved older boy wind up consuming his bunkmate . . . and the boys took this threat seriously. Not quite an act of derring-do, then. (Although even we, skeptics of Master Twist's rightful place in the pantheon of heroes, will indeed applaud politely for his subsequent assault on a noxious older lad who spoke disparagingly of Oliver's mother. Then again, there are lines that even the most whimpering of boys will not see crossed.)

So there is the classic image of young Oliver in your mind's eye: a failed beggar with an empty bowl. Now set next to it your mental picture of the Artful Dodger, described by Mr. Dickens thusly:

He was a snub-nosed, flat-browed, common-faced boy enough, and as dirty a juvenile as one would wish to see; but he had about him all the airs and manners of a man. He was short of his age with rather bow-legs and little, sharp, ugly eyes. His hat was stuck on the top of his head so lightly that it threatened to fall off every moment and should have done so, very often, if the wearer had not had a knack of every now and then giving his head a sudden twitch, which brought it back to its old place again. He wore a man's coat, which reached nearly to his heels. He had turned the cuffs back, halfway up his arm, to get his hands out of the sleeves: apparently with the ultimate view of thrusting them into the pockets of his corduroy trousers; for there he kept them. He was, altogether, as roystering and swaggering a young gentleman as ever stood four feet six, or something less, in his bluchers.

Two questions immediately come to mind. The first, of course, concerns the definitions of "roystering" and "bluchers." The former means "blustering," and the latter are half-boots, typically of leather, so that puzzle is easily attended to.

Of greater curiosity is this: Why did the adventures of such a memorably described, thoroughly engaging, and far more captivatingly visualized young man—always pictured with a cocky smile and upraised, mocking eyebrow rather than tears of pathos trickling down his face—play second fiddle in the great orchestra of fiction to the perpetually sobbing Master Twist?

The answer is profoundly deep and disturbing and involves something that most normal people would find deeply impossible to accept.

What is that thing?

Vampires. Or, as it was spelled at the time, *vampyres.*

Yes, we know: It is difficult to accept, a strain to wrap your head around. Go and take the time to do so. Watch some television programs, or read some books in which vampyres are heroic and charming and sparkle in the daylight, and then return here and brace yourself for a return to a time that vampyres were things that went bump in the night.

It is our speculation that Mr. Dickens, despite his having taken up the unsavory profession of writer, nevertheless considered himself a gentleman, and there were some aspects of life that gentlemen simply did not wish to address. As such, he might have constrained himself to the rather mundane story about a boy named Twist, if only to pay respect to the delicate social mores of his time regarding all things truly detestable, such as politicians or, as is the case of Dodger's full history, vampyres. For that matter, it was entirely possible that he simply did not wish to alarm the citizenry of London and its surroundings with the knowledge that vampyres lurked within their midst. It was tragic enough for the average citizen to know that bloodsucking monsters known as tax collectors already existed; to be informed that there were *other* inhuman bloodsuckers stalking the night as well, desiring to sink their fangs elsewhere than bank accounts, might simply have been too much for people to bear. It was one thing for Mr. Dickens to be able to acknowledge the existence of the supernatural, as he did in *A Christmas Carol*, for that could easily be seen as a fairy tale rather than the exacting biographical study that it was. (Indeed, had Scrooge possessed the Artful's contacts and resources and used those to avail himself of the services of an exorcist, then the tale might well have concluded very differently for Scrooge, Tiny Tim, and the ill-fated Christmas goose.) But *Oliver Twist* was far too much of a genuine slice of life to allow the *unlife* to intrude, at least substantively.

Which is not to say that the original story does not *hint* of the existence of vampyres. Any conscientious reading of the text will make it plain. We will provide two examples for any who may doubt us, both of which will be particularly germane to the tale you are about to peruse.

First, though, it should be noted that in order to spare private citizens embarrassment, whether deserved or not, and very likely legal actions against himself for libel and slander, whether deserved or not, Mr. Dickens tended to assign whimsical and entirely descriptive fictitious names to his cast. So renowned for this was he that to describe a name as "Dickensian" is to say that it is aptly ironic. In other words, there is a truth to it that may well be obscure to the owner, but evident to observers.

Consider, then, young Oliver's antagonist in Chapter XI of the original volume: a formidable, powerful, and utterly cruel police magistrate with the name of Mr. Fang. Let us dwell upon that name and evoke it yet again: Mr. Fang, who slunk through merely the one chapter of Mr. Dickens's tale, but will be allowed to assume the full measure of his villainy in this recounting.

It staggers credulity to think that the name is a random happenstance. With a name like Mr. Fang, what else *could* the magistrate be *but* a vampyre? His subsequent dealings with Jack Dawkins, the Artful Dodger, who—as we will see in these pages—becomes inadvertently drawn into the web of Mr. Fang's plots through an act of consideration while momentarily forgetting that no good deed goes unpunished, could not be ignored if one is to give a fair and accurate recounting of Dodger's activities.

And then there is the matter of Fagin, routinely referred to as "the Jew." I needn't remind you that this was back in the day when the mere act of not being a Christian was to make one suspect, if not an outright potential criminal. These, of course, are far more enlightened times, when it is only acceptable to believe that not being a Christian is likely to mean one is a criminal only if one is a Muslim (or at least so we've been assured by people who claim to know such things), and therefore we shall refer to Fagin merely by his surname.

This would be the selfsame Fagin who prefers to hide within the shadows and never faces the harsh light of day.

This would be the selfsame Fagin who is shown preparing food from time to time, but never consuming it.

The selfsame Fagin who sits in a commons house and, while others are drinking, is reading a magazine.

The selfsame Fagin who, when handed a glass of wine by the evil, but decidedly human, Bill Sikes, is described as putting it to his lips, drinks not from it, and then claims he has had a sufficient amount to quench his thirst.

So let us consider the name itself: A simple rearrangement of two letters provides "I Fang," delineating a distinct connection to the other gentleman named Fang already extant in the book.

As for his clothing: all in black. A hat, broad brimmed to keep the damaging rays of the sun at bay, should he be unlucky enough to be dragged from the confines of his hidey-holes, as indeed happened in the course of the original novel.

And his physical description: "And as, absorbed in thought, he bit back his long black nails, he disclosed amongst his toothless gums a few such fangs as should have been a dog's or rat's."

Damning evidence? Superficial at best? Many men, not to mention boys, were transported or hung on far less substantive testimony than that. There were many courts in London where the above would be more than sufficient to see Fagin with a wooden stake driven through his heart . . . presuming the officers of the court professed to believing in such things. I can merely present the evidence; you, dear reader, must be the judge and jury.

We must, then, show how these matters will intersect, and how Dodger wound up encountering his true destiny as a challenger to creatures seen and unseen; that will be the subject of the following tale. We know that these are disturbing subjects, and only hope that Mr. Dickens and his heirs and descendants— not to mention his long-departed shade who may well be dwelling nearby and reading this narrative over your shoulder and shaking his head and muttering, "The Dickens, you say," and urging his long-desiccated body to spin in its grave—will not take too much offense in the unsavory, but no less true matters, being brought into the sort of light that they typically loathe.

ONE

In Which We Start With the Artful as He is Now,
Then Go to Where He Was, But Not So Far Back
as to Where He Began, Because That Will Be
a Matter of Later Interest

J ack Dawkins, since we had seen him in his last appearance
in *Oliver Twist,* had grown both older and wiser, although
a bit more of one than the other, and in height not much
at all. It was never a certainty as to his age, for he was
uncaring of such things and considered them rather limiting to
a gentleman of his disposition. Indeed, on occasion when his
age was asked after, it was a flexible commodity to be traded as
needed for personal gain. Even when he was a child, he was not
truly a child, if you catch our drift, and so it is simplest to say
that at this particular point, young Jack—though not yet having
been inflicted with that terminal disease customarily referred to
as manhood—is exactly and precisely as old as you require him
to be, which we think is very much how he would want it as it
would be consistent with the way he lived his life, if naught else.

Mister (or Master, as it suits you) Dawkins had picked up
any number of nicknames since his return from near transportation to Australia: Clever Jack, Jack B. Nimble, Jack-of-All-
Hands. But none of them were as apt as the old standby of the
Artful Dodger, and so Artful it remained and shall be, especially
as it's best to avoid any possible confusion with the notorious
Spring-Heeled Jack, of which more later.

The streets of London to which he returned were remarkably different from those that he had left not very long before, which simply goes to prove how quickly life can and does change. At the point when he was hauled in and thrown into the choky, Fagin and his band of young thieves still ranged about at will, snatching gentlemen's handkerchiefs and whatnot whenever and wherever they chose. The formidable Bill Sikes glowered and menaced and planned robberies. Oliver Twist—to the best of Dodger's knowledge—was lying in a ditch somewhere and might well be dead. And Nancy, that tragic woman whose fundamental goodness of femininity had been diminished and dimmed, but not destroyed, by her life as a slattern whore, was still practicing her trade while worrying that her devotion to Bill Sikes would end tragically in her demise.

So it was that when the Artful emerged from his aborted incarceration, he discovered the following circumstances had transpired.

Fagin had been arrested, tried, convicted, and hung before a courtyard full of entertained well-wishers.

Having been the center of gravity for his band of rapscallions, the youngsters had quickly dispersed, most of them putting London to their back as hurriedly as possible lest their association with the late overseer of cutpurses and pickpockets wind up with their sharing his fate. One of them, Charley Bates, had been so appalled by what he had witnessed that he absented himself from the life of a criminal. We will currently not trouble ourselves on bringing up his occupation save to say that, if it becomes relevant, we shall inform you of it thusly: "There stood Master Bates."

Nancy, she who had represented the ultimate in female pulchritude to Dodger, despite the fact that any true gentleman—as opposed to the faux gentleman that the Artful made himself out to be—would have taken one look at her and been repulsed because of her low office—unless, of course, he was prone to take advantage of her services and thus employ her briefly for higher office . . . alas, poor Nancy's premonitions had been all too real, and she had been bludgeoned to death by the man in whom she had misplaced her trust and faith. She had always believed he would be the ruin of a woman already ruined, and in that regard, her trust and faith in him were, in fact, well placed.

That man, of course, was Bill Sikes, whose escape attempt from the mob baying at his heels went amiss when he inadvertently hung himself with the very rope he hoped to use to scamper to safety amidst the rooftops. This greatly frustrated his pursuers because failing to capture him alive meant that he could not be executed at their convenience and on their schedule—this being the same crowd that would not have given a halfpenny for Nancy's life while she was living it. Thus it has always been: Only in death do worthless people have worth.

And then there was young Oliver, whose entire association with Fagin and his band was the result of Dodger's own actions, when he had come upon the lad in the little town of Barnet on the outskirts of London. Dodger had seen possibilities in the boy, perceiving the perpetual sorrow Oliver wore around him like a greatcoat as a distinct advantage, and was sure he would make a splendid beggar and even better source of distraction. The plan had been, as Dodger hatched it in his constantly scheming mind, that young Master Twist would stand at curbside or accost pedestrians while looking limpid-eyed and pathetic, making them easy pickings for Dodger to relieve them of their valuables. As you well know, matters did not pan out for Dodger as he had planned, though—a rare misfire in his normal calculations. Indeed, things had gone so completely awry since the appearance of Oliver in Dodger's life that the Artful was inclined to wish he'd never set eyes on the creature in the first place.

Yet for all the disaster that had befallen everyone who came within the influence of Master Twist's orbit, Oliver himself had landed upon his feet in a manner that any plummeting cat would have envied. Indeed, the Artful had espied the aforementioned felinesque Master Twist in a hansom less than a week after he had managed to extricate himself from the hospitality of those in authority (yes, yes, we are aware we have not yet explained how the Artful managed to escape transportation to Australia; we shall do so in the very next chapter, and so ask for your patience until we arrive at that point in the narrative). So on the side of the curb stood Dodger, aghast, as there—on the side of a smiling older man—sat Oliver, who was so ebullient that one could have leaned against him in pitch-blackness and had sufficient illumination to read a book. Oliver looked neither right nor left and took no notice of Dodger at all as the cab rolled by.

To be charitable to Oliver (or *more* charitable, as has been explained above), the Artful's greatest weapon had always been his invisibility. Indeed, it was a power shared by all children who lived upon the street, for no one of any substance gave them even a first look, much less a second. But Dodger had honed his illusion of absence far beyond anything that others of his ilk could aspire to. Yet now he became a prisoner of that selfsame ability he had exploited, for though he waved frantically from the curbside and even shouted Master Twist's name once or twice to attract his attention, it was to no avail. Whether it was the wind and the hustle and bustle of the crowd that drowned Dodger's words or that Oliver's interests were so upon the man who had recently adopted him as his own son that he failed to notice his former friend, Dodger couldn't be sure. All he knew at that particular moment was this: He might well have been a pane of glass, so thoroughly transparent was he.

Dodger considered sprinting after him, for there was none fleeter of foot than the Artful, and it was possible that he might have caught up. But then what? Ask whether Oliver remembered him? Beg for tuppence?

In the words of a man with his own disturbing tale (which must wait for another time): "Bah, humbug."

The Artful straightened his coat, snapped his chin up, kept his wavering top hat in position with that customary imperceptible tilt of his head to which we earlier alluded, and declared briskly, "I have my pride; yes, I does. A gen'leman don't have no need to be runnin' after the attentions of some former street urchin aspirin' to move up to a class what he don't belong in. That"—and he snapped his fingers—"for Oliver Twist."

Thus having wrapped himself in a cloak of self-delusion that one normally had to reach full adulthood to acquire, Dodger went upon his way without once looking back (save for the three or four times he looked back until the cab vanished into the gathering evening).

And so it was that the Artful Dodger reclaimed his rightful place upon the street. His first order of business was to seek shelter; sleeping in the streets or in back alleys had quickly worn thin. His natural inclination was to hie himself back to those domiciles that had served him for so long, namely the beloved run-down pit of squalor that had been Fagin's den of thievery. But he dared not, for the whispers in the wind declared the nature of the place public knowledge. This made the prospect of taking up residence therein dodgy for Dodger.

"What if Fagin peached on us," muttered the Artful to himself, "in the hope of savin' his scrawny neck from being drawn even scrawnier? And what with me just having taken my leave of that fine 'stablishment, which is to say the jail, they might come lookin' for me here, if they was having a reason to come lookin', such as Fagin's peachin'." Having come full circle in his speculations, Mr. Jack Dawkins did not hesitate to turn himself from his path and head instead in another direction entirely, one that he had not walked for a good long time but now found himself drawn to slowly and inevitably because it was his personal starting point, the place where his life had begun. All of it had started there, and so it was that it was there that he went now, the place being Drury Lane.

Night rolled in and brought the fog with it, and the Artful sank into its embrace like a child clinging to its mother's bosom. He always enjoyed the fog. It had served to cover his criminal activities any number of times. Thanks to the fog, he had been able to sneak up on people without their seeing him, and then vanish with their purses or snuffboxes securely in his pockets. Once again he felt momentary gratitude for having escaped from being shipped off to Australia. He knew very little about the continent down under, but he doubted that the atmosphere would have been at all as suitable as his preferred environment.

The cobblestones were uneven, the cracks thick with dirt. Ladies of the evening were gathered at street corners, and some cast speculative eyes upon Dodger as he approached, for the fog obscured his age and his high hat and long coat gave him the appearance of a fine gentleman and potential customer coming their way. When he drew closer, of course, the painted ladies laughed and winked at him, but offered him nothing beyond that. Dodger, for his part, would remove his hat and bow deeply, even as sorrow panged at his heart.

For in every one of them, he saw poor, dead Nancy.

Nancy had been his solace, his escape from an even greater sorrow buried deep within him. When he had looked upon Nancy, so alive, so nurturing to him, his mind had a brief respite from memory of the woman in his past who should have been doing that very nurturing: his own mother, so cruelly and strangely snatched away from him.

The flame of his mother's murder had burned less brightly with Nancy in his life. Now, with Nancy gone, not only was the pain not mollified, not lessened, but instead it was doubled.

Nay, quadrupled. For before he knew it, his feet—all on their own—had brought him to that very place that he had sworn he would never go to again, that pathetic little building that had been his family's refuge from the hardships that the streets had to offer. He had not known what to expect when he came to it, and once he had, he stared upon it in confusion and looked around to make certain that the address was as he had remembered it.

At its best, the collection of tiny flats within the rundown tenement had been barely livable. But at some point, fire had swept through the building and gutted it. The walls were stained with blackened soot, the windows gone, half of the door hanging stubbornly upon the hinges as if refusing to acknowledge that its days as a useful portal were long gone. The roof was mostly intact, which was the most that the building had to recommend it.

For one such as Dodger, that was tantamount to a three-star endorsement from a board of governors.

Leaving the door to its solitude, he clambered in through one of the windows. There was no one around, which was a relief as he had been concerned that someone else might have seized upon the structure. Such was not the case, confirming for the Artful that, at least at this particular point in time, he had actually managed to find someplace in London so pathetic that no one could possibly want to reside there. He squared his shoulders and smiled in pride. "That's something of an accomplishment of one sort or another, innit?" he asked no one save himself, and nodded in reply.

Thus did the Artful Dodger find a place for himself where he was not always in residence, but was more often than not.

Whether the landlord had abandoned it or the city had taken it over and simply could not be bothered to attend to it, he neither knew nor cared. He had found a new home, which was his old home, and was thus content. The memories of his mother remained vivid to him, and at first he had trouble sleeping at night because he could not get past his recollections. He would wake up crying out as he would see the events of her death played out in his sleeping mind. However, as time passed, they faded sufficiently so that he was able to rest in relative peace, and awakening was a much rarer—albeit consistently traumatic—circumstance.

TWO

In Which the Reader's Patience is Rewarded by
Explaining the Seemingly Inexplicable and the Jailer
is Introduced for as Long as He Suits Our Purposes

By now, you are doubtless becoming impatient in wondering just how it was that the Artful was walking the streets of London rather than striding the deck of a ship bound for the land of Oz (an excursion not to be confused with his later unexpected journey to the Land of Oz, an astoundingly unlikely sequence of events that will remain unexplored for the duration of this history). Lest this curiosity become so consuming that it impedes your ability to become wholly involved in the narrative, be aware that it transpired thusly:

The Artful was only minutes departed from the courtroom, wherein he had laced into the judge and given him what for. The jailer was in the process of escorting him back to the lockup, there to wait for collection and enforced escort to the ship that the Crown's representatives had arranged. Their intention was to make sure that the charm of Dodger's acquaintance could be made with the savages, roughnecks, and criminals who largely comprised Australia's population. The Crown's representatives apparently felt that because the Artful was such a unique individual, it would be positively unjust to keep him to themselves.

The jailer was two heads taller and five heads wider than Dodger, waddling rather than walking, quacking rather than talking, so much so that Dodger was quite certain that if the man's boots were removed, they would reveal webbed toes. By contrast, Dodger walked with his customary swagger, and this seemed to sorely annoy the jailer, although whether it was because he considered it an inappropriate attitude for a rapscallion such as the Artful, or he was simply jealous because he would have been physically incapable of emulating it, is impossible to say. "Show some respect for your situation, you rascal," he snarled at him. "Bedad, you should! What right have you to act like cock of the walk?"

"The right of all free men and gentleman to behave the way God meant us to."

Angrily, the jailer lashed out with one meaty, oversized fist and struck the Artful squarely in the back of the head. The startled Dodger went down upon the unforgiving floor, scratching his hands; scraping his knees; and, most catastrophic of all, failing utterly to prevent his hat from tumbling off his head.

"Know your place!" thundered the jailer. He hauled the lad to his feet, scarcely allowing Dodger the time to grab up his fallen hat, and shoved him forward with such force that Dodger nearly fell once more before he righted himself at the last second.

The jailer guffawed loudly as he approached Dodger's cell. He reached into his pocket, extracted the keys, and opened the cell door with a rickety creak. "In ya go!"

The Artful strode in, but then, once having crossed the threshold, his shoulders slumped mightily as if the air had just been let out of him. The jailer slammed the door shut behind him, and then Dodger said something so very softly that the jailer could not hear him properly. Naturally expecting that it was some sort of imprecation, he snapped, "What said you, boy? Bedad, I'll beat you senseless, even through these here bars—see if I don't!"

Still not turning around, Dodger said, "I simply wish to offer my fart-helt apologies, sir, for you're just an honest man doin' your job, and I'm a dishonest lad doin' mine, and of the two, you have far more reason to hang your head high than does I."

"Well," harrumphed the jailer, "it's nice to see that in the twilight of your criminal career in our lands, you have some slight ability to see things as they are instead of what you wish 'em."

The Artful turned to face the jailer then, and to the shock of that rotund individual, there were tears streaking the boy's dirt-stained face. The jailer took a step closer to make sure he was seeing aright, and with an agonized sob that only the truly repentant could expel, Dodger shoved his arms through the bars and embraced the startled elder. "God bless ya, sir! And may ya get everythin' that's comin' to ya!"

"And you, my lad," said the jailer, unsure of what to do and settling for awkwardly patting the top of Dodger's hat. "Look at this new chapter of your life not as a punishment, but as a great adventure and a chance to start off with a clean sheet."

"My sheets will be of the cleanest, sir—I swear it so!"

The Artful then stepped back, having removed his hat and holding it in front of him and bowing so deeply that he could well have looked between his own legs.

The jailer waddled away then, swaying with the sort of pleasure that only comes from a bully having satisfaction from the powerless. As he did so, though, he began to become aware ever so slowly that something was wrong or out of place or out of joint, but could not quite determine which one or the other. And then, with the force of a thunderclap, it came to him. The side-to-side gait that was his customary method of locomotion was unaccompanied by any sounds other than the rubbing of his thighs and his own labored breathing. And the particular sound in question that was conspicuous by its absence was the jingling of his keys. By a startling lack of coincidence, the absence of the sound of keys was accompanied by an absence of actual keys.

The jailer voiced a roar that was intended to be on par with that of an infuriated lion, and indeed sounded like that to him in his own head (but to an observer or listener was much more akin to a consumptive mallard) and sped—which is to say moved with slightly less slowness than he typically did—to the cell that he had just absented.

This gave the jailer something in common with the Artful, who had likewise absented the cell. That was where the similarity ended, for the jailer knew where he himself was, but was clueless as to where Dodger had gone.

He sounded an alarm, which made it sound as if the consumptive mallard had acquired severe agita, but in the end it accomplished nothing. Dodger was long gone, and it was only subsequently that the jailer realized his purse had decided to provide Dodger some company in his sojourn from His Majesty's tender embrace.

"This cell will not remain unoccupied long—I swear it, bedad!" bellowed the jailer, and in that, he was right. He wound up spending the next six months in it himself for his rank incompetence.

THREE

In Which We Continue in the Spirit of the Preceding Chapter by Explaining How Someone Who Should, by No Rights, Be Walking the Streets of London, Nevertheless is Doing Precisely That

I t is extremely unusual for anyone to interfere with, interpose upon, or in any way impede the progress of an undertaker, because the average person, of whom there is an insufferable number in the world, prefers to distance him- or herself from anything having to do with that inevitable end result of life, that common condition in which we all find ourselves at some point or another, and from which none of us has a hope of getting out alive.

An undertaker's wagon—typically drawn by a horse who appears to have one or more hooves already settled within that six-foot-deep hole to which the horse is journeying toward, so there was some measure of poetic justice intertwined with a mute commentary on inevitability—makes its way down the middle of a street. All stand aside or watch in silence, sometimes even doffing their hats out of respect, particularly if they know the occupant or if there is a sufficient number of mourners trailing behind to indicate that this was someone of respect or status.

This particular early evening, behind this wagon to which we now turn our attention, there were no mourners. Not even a small child trailing behind, with a tear in his eye, typically in the hire of the undertaker to foster sympathies upon onlookers (which as it so happened was Oliver Twist's very first job once he had been shunted from the confines of the workhouse, because crying came so easily to him).

If anyone *had* been predisposed to follow behind the wagon, he would have been cheering or hooting or catcalling over the demise of the occupant, and holding up his passing as proof that there was indeed a benevolent God looking down from on high, despite the fact that it often seemed the perpetual cloudiness that hung over London obscured the city from His attention and left the residents therein more or less on their own. In fairness to the Almighty, though, it should be noted that lack of attention from God is not necessarily a bad thing, as the former residents of Sodom, Gomorrah, and the entirety of the Earth prior to Noah's construction of an ark would have been able to attest. This would run counter to the desires of many former occupants of London who would have been delighted to see London, upon their departure, erupt in a tower of flame, cleansed by the wrath of God . . . .

We have wandered from the horse and will reorient ourselves.

Guiding the horse was one Mr. Sowerberry, a cadaverous individual whose stock in trade was cadavers. Mr. Sowerberry's thoughts were his own, and not of overmuch interest to our narrative, other than that they were interrupted in a rather odd manner.

The street down which the wagon proceeded was narrow and darkened and not particularly pleasant. It would be relatively easy for a single man to impede the progress of anyone coming down the street in a vehicle of any width, and that so happened now to be the case.

It was odd, this man, that he was in the way, for a moment before he had not been there at all. Instead, he had been securely in the embrace of the shadows, and they had now apparently disgorged him for the explicit purpose of making certain that Mr. Sowerberry could not continue upon his path.

It was odd, too, that he was tall—unusually so—but stoop shouldered and hunched, which served to undermine his natural height. He wore a black greatcoat that hung loosely around him. His face, or what Mr. Sowerberry could see of it, seemed to be composed almost entirely of chin, and a cap pulled low over his brow served to obscure his eyes.

"How now!" called out Sowerberry. "If you're seeking to rob me, I have barely two shillings to rub together, and I assure you that my sole passenger is traveling light in the pocket."

"I would imagine that he is," said the man, in a voice that was low and unpleasant and brought to mind images of worms wending their way through the occupants of the great dirt collective. "To where do you travel, if I may ask?"

"You may not ask," said Sowerberry stiffly, but then he shrugged and said, "but I may answer if it will satisfy your curiosity and send you on your way. Common sense would dictate that I am on my way to the graveyard."

"I am not asking common sense. I am asking you."

"Very well," said Sowerberry with unrestrained impatience, "I am on my way to the medical college. This fellow has a date with an interested student of human anatomy."

"For which you will be paid handsomely," said the man.

"That is none of your concern. You are not my agent in these matters."

"True. I am an agent of altogether a different nature."

"And what nature would that be?"

At that moment, the horse suddenly reared up, astounding Mr. Sowerberry, who would have guessed the animal had as much ability to make such a movement as did the wagon's cargo. The horse's panic distracted Sowerberry from the man who had been blocking him, and so it was with astonishment that he discovered the man was no longer in his path, but at his side on the rig.

"The nature of which will bring about your death," said the man, who had actually known the entire time what Mr. Sowerberry's destination was and had simply been engaging him in conversation until the sun was sufficiently receded for him to be at his full power. With this declaration of his agency, he drew back his lips to reveal a pair of glistening fangs that seemed to elongate as Mr. Sowerberry looked upon them, and now he could see the man's eyes, burning red with the power of inner fires that reflected his hellish origins. Sowerberry's mouth moved, but no words emerged, which was a tragedy because a man's last words are important, and Mr. Sowerberry's were the utterly forgettable inquiry as to his killer's nature from moments earlier.

The man's head speared forward, his fangs sinking deep into Sowerberry's neck. Interestingly, the horse calmed, as if realizing that it was not the target of the monster's appetites and thus was content to let matters run their course.

Blood trickled down the sides of the man's face, and Sowerberry was too terrified to do anything other than provide a small, pathetic whimper of protest. Then his head slumped to one side, and his skin went ghastly pale, drained of the juice of life, and in less than a minute, he was gone.

The new commander of the vehicle wasted no time at all. He tossed the empty sack of meat and bones that had once been Sowerberry in the nearest alley and turned his attention to the back of the wagon.

The sun, already low upon the horizon, had set completely, leaving the shadows to lengthen at will and consume the entirety of the street. Yet the man within moved with the assurance as one might if he were striding through daylight or—more accurately in this instance, because a stroll under the nurturing rays of the sun would be less than salutary to him—a cat padding through the midnight hour.

Yanking open the back of the hearse, the man gripped the end of the simple coffin within and pulled. It was a mere pine box with handles on either end, and yet one would have thought it would have some weight. But the man did not grunt or exert the slightest effort. The coffin slid out, and he angled it so that one end rested upon the street and the box leaned upright against the wagon that had been its conveyance.

The top was fastened with a simple padlock, and the man gripped it firmly and snapped it off with his bare hand. Then he threw open the cover and looked inside.

The deceased lay within, his head at an odd angle, the imprint of the noose still fresh and impressed upon his throat. His blazing red hair was sticking out untamed in a variety of directions, and his beard was bristling. His eyes were closed. His chest was not moving. He wore black, threadbare clothing upon a frame so thin and frail that it was a wonderment he had ever been alive at all.

"Fagin!" snarled the man.

The corpse started awake, his red-rimmed eyes snapping open.

Yes, they snapped open. We know that this may well be startling for the reader who was unprepared for this moment, despite all our previous warnings. This constitutes our first actual foray into the world of the living dead. If the more faint-minded of you need to take a few moments to compose yourselves, we will wait.

There. That should constitute sufficient wait time. Onward.

The eyes actually moved independently of each other for a few moments before finally coming to focus upon the man in front of him. "Sanguine Harry," he whispered, "as I live and breathe."

"You do neither," Sanguine Harry reminded him. "Get out of the coffin, you lazy good-for-nothing."

"Coffin? Why am I in a coffin?" He put his hand to his throat. "What's wrong with my voice? Why are you sideways, my dear?"

"You strangled. You took the short drop and sudden stop."

"Did I?" said Fagin, and then slowly the memories crept back to him. "Ah. So I did. So I did."

"Come here, you old fool!" said Harry. He reached over, gripped Fagin's skull firmly with either hand and then snapped the dead man's head upright, a movement that was accompanied by a very distinct crack. Fagin let out a cry of pain and then slowly, experimentally moved his head this way and that. It flopped a bit, but otherwise appeared to be in normal, functional order.

"Thankee, Harry. You was always a kind one, you was."

"I was never anything of the sort," Sanguine Harry retorted. "And if you believe that, more fool you. Come. Come quickly." He returned to the alley, retrieved the body of Sowerberry, tossed him into the coffin, then shoved the coffin back into the hearse and secured the door. Then he clambered back into the driver's seat, Fagin slowly climbing up to sit at his side. Snapping the reins, Sanguine Harry continued the route upon which the late Mr. Sowerberry had been engaged.

"I thought I was done for, my dear, I truly thought I was," said Fagin, his hand going to his throat. "I wasn't sure that I, in my frail condition, could possibly survive. Not in the full light of morning. Eight in the a.m. An ungodly time to ask someone to give up their life, even if they had one to give up, which was not the case with me. Still, at least I had the black hood on; that was a blessing," he said, speaking of the typical headwear placed upon the condemned so that he was allowed that small measure of dignity and so that the onlookers did not gaze upon the final death agonies as reflected in the condemned's twisted countenance. "Kept the sun from doing me a treat, it did—"

"Shut yer yammering mouth," ordered Sanguine Harry. "There was no sun that morning. Darkness and clouds. Even the Lord didn't want to waste His time looking down upon you, nor does your brother, nor do I. Yet here am I, the only one forced to looked at your wrinkled, ghastly hollow of a face, so at the very least, spare me the endless array of useless verbiage that spills out of your mouth like sewage from a pipe!"

Fagin attended to keeping quiet for as long as he was capable, which happened to be just over a minute, and then he asked contritely, "My brother is put out with me, is he?"

"The right honorable Mr. Fang almost wishes that the noose had torn your fool head off." And then, with something almost akin to sympathy, Sanguine Harry emphasized belatedly, "Almost."

"Well . . . that's something, I suppose, isn't it, my dear? That my beloved brother allows for some small joy that I'm not bereft of my head?"

"It's not as if you were putting the damned thing to any useful purpose. What were you thinking, Fagin, to let yourself wind up in such a folly?"

"It weren't my fault, Harry—I swear to the living God what made me and turned His back on me, it weren't," Fagin said with such urging that he sounded not unlike a plaintive child. "They were lookin' for a scapegoat, is what they wanted, and that's no lie. Nancy, poor Nancy, old Sikes gave her what for. Murdered her in cold blood he did, and he died by his own hand, and that's not what the mob wanted—no, it wasn't. They wanted a warm body that they could hang for themselves to believe that they and they alone had brought proper vengeance to the situation. And who do they turn to as the object of their hatred and receiver of their unjust justice?" He thumped his chest in indignation. "The Jew. Always the Jew. You dislike the way of things? Grab the nearest Jew and vent your spleen upon him. It was a grouse miscarriage, is what it was. A grouse miscarriage."

Sanguine Harry suddenly pulled up on the reins, and the horse, which needed very little incentive to come to a halt, obliged. Fagin looked up and saw that they had arrived at the medical college, a rather undistinguished brick building with gargoyles leering down at them from the drainpipes overhead.

"Wait here," Sanguine Harry ordered him.

At first, Fagin was inspired to ask why and, for that matter, inquire as to why he could not simply be on his way, but when he opened his mouth to speak and made as if to depart the immediate area, Sanguine Harry glared at him with that evil eye of his, and Fagin kept himself exactly and precisely where he was, murmuring, "No reason not to be keeping peace in the family; no, there isn't." So he kept his peace—and while he was at it, kept himself in one piece—while Harry offloaded the coffin and, hoisting it onto one shoulder, strode into the college as if he were delivering a box filled with bread. He was there for several minutes, and when he emerged, it was with a black purse that jingled when he walked. He vaulted to the driver's seat and once again snapped the reins. Had the horse been a man, he would have groaned audibly upon being made to start walking yet again, but the horse had been given no say in the status or social ranking it had achieved thus far, and so offered no protest, correctly judging that it would serve no purpose.

"You have to be getting out of London, Fagin."

Fagin nodded. "Yes. Yes, taking a short break could—"

"Not short and not a break neither. You need to get completely out. For the love of all that's unholy, you old fool," he continued, running right over Fagin's attempted protest, "you were dragged out into the street. Dozens of eyes saw you. You were hung. All London knows you were hung. The bloody newspapers wrote of it. If you're seen as alive, it's going to raise all manner of questions that no one wants asked, most especially you and me, and even more most especially, your brother."

"Then it's my brother I'll be approaching to learn his opinion of this wretched notion of exile."

"It isn't a matter of opinion, Fagin. This is what your brother wants of you and for you. You're toxic to him and to all our kind right now. The citizenry can't know that dead don't always mean dead, or it could ignite a witch hunt the likes of which we've never seen."

"Witch hunt?" scoffed Fagin. "Nonsense, Harry. People are more forward-thinking than that. More enlightened. This is not the Dark Ages. This is the nineteenth century."

"And we—all of us—desire to see the twentieth century, and will do nothing and allow no one to endanger that."

"I don't pose any sort of threat."

"And if you'd been allowed to be delivered to the college? Lying there on the slab, still sound asleep, the moment they cut into you, you'd have sat up and started shrieking like a banshee. You think such a thing wouldn't have gotten some small bit of notice, eh? You think they wouldn't have backtracked every step of the trail you left behind, and where do you think that trail could lead? Ah, you're silent in response to that, eh? Finally! I thought nothing save ripping the tongue from your withered head would accomplish that. Gods, Fagin, look at you," he said, shaking his head in disgust. "Why have you let yourself get this way? You've near to starved yourself! Let yourself become a withered shell of what you should be!"

"If my dear brother is concerned over my drawing attention to myself," said Fagin defensively, "I'd think he'd be appreciative that I've been restrained in my appetites."

"There's restraint and then there's self-deprivation!"

"Just haven't been as hungry as I used to be. It's none of your concern, my dear Harry."

Sanguine Harry said, "What concerns me is what the Magistrate says concerns me."

"And he's concerned about my getting out of London, is he?"

"He's concerned about you getting your priorities in order, and he's concerned about you doing it nowhere near him. He has long-term plans for you, for us, for our kind, for the whole of London and our influence, and he don't want you being in the mix as some sort of wild card. Not gone forever, you understand. Just gone long enough so that people have time to forget Fagin. Come back as someone else."

"Someone else?" Fagin stared at him, swimming in confusion, drowning in bewilderment. "I am what I am, my dear."

"And whatever that is, we need you to be it somewhere else. It is"—and his voice dropped to an appropriate sense of gravity—"what Mr. Fang requires. Who are you to act in contravention of that?"

"Who am I indeed? That is the question in front of us, innit? And I have to be findin' that out for meself, it seems."

"It seems so, yes."

When they reached the outskirts of London, Sanguine Harry drew the horse up and extended the purse to Fagin. Fagin stared at it, and Harry said to him with a sneer, "Why starin'? Flummoxed by someone just handin' you a purse, rather than you tryin' to pluck it out of their pocket unawares?"

Fagin snatched it from his hand and jingled it slightly, putting it against his ear. "Decent pay just for deliverin' bodies. Perhaps I've been spendin' me time in the wrong line o' work."

"Then find a better one elsewhere. You'll have somethin' in your pocket just to attend to basic need. Creature comforts." He gave a short, strangled laugh, amused at his own comment. Then he leaped down from the driver's seat and watched as Fagin slid over to take the reins. Pointing, he said, "Give yourself the distance of time, of geography. Hie yourself to the Midlands. Scotland, perhaps. Make something new of yourself. Mr. Fang will see you anon."

"As you say, my dear," said Fagin softly.

He snapped the reins, and the horse began its slow, steady movement toward the King's highway. Sanguine Harry remained where he was, his arms folded, not trusting Fagin for a moment, not moving from where he stood. A statue would have been more lively.

Finally, when Fagin had dwindled to little more than a speck, Sanguine Harry growled, "Idiot," in that low manner that was the very antithesis of mellifluousness, and shoved his hands into his pockets as he turned away.

It was at that point that he realized his handkerchief was gone, along with his own purse, at which point he howled Fagin's name in white fury, and Fagin, who by all rights should have been much too far away to hear, nevertheless did, and his toothless mouth smiled in amusement.

"Idiot indeed," said Fagin, and kept on going.

FOUR

IN WHICH IS TREATED THE BEGINNING OF THE UNUSUAL
EVENING WHEREIN THE ARTFUL DODGER MEETS THE
FIRST OF TWO YOUTHFUL INDIVIDUALS WHO SHALL
BE OF SIGNIFICANCE

H aving explicated in detail the circumstances that enabled several of our dramatis personae to leave behind
the dire predicaments in which their previous biographer stranded them, it is now time to move forward an
indeterminate amount of time—months, years, who can say?
For time, like memory, is malleable to the needs of those who
observe it. But we say again, as we already have, that the Artful
Dodger is both older than when we left him and not as old as he
will be when we eventually take our leave of him.

His body had not grown tremendously in stature, but he was
fast and wiry, lean, and with not an ounce of fat upon him. He
had taken to carrying a walking stick, having helped himself to
it when a swell had been discourteous enough to leave it leaning against the wall of a shop, a truly insulting action as it displayed an utter disregard for the talents of upstanding thieves
such as the Artful. It was a clouded cane, made of malacca, with
a rounded metal grip and a small strap which he could loop
around his wrist to make certain that it did not slip away. It became a permanent part of his appearance, the gentle tap-tapping
of its end signaling his approach when he was predisposed to
make his imminent arrival known to all within hearing.

As for his face, it became less rounded and rather more mature, whereas his eyes—uncharitably described in the past as ugly—became more thoughtful, although they were still capable of narrowing in thought or calculation when the opportunity called for it.

But however much his physical stature may have remained unchanged and unimpressive, the same could not be said of his reputation amongst the more lowly denizens that populated Drury Lane, particularly—it should be noted—amongst the ladies of the evening who worked their wares there. With them, the stature of his reputation continued to grow, and one had been heard to comment—not without cause—that the Artful Dodger stood fully six feet tall if he were perched atop his own charisma.

Just so you do not misapprehend: The Artful did not make arrangements for the ladies or profit in any manner from their activities. Mostly what he did, the service that he offered them, consisted of nothing other than treating them with simple respect. You might think that this would be their birthright as living beings, but ponder: With how much respect do people treat slabs of beef? Beef is pounded, sates the appetite, and is extended no particular consideration beyond that. The sad truth is that oftentimes the ladies are seen as similar objects in that they are pounded in a variety of ways for the purpose of satisfying certain appetites, albeit unwholesome ones, and the remains are left behind for someone else to worry about.

And the ladies were accustomed to this. What they were unaccustomed to was the Artful's consistent treatment of them in his daily interactions. He would routinely bring them little sweets and trinkets that happened to come into his acquisition, courtesy of the inability of London's more prominent citizens to be wary about who happened to be dipping his fingers into their pockets. Snuffboxes; small bottles of perfume; and, of course, handkerchiefs were always popular and gratefully received. Of particular pleasure and interest to the ladies was that the Artful expected naught in return for all his favors, which was something of an unusual experience for them. In fact, a few of them even offered to compensate Dodger for his efforts in the only way they knew how, and every time the Artful explained to them that, while he appreciated their generosity, it was of no interest to him. "It is not," he would say, "how a gen'leman behaves." This caused great merriment to the ladies, whose primary clientele consisted of gentlemen, and when they pointed that out to him, Dodger said airily, "The measure of a gen'leman is how he treats ladies. They can call themselves what they wants, but if what they says don't match up with how they behaves, well, what they do says far more of who they are than what they says they are does, if you gets my drift." Which the ladies did—or thought they did—and that was generally sufficient.

So did Mr. Jack Dawkins live his life, without any general direction or clear idea of where he was going or what he was doing. He made some effort to check into the whereabouts of his former fellow gang members, but had no luck in locating any of them save one: He discovered where Mr. Brownlow had taken Oliver Twist to live out the remainder of his youth (as was detailed in his biography by Mr. Dickens. Anyone wishing to learn more can seek out the book, which can be found more or less anywhere). This he found to be ironic, learning the whereabouts of the one individual he did not particularly care about.

One day was very much like the next, as he continued to reside in the crumbling digs that represented a link to his former life. From time to time, he fancied that he could perceive ghosts long gone dwelling within, watching him, pinking his memory, and there were some days—the night being the Artful's preferred time of doing business—where sleep did not come easily to him. It was during the evening that he stole food where he needed, purchased it when he was flush enough to do so, and on rare occasion wondered if there was any sort of grand scheme or plan for him, and kept returning to the conclusion that it was not terribly likely. He was what he was, and if there was indeed a God—a proposition that the Artful was dubious over at best—then He certainly counted on men of far greater rank and position than the Artful Dodger to implement His grand plan.

It should be noted, however, that the Almighty has a wicked sense of humor, and often had little concern for whether or not one such as Artful paid obeisance. Indeed, He occasionally delights in sending one of His pawns in the chessboard of life into the thick of the fray. And in the unlikely event that the pawn should happen to reach the far side of the chessboard, well then . . . anything can happen. And has been known to.

So it was that late one evening the Artful Dodger was returning from his nightly perambulations when he heard the sounds of a scuffle from a corner of Drury Lane, and a female cry of protest, bordering on outrage.

He knew the voices of every female who did her business thereabouts, and the voice he was hearing now was certainly not one of them. He quickened his step, and when he rounded the corner, he came to a halt, his eyes simultaneously widening in surprise and narrowing in suspicion, which was certainly something of an accomplishment that no one save the Artful Dodger could likely have carried out.

A rotund man in a patchy gray coat, sporting a head of hair that was mostly head rather than hair, was accosting a young woman whom Dodger had never seen before. Younger than the age of majority, certainly, although perhaps not by much, her face was round and not exactly lovely, but possessed of a vague prettiness. She was hatless, which was surprising, with brown hair parted down the middle and drawn tightly on either side of her head. She wore a simple brown dress with a white shawl tossed over it.

Yet for all that made her seemingly unremarkable, Dodger was still struck by an ineffable something about her. She held herself with a pride that was typically absent from those with whom Dodger spent his time, and although she was shorter than the man who was currently trying to engage her services, nevertheless she seemed to tower over him through the sheer force of her personality.

Not yet intervening, Dodger sidled over to one of the girls, Mary by name, and inquired as to what was transpiring and whence the girl had come.

Mary shrugged beneath the folds of her cloak. "Ne'er seen 'er b'fore. Just showt up from n'where, standed on that corner, lookin' around like she ain't ne'er seen a street b'fore."

"Must be new to the life," opined the Artful.

"Bloke's doin' her a favor, ya ask me," said Mary, tilting her chin in the direction of the fellow who was continuing to ask after the girl's services. "That there's Sarah's corner. Sarah's with a client, she is, but when she comes back, she'll do that little tart up a treat. Look at 'er, standin' there,"—and her voice dripped with contempt—"puttin' on airs like she's so much better'n the rest of us."

The Artful did look, and the longer he watched the exchange between girl and man, the more he started to think that perhaps this was a mistake. She did not dress or act like any of the ladies of the night with whom Dodger had familiarized himself. She didn't look hungry; clearly, she had regular meals. Her clothing was immaculate, and there was no pox or any sign of disease upon her. The girl had been standing on the corner for a prolonged time, yes, and that had been the basis for the man's clear misunderstanding. And now she was in deep because the man had taken a fancy to her, and he didn't seem inclined to consider "no" an acceptable response.

Mr. Jack Dawkins knew the type of brute all too well, and there was something about the girl's attitude that appealed to him. He was not able to articulate for himself what it was, although we are not so limited: Clearly, it was the fact that the girl affected great airs to act as if she were above her station, and because Dodger customarily did the same thing, he felt that connection to her. At least, that is our surmise, and it seems a reasonable one given the circumstances, although it is certainly not intended to supplant whatever conclusions the reader might draw on his or her own.

Whatever the reason, the Artful was moved to cross the street as quickly as possible. He briefly considered challenging the man directly, perhaps battering him with his walking stick, calling him a bounder or cad, doing whatever was required to let the chap know just how little Dodger thought of him and his ilk. Still, as much pleasure as that might give him, it wouldn't really serve to accomplish the most important and pressing matter, which was to make certain that his interests in the girl were distracted and diverted as expeditiously as possible. Besides, the man also had a walking stick, and it was entirely possible he was quite proficient in its use.

So it was that Dodger settled on another stratagem: He drew within range and reached into the man's pocket for his handkerchief.

Under ordinary circumstances, the man would have felt and noticed nothing at all. The inestimable Fagin had trained his pupils quite thoroughly in the art of relieving gentlemen of their handkerchiefs, and in that particular schooling, the Artful Dodger had been a valedictorian.

This time, though, Dodger made no effort to mask his presence. He kept his hand in and fumbled about for what seemed an age to the lightning-fingered lad, and then the man turned and his face purpled as he shouted, "Hey, there!"

By that point, the man's handkerchief was already in Dodger's possession. It was, Dodger had to admit, quite a beautiful one, silken with lace around the edges. Dodger had already taken several steps back, and he bowed slightly. "Pleasure doin' business with ya, saaaar," he said, dragging out the honorific to such a degree that he sounded nearly piratical.

The oaf lunged for the Artful who, living up to his *nom de street,* eluded his grasp quite easily. "Get back here, rapscallion! Guttersnipe! Return that at once, do you hear?"

The oaf's hand pulled at the top of his cane; there was a sharp sliding noise of metal on wood, and abruptly a blade, two feet long, produced from within hiding in the cane, glittered in the evening light.

Dodger gasped, momentarily startled. The first thought that went through his mind was a twinge of jealousy, for he had never seen the like and now desperately wanted one. The second thought was that it behooved him to put himself beyond the blade's reach as expeditiously as possible.

Moving with far greater speed than the Artful would have credited him, the man swept the blade at Dodger. The extended reach provided him by the blade brought him far closer than the current geography of the situation would have allowed were he unarmed, and Dodger bent himself in half backward, watching the blade as it passed directly overhead and within mere inches of his face. The man swung again, and this time Dodger batted the blade aside with his own cane, but an extended engagement of simple wood versus cold steel did not seem to be in Dodger's best interests.

For a moment, he entertained the notion of throwing down the handkerchief and leaving the girl to her fate, but the notion was repulsive to him, not squaring with his view of how a gentleman should behave . . . so he turned and ran. Which was hardly the actions of a gentleman as well, but at least it made some contextual sense in planning the encounter.

The larger man did not hesitate to follow, once again moving a bit faster than the Artful would have thought him capable.

He ran a block, then two, and the man pursued him, continuing to shout a string of imprecations, although, the Artful couldn't help but notice, he was not howling for the intervention of the police as his sort was wont to do. Dodger considered that curious and wondered if the man had some reason to be opposed to the constabulary sticking its collective nose into his business.

He darted down a darkened alley, still significantly in the lead. The alley was sufficiently narrow for his purposes as Dodger used his walking stick in a manner similar to the way a vaulting man would use a pole. It provided him just enough lift that he was able to bring his feet nearly horizontal and his arms across from them, wedging them on either side of the alley, stretching his body across it. With a deft motion, he gripped his walking stick sideways in his teeth and made his way up the wall. Five feet from the ground—six, then seven, then eight— all in a matter of seconds the young man's arms propelled him upward, his body rigid.

Then he froze as his pursuer entered the alley at a full run. The man was wide and the alley narrow, but fortunately enough the man was not so wide that the alley was too narrow. He sprinted down the length of it so quickly that it scarcely seemed a handful of breaths before he was gone; not that the Artful would have known firsthand, as he was holding his breath the entire time.

Now here, now there—and then the man was gone. The Artful wasted no time in releasing his hold and dropping to the ground, landing in a crouch that made him appear similar to a frog for a moment. He hastened back to the corner where the young girl had been, certain that she would be long departed.

He was quite wrong. Instead, the girl was there and, even more problematic, Sarah had shown up. Sarah who was as soft as taffy to a potential client and hard as brittle to a perceived threat. She was looking the young lady up and down and demanding that she leave her corner forthwith.

"*Your* corner?" said the maiden. "Woman, this is a public corner, and I will stand where I like."

"Then I 'ope ya like standin' on yer arse!" declared Sarah, and she came at the maiden with her nails extended, fully prepared to rake them across the interloper's face while the rest of her ilk cheered her on. The maiden was so astounded at the prospect of physical assault that she did nothing to defend herself, perhaps because she could not conceive of the reality with which she was faced. As such, she would have borne the marks of Sarah's wrath of a certainty if the Dodger had not, at the last moment, abruptly pulled her out of the path of the territorial harlot and raised a chiding finger.

"Here, now, Sarah!" said the Artful scoldingly, as if dressing down a child. "Is that any way to be treating a guest?"

"Guests have to be invited! This one's a 'truder, she is, and the only thing what's bein' invited is trouble, and she's the one doin' the invites, and I'm the one answerin' it!" She moved as if to come at the maiden yet again, and only Dodger's bodily intervention prevented her from scoring upon her target. This would not have gone on indefinitely, for as beloved and appreciated as the Artful might have been by the ladies, business remained business, and if he got in the way of it, he was as subject to the penalties as anyone else.

Fortunately, his knack for distraction remained unmatched. "Care for a pretty, pretty?" said Dodger carelessly, and he waved the filched handkerchief at the irate Sarah.

Her ire evaporated like the morning dew. "Oooooo, Dodger!" said she, and she snatched it from him and ran the silk across her face. There was more oohing and aahing, and by the time she remembered that she had been put out by the presence of a newly arrived young woman who posed a potential threat, both the maiden and the pickpocket had departed the area.

The Artful hurried the maiden down the street and said cheerfully, "Well, you seem to have quite the knack for makin' friends, don't'cher?"

"What in God's name was wrong with that old woman? Who was she? What was she going on about?" demanded the maiden.

"She felt you were threatenin' her livelihood."

"Livelihood? Standing on a street corner is a livelihood?"

Her voice was polished, refined, but there was a sense of wonder to it that the Artful found remarkably appealing in its freshness. "You don't know? You truly don't?" She shook her head. Dodger opened his mouth to explain it to her, but the words would not come. He stood there that way for a few moments, gaping like a beached fish, and then his mouth closed with an audible click. "Sorry. Can't. Not for a gen'leman to discuss with a lady, don't'cha know?"

She stared at him, mystified. "You," she said, "are such an odd fellow."

"I've always taken great pride in me oddity," proclaimed Dodger. He bowed slightly and said, "Jack Dawkins, at'cher service, miss."

"And indeed you have been at my service twice thus far this evening, Mr. Dawkins," she said. She spoke with such grace, such elegance, that it appealed to the gentleman's soul that resided within the Artful but was frequently threatened with strangulation by the nature of the world in which he resided.

"My pleasure, miss."

"Did that old woman call you . . . 'Dodger'?"

"Dodger by street nature and nature of the street. Artful Dodger in full, as I'm reg'larly addressed by me more intricate friends."

She frowned a moment and then said, "You mean 'intimate'?"

Dodger blinked and then said cheerily, "Much the same thing."

"Not truthfully, but I am not of a mind to argue with he who has been twice my savior this evening, from that man and from the old woman."

"Ya keep calling Sarah 'old.' She ain't but much more than a summer or so ahead of you, truth t' tell."

The maiden was clearly astounded at this intelligence. "She looks so much older!"

"Life on the streets can do that, and does."

"I . . . had no idea."

"No," said Dodger, looking at her sidelong. "No, I'm fain to think you would'na. It's like—no offense intended, miss—but it's like ya just dropped into the middle of the world out of nowhere. If ya told me right here and now that you descended from the moon and were new to this sphere, I'd say that makes as much sense as anythin' else."

"I've . . ." She hesitated, as if searching for the best way to express it. "I've led a rather sheltered life."

"Are ya a novice escaped from an abbey before taking your solemn vows?" He said it partially in jest, but even as he did, he realized that it was a sensible explanation, plus it had the additional merit of being relatively earthbound as opposed to relying on lunar visitation.

She looked as if she wanted to laugh at that, but wasn't entirely sure how one was supposed to go about laughing, as if the entire business of enjoying a joke were alien to her, which seemed to go a ways toward reinvigorating his lunar visitor theory once more. "Hardly," she said finally. But she volunteered nothing beyond that. Still, she kept staring at the Artful as if she found him worth studying in some academic manner.

"Do you have a name, at least?"

Even in that regard, she hesitated. "Alexandrina," she said at last.

"That's far too much of a mouthful for the street life," said Dodger. "Takes too long to shout out if you're in danger. 'Alexandrina, look out!' By the time you get through all the syllabubs of the name, whatever's after you is already on you."

"I had no idea," she said, "that just a handful of . . ." She paused and then there was the slightest—ever so much the slightest—hint of an upturn at the corners of her mouth, "*syllabubs* . . . could constitute the difference between life and death."

"Now ya know. To wit,"—and he pondered the matter— "Alex is a boy's name and not a fitting way for a gentleman to address a lady, and so Drina it is, if it suits your fancy."

"I am . . . not sure. No one has ever addressed me as such." She rolled it about in her mouth for a few moments and then said with a firm nod of her head, "Very well. Drina, then."

As they walked, he saw that she was looking to the right and left and behind and in front of herself, and there was a wariness in those glances that spoke volumes to him. It told him that she was on the run from someone, and it wasn't simply that boorish fellow who had endeavored to force his attentions upon her. There was someone—or some*ones*—else.

They reached a place where the road crisscrossed with another, and they stared at each other for a long moment of silence.

"You have been too kind, Dodger," she said after a time. It was odd, for there was no nervousness about her, even though she was clearly out of her element and concerned that she was being followed. She was one of the most self-possessed individuals he had ever encountered, yet there was that paradoxical caution about her. "But I would soon as not put you at any continued risk defending my honor."

At that, the Artful laughed, said noise serving to startle Drina. "Of all the dangers I face every single day and every single night, from jail to transp'tation, to the noose, defendin' the honor of a young lady is the least dauntin' and the most rewardin'. It was me pleasure is what I'm sayin', miss."

"Well . . . thank you, then." She curtsied slightly and then turned away.

The reasonable thing for the Artful to do would have been to let her go without any further word, for he had been in her presence less than five minutes and had found himself deep in it twice already. There was no sense in him risking his own neck. No sense in it at all. The only actions that young men undertake that have nothing to do with sense typically relate to affairs of the heart, and in that regard the Artful Dodger knew himself to be unassailable, for his heart was a dark and mysterious thing locked away in a high tower.

And yet he heard his own voice saying, as if he stood a distance from it and overheard it merely as an interested observer, "Have you lodgings?"

She turned and looked at him in a curious manner. "Not . . . hereabouts," she said at last.

"The streets can be fierce for a young woman with no protector and no place to stay. If you be in dire straits—which is how it seems to me, what with me being merely an onlooker—if that's the case, and you need a place to hang your hat—not that you have a hat, but if you did—I have a shelter which is not much of anythin' at all, but it does me all right and should do you as well . . . ."

His voice trailed off, and he felt abashed, for he could not recall a previous time where such a nearly unconnected string of words had tumbled from his mouth, associated with each other only in the fact that they were in each other's general neighborhood during the period of their utterance.

She was regarding him with wide eyes. "That is . . . very kind of you, but I am not certain that it would be proper."

"Were I not a gen'leman, I could see reason for that worry, but I am and therewise there is not," said the Artful Dodger with as much pomp as he was capable of pomping out. "You simply strike me as someone who needs a place to stay, and I gots a place that needs stayin'."

As if to urge them on their way, there was a faint rumbling from on high, and the first of several fat raindrops—with the promise of more to be forthcoming—descended and landed squarely upon their faces.

"Any port in a storm," said Dodger with a grin, and so it was that Drina followed Dodger as quickly as they could to the burned out, run-down façade that served as his shelter and place of residence.

She hesitated outside it, scrutinizing the dilapidated structure, and said cautiously, "Is it safe? Truly?"

"You ventured out into the streets of London with little or no knowledge of the ways of survivin' on them," the Artful pointed out to her. "A bit late in the day to be concernin' yourself over matters such as safety, wouldn't 'cha say?"

If the wisdom of his words were not sufficient incentive, the flash of lightning and crack of thunder overhead and the increased velocity of the rain were enough to propel her inside.

And it was in that manner that a young, desperate woman accepted the hospitality of Jack Dawkins, the Artful Dodger, and set his life on a very unexpected course.

FIVE

In Which We are Relocated to a Site of Some
Villainy Cloaked in Justice, Before Returning
to the Dodger's Circumstances in the Next Chapter

Mutton Hill was the location of a particularly infamous metropolitan police office, notorious for the parade of hardened criminals, accused criminals, and non-criminals, all of whom received more or less the same treatment and level of punishment, for the reasoning by the magistrate in question was that if one was truly innocent, one had no business being brought into the police office in the first place, and that to be there was to be guilty, and only the expeditiousness of the sentence was worth considering.

Suchlike was the province of the Magistrate Mr. Fang, about whom we have presented you some intelligence already, and who has been waiting with some impatience to be brought directly into the heart of the story. And when an individual such as Mr. Fang demands attention, then by rights and for the safety of all concerned, attention must surely be paid.

The police magistrate did not have a courtroom so much as he had an overlarge, paneled front office with a bar at one end, behind which he sat perched like the vulture that he was, every evening, without fail, navigating through the human Sargasso of lost souls like an excessively deft mariner, steering his way without allowing them to touch him in any way or pose any manner of threat to him.

One after the next after the next, the police would bring their various examples of gallows bait before Mr. Fang, and he would listen (barely) and pronounce sentences (quickly) in the best tradition of the sort of mercy that far more human individuals than he had displayed with equal facility.

This had been a particularly busy evening, for when rain was coming down, police tended to be particularly aggressive at nabbing miscreants, or suspected miscreants, the latter requiring nothing more than looking as if perhaps, at some point in the future, they might be inclined toward considering some manner of mischief, and therefore such activity should be nipped solidly in the bud. The reason, of course, was that it was far drier in Mr. Fang's parlor than it was outside, to say nothing of far more temperate, basked as they were in the warmth of Mr. Fang's generosity of spirit. Not toward the plight of those brought before him, of course. No, lack of generosity of spirit would have been the more accurate way in which to put it. But that very lack of generosity, the no-nonsense manner in which Mr. Fang dispatched villains of all kinds, was more than enough to warm the hearts of the police officers.

This particular evening, the officers were clustered, dripping and wet, in the parlor, trying not to step on each other, holding firm to their various charges, hoping that their business would require as much time as possible so that the rain would have the chance to cease its pummeling of the streets. This gave them opportunity to observe Mr. Fang, who was in a rather dyspeptic mood, which was a bit of a change from his typically foul mood, so at least some measure of variety was being provided.

A police officer had just had his latest acquisition, a starving child who had snatched an apple from a merchant, sentenced to six months in jail, and was ushering the sobbing youngster out of the room when all of the brave officers were jolted to their feet by a barking so loud that it sounded as if a hound spat from hell had honored the gathering with its presence. Shouts and protests and threats of arrest were all topped by a thunderous demand from the magistrate himself: "What is going on here! What is the meaning of this!"—both not questions so much as demands for explanation.

The demands were aimed at a tall, broadly built man, who had a thick gray cloak draped around him and a high-topped hat that gave him a faint resemblance to an old-style Calvinist. His height enabled him to dominate the room, which promptly fell silent. He had strong, chiseled features and a black Van Dyke beard with flecks of silver at the edges. The beard was so bristling that it seemed to have a defiant life of its own, sticking out as if challenging someone to comment upon it.

He had one hand firm upon a leash that was keeping in place an extremely sizable German shepherd, with fur of brown and black and a sizable piece missing from its left ear, no doubt torn off by some animal. The remains of the left ear, and all of the right, were drawn back, and the dog was snarling softly, with its gaze fixed upon the magistrate. The magistrate shifted uncomfortably in his chair, finding himself disconcerted by the dog's attention.

The dog's master was carrying in his other hand the distinctive black satchel of a practitioner of the medical arts. And when he spoke, his voice was oddly accented. "I apologize for my dog's enthusiasm. Silence, Jacob!" And he snapped the leash once. The dog quieted, but its attention remained focused upon the magistrate. The police officers were looking at each other with concern, clearly trying to convey mutely their opinions to each other as to whether they should do something to intervene and force either the man or mastiff or both from the police house immediately. No one, however, took the initiative, each of the officers doubtlessly so modest that none of them wished to make their bravery conspicuous.

"You are German, sir?" asked Mr. Fang.

"Dutch, actually. It is a common mistake."

"Either way, sir,"—and Mr. Fang thumped his hand upon the bar impatiently—"you are a guest in our land, and as such, are displaying deplorable manners. You will bring that . . . that animal"—and he pointed at the German shepherd, whose growl had dwindled to a barely controlled rumble—"outside immediately, and then wait your turn behind all these good gentlemen."

"I have no doubt that will happen," said the doctor coolly, "should another man who has business here, and who is accompanied by a dog, choose to stop in. As for me, neither of those requests, sad to say, will be honored."

Mr. Fang was so flummoxed, so outraged, that at first he could not summon a response. When he did, it was to thump the bar yet again and bellow, "Insolence, sir! Insolence most intolerable!"

The newcomer looked chagrined. "I see the cause for your ire, sir. If it will mollify the situation,"—and he reached into his bag—"I will happily apologize . . ." He drew a large silver crucifix from his bag. "And in fact, if you will join me by gripping this symbol of forgiveness, then all will be well; I swear to every good and true servant in this room, it will be."

The magistrate drew in breath with a sharp hiss and let it out slowly. When he spoke again, it was in a different tone, one that was far more cautious and wary, with an undercurrent of danger. If a cornered lion, or more accurately a jackal, were able to engage its hunter in conservation, it would have likely sounded similar. "I do not believe you offered your name, sir."

"I do not believe it is necessary."

"You are quite right. I believe I know you, inasmuch as to know *of* someone is to know him. A doctor of some notoriety, yes?"

"Yes. And your notoriety has reached me as well," said the Dutchman. He shook his bag ever so slightly, and there was the sound of something clattering in there: wooden objects, it seemed to everyone in the room. "And because we see each other plainly, then I believe you are aware that we have business requiring attention."

"Yes. Yes, we do," said Mr. Fang.

The officers of law enforcement were becoming increasingly perplexed, aware perhaps that there was some aspect of the conversation that was remaining obscure to them. Mr. Fang settled the matter quickly, however, when he stood slowly, like a shadow rising, and gestured behind himself. "It would be best, I think, if we talked in my private office."

"If I am acceding to your request, then these good gentlemen," said the Dutch doctor, "are all bearing witness to the fact that I am doing so."

"Yes. Freely and of your own will," said Mr. Fang. "You may leave your dog."

"I may. But as it happens, I shall not."

The magistrate shrugged imperceptibly, and so it was that several minutes later, Mr. Fang and a man who was in a position to give him a good deal of difficulty were facing each other in the small, spare room that served as the magistrate's private office. There were no windows and only one door, both aspects of which the doctor silently apprised himself. He had replaced the crucifix into the bag, but it was still visibly protruding and thus easily accessible. Nor was the dog seemingly inclined to shift its attentions away from Mr. Fang, who returned the animal's level gaze but otherwise maintained an impassive face.

"Are you enjoying your stay in London?" asked Mr. Fang.

The Dutchman tilted his head slightly with a puzzled expression. "I had in my head the envisioning of several ways that this would proceed, but I can say in all honesty that that was not amongst them."

"What did you envision? That I would beg for mercy certain not to be forthcoming? That I would attempt an assault which would most surely be thwarted by your hound there and whatever tools you have in your bag? Stakes, I presume? Holy water? Garlic, perhaps? Mirrors?"

"I pride myself on being prepared for whatever I encounter." The doctor leaned forward, resting his fists lightly upon the desk behind which sat he who was his mortal enemy simply by dint of his nature. "My agents are everywhere, Magistrate. Your activities have been brought to my attention."

"As have yours to mine," Mr. Fang rejoined. Still the picture of calm, as if unaware that his imminent death stood before him, he reached into a drawer and produced a thick file. He opened it and studied it with a raised eyebrow. "Doctor Isaac Van Helsing: Doctor of Medicine, Doctor of Philosophy, respected scientist or, should I say, once respected. According to these files, you went a bit mad after the murder of your beloved sister, Rachel. A tragic business, that."

"A tragedy committed by one of your kind," said Van Helsing, and his voice nearly choked with fury.

"I should imagine." Mr. Fang made a great show of studying the papers before him. "Simply to drain prey for sustenance takes a matter of seconds, but apparently one of my kind decided to give your sister the honor of turning her into one of us."

"The *honor*?" Van Helsing reached into his bag and produced a stake, as if to emphasize his incredulity.

The magistrate's gaze flickered to it for a moment. "Mahogany. An excellent choice. Quite sturdy. But you'll find it difficult to strike cleanly if your hand continues to shake with rage, as I notice appears to be the case." Then, as if Van

Helsing's anger were of no relevance, he returned his attention to the file. "It must have been agonizing for you, watching her deteriorating, turning into one of us. And during that time, at first you must have denied the reality of what was happening to her, because truly, what sane person would accept the existence of the vampyre? Our superior strength, our fangs . . . with all these weapons at our disposal, the single greatest defense we have is the mind of the rational man. What persuaded you to accept the reality, I wonder? Your readings upon the subject? An unimpeachable source?"

"With eyes red as flame, she tried to sink her fangs into my neck."

"That would go a long way to convincing you, I should think. Of course,"—and Mr. Fang sighed heavily, as if he were in tremendous sympathy with Van Helsing—"had you managed to find the vampyre who had committed the deed and slain him in time, you could have salvaged the situation. But your own skepticism, borne of a lifetime of scientific training, undid her."

"I did not undo her!" And Van Helsing pointed at him with the stake. Sensing its master's rising anger, the German shepherd's hackles rose, and it growled more loudly. "One of your ilk did! It was his monstrous acts that turned her!"

"And it was your hand that destroyed her." Mr. Fang's finger rested on one line of one document in the file. "After a yearlong search for her, because she fled from your 'care' and you had to track her down. How brutal that must have been for you. By that point, your reputation in the serious medical community was destroyed. Thank God for your considerable personal fortune that you could proceed to waste in endless pursuit of my brethren."

"You think to make me act precipitously. To make me sloppy," said Van Helsing, his voice quivering with barely contained fury. "It will not work."

"It is already working. You cannot focus yourself sufficiently to strike home with your stick."

"You underestimate the strength of my hand."

"As you do mine."

The magistrate's hand had been in his pocket. Now he withdrew it and carefully lay something upon the desk with a gentle "clink." He then draped his hands behind his back and kept his gaze fixed upon Van Helsing's face. "You are reluctant to divert your attention from me, perhaps thinking that I will spring across the desk at you like a snake, uncoil, and strike home. Do not concern yourself. You have naught to fear from me, just as I have naught to fear from you."

"If you believe you have naught to fear from me," Van Helsing began to say, but then, despite his desire not to, he looked down at that which was lying upon the desk, placed there by the magistrate's hand. He tried not to gasp when he saw it and did not succeed.

A golden ring with a crest, sized to fit upon a child's hand, lay upon the desk. "A family heirloom, surely?" said the magistrate so softly that, in keeping with his allusion to reptiles, it was barely above the hiss of a snake. "Your father gave it to you, I take it, when you were a child? And you, in turn, presented it to your son?"

Van Helsing endeavored to speak but at first was unable to produce the slightest noise. Finally he found his voice. "Where is he? Where is my son?"

"You made him quite difficult to find, I will admit that," said Mr. Fang, as if Van Helsing had not spoken. "And very well guarded. I believe, though, that you will discover your guards are no longer amongst the living. Tragic, really, to die for something as inconsequential as a boy."

"Is Abraham . . . ." Van Helsing did his best to steady himself. "Is Abraham still alive?"

"Of course he is. What use would he be to us if he were dead? Or like us?" he added, apparently in anticipation of what Van Helsing was thinking. "If you knew him to be turned, then you would give up hope. Your hope is of terrific utility to us. As long as you hope that he will be returned to you, safely and unharmed, you, Doctor Van Helsing, will do nothing to stop us. Nothing to interfere with us. You will return to the small inn where you were staying, and you will wait, and you will do nothing. If you do not return there within a fairly brief period of time, then the return of your son will commence immediately, but only one piece at a time. If you wish to receive him whole, rather than as a young man of many parts, you will do precisely as instructed. And I assure you that when and if we decide to release your son, you will be the very first to know. Good day to you, Doctor Van Helsing." And when Van Helsing did not move immediately, Mr. Fang repeated, "I said good day, sir."

Looking as stunned as he felt, Doctor Van Helsing allowed the stake to slip from almost nerveless fingers back into the bag. The dog actually seemed to display a human reaction upon seeing the weapon restored to its place of residence without being used to deliver a well-deserved death to the creature on the other side of the table. Disappointment appeared to register upon its face, and then it swung its attention back to Mr. Fang and seemed poised to try and go for the magistrate's throat. It was with tremendous emotional effort that the doctor pulled on the dog's leash, restraining him from attacking the magistrate, as much as that would have given him some measure of satisfaction.

"Keep a hold upon your animal, Doctor, if you know what is good for you and for your son," warned the magistrate. Van Helsing, still numb because of the manner in which matters had gone so entirely differently from what he had expected, managed to nod as he pulled hard on Jacob's leash. The dog fought its master's will at first, but then acquiesced, albeit reluctantly.

And so it was that a frustrated, terrified, and thoroughly chastened Isaac Van Helsing departed, although not the way he had come, for the way he had come had been brimming with confidence and a certainty that the force of his righteousness would easily triumph over the pestilent evil represented by Magistrate Fang.

As for Mr. Fang, he was in one of those very rare states: a good humor. His evening had not begun that way, but he was surprised to discover that it was going to end in that manner, for he had thoroughly enjoyed being in anticipation of Van Helsing's intended assault and thus prepared for it.

In so good a mood was he, in fact, that he was in no hurry to return to the bar and render judgment on the inevitable parade of miscreants that would be his duty to attend to. So he allowed himself several minutes to simply remain where he was and bask in the lack of presence of Doctor Van Helsing, who had himself departed the police station and hurled himself back into the oppressive darkness and rain that pervaded London.

As it so happened, before he could then return to his duties, there came a knock at the door, and a familiar face peered in.

"My dear Harry," said Mr. Fang, much to the open astonishment of Sanguine Harry, for it was indeed this disreputable personage who had presented himself unannounced, and the sanguine one would never have anticipated any manner of joviality from this man to whom he had pledged fealty. "Your timing could not have been more unfortunate, for if you had been here only a few minutes earlier, you would have been able to witness the humbling of the famed Doctor Van Helsing, self-proclaimed stalker of our kind."

"I wish I could have seen that, yes," said Sanguine Harry.

"Would that you could have. The look upon his face when he learned that we have his mewling son was simply beyond price." He rose from behind his desk. "Come. Come and see me dispense justice, for it will surely be entertaining—" Then he saw the look upon Harry's face, and a wariness crept into his tone. Slowly he sat back down behind the desk. "Tell me," he said.

Sanguine Harry would dearly have preferred to find some other manner in which to approach the topic, but the dour look upon Mr. Fang's face precluded any approach save that of being as straightforward as possible. "There are a couple of things you should know. First, and of most immediate concern: The boy escaped."

"The boy."

"Yes."

"Escaped."

"Yes."

"*The boy escaped!* Where is he now?"

"We do not know."

"What do you mean, you do not know?" He was now fighting to keep his voice down, lest a note of alarm bring unwanted attention from the police officers gathered outside.

"Well, there are times when we know where people are, yes? This would not be one of those times."

"I don't understand! We had two vampyres guarding him."

"As it turns out, 'guarding' may have been too generous a word for what they were doing."

"What *were* they doing?" inquired Mr. Fang in a fury as cold as the body that he inhabited.

"Ignoring him, mostly. They acquired a flat, and they locked him in a closet and ignored him, figuring that he would be safe there."

"And instead—?"

"Apparently, in the back of the closet there was a panel in the wall that led into a crawl space. He was able to access it and escape in that way."

"And neither of them saw it before they put the boy in there?"

"So it would seem." He hastened to add when he saw the expression on Mr. Fang's face, "They are tracking the boy down even now. He is alone and in a strange city, and his father has certainly told him enough about our influence in society for him to be afraid to seek out anyone in authority, for fear he will simply be returned to our keeping. He will be found and retaken."

"We cannot assume that," said the magistrate. "We cannot assume that at all." He gave the matter some brief consideration. "We may have to accelerate our plans."

"Accelerate?"

"The Princess Victoria."

Sanguine Harry drew in a sharp breath.

"Yes," said Mr. Fang, nodding his head in reply to Sanguine Harry's unspoken response. "It is time for us to extend our influence to the highest level. It is time to send in our people and turn the princess so that our interests and hers coincide. At least," he said with satisfaction, "we know where to find *her*."

"Yes, well . . ." said Sanguine Harry slowly.

"Well *what*?"

"Do you recall that I said there were a couple of things I needed to discuss with you?"

Mr. Fang stared at him. "You cannot be serious."

"Yes, well . . . the princess is gone as well. She managed to take her leave of the palace. Slipped out. Escaped. No one knows where she is, either."

"So the one means of leverage we have over Isaac Van Helsing is wandering around, whereabouts unknown, and the maiden upon whom we are counting to extend our influence to the highest reaches—Princess Alexandrina Victoria—is also wandering around, whereabouts unknown. That is what you are telling me."

"In short: Yes."

"In short: Find them. In even shorter: Now."

"Yes, sir," said Sanguine Harry.

Mr. Fang tossed him the ring and said, "Use this in order to get the boy's scent."

"Yes, sir."

Harry then hastened from the room, as Mr. Fang was still barely managing to repress his rage. Once he had departed, Mr. Fang leaned back in his chair and rubbed the bridge of his nose between two skeletal fingers.

"The dangers," he said to no one in particular, "of allowing myself to be in a good mood for even a few minutes." With that, he then let himself back out into his parlor so that he could exercise his foul temper upon whatever unfortunates were being hauled before him that evening.

SIX

IN WHICH DETAILS ARE PROVIDED OF THE ARTFUL'S
EVENING WITH DRINA AND THE UNTOLD STORY,
NOW TOLD, OF THE ORPHANING OF JACK DAWKINS

A s unaccustomed as the Artful Dodger was to guests of any sort—and by "unaccustomed" what we truly mean is unused to in any way, shape, or form—that did not mean that he was bereft of the social graces required should such a happenstance present itself, nor likewise lacking in the resources necessary for a gentleman to treat a lady as she was rightly due to be treated.

There was a small fireplace in one corner of his lodgings—his lodgings, someone else's ruins; but there it is for you—over which he had a small kettle heating up water for tea, as he felt that ginger beer, the only other libation available to him, wasn't suited to the occasion. *Not genteel enough,* as he put it to himself. He also put several sausages in a frying pan and was in the midst of cooking that as well, while Drina looked on with curiosity.

"You are very resourceful," she said, turning her interest to the rest of the Artful's lodgings.

"You has to be when you got no resources," he said modestly. "I do what I can to squeak by."

"That smells quite good," she said of the sausages.

"I've found that the longer you don't eat, the better it smells. When was the last time you ate, eh?"

"I don't recall."

"Ah. Now you're lyin'." She looked flustered when he said that, but he shrugged it off. "If you really couldn't recall, you'd be right here next to me, watchin' the food cook and maybe downright satiatin'."

She frowned slightly and then said, "Salivating, you mean?"

"I always say what I mean," Dodger said archly, and then went on, "Just tellin' you that you don't have t' spare me feelings, is all. Maybe the ladies out there,"—and he gave a general tilt of his head in the direction of the streets—"maybe they think that you were trying to start up in their trade, but me, I know better. I think you're new to the streets and don't know what you want."

Drina took all that in and then smiled in a rather wan fashion. "You're right," she admitted. "About that I was lying to you, I mean. I took some food with me last night when I left the . . . when I left home."

She moved toward him and stood by the fire, although she did not crouch. She removed the thin gloves she had on and held her hands to the fire, enjoying the warmth. "I made the food last through breakfast and part of lunch, but I had nothing else. I was beginning to get nervous, thinking I was going to have to return home."

"Leastways you gots a home to return to. More'n lots of folks can say. Truth t' tell, at first I figured you to be a servant somewhere. Got the right garb on for it. But your hands look too soft. Not," he added quickly, his face flushing slightly, "that I was lookin' too much at'cher hands, or thinkin' about holdin' 'em, ya understand. Wouldn't want'cha to think I was being forward or nothin' like that."

"No, not at all," said Drina with a small smile. "You're the perfect gentleman."

"'S'truth," he agreed. "So I ain't sure what to make of you, really. If I didn't know better, I'd think you was some rich, pampered girl who got her hands on some servant's clothes so you could sneak out easier. Which don't make no sense, 'cause you seem in your right mind, and who in 'er right mind would do that?"

"Who indeed. You're quite wise to be able to see the truth of things so ably, Artful Dodger."

"Just 'Dodger' will do. So why'd you scamper, if you don't mind my askin'? Your father beat'cha, did he?"

"I never knew my father. He died not long after I was born."

"Ah. Well,"—and he shrugged—"might well be better off, ya ask me. Don't have no recollect of my father, neither, but to hear me mum tell of it, he was a righteous lout who took the back of his hand to her whenever things weren't goin' right for 'im, which was most times. He lit out long ago. No loss." He glanced toward her and saw that she was looking at him in what seemed a pitying manner, and inwardly he cringed at the notion. He absolutely did not want her pity. "What of your mum, then. She beat you?"

"All this talk of 'beating,'" she said. "Do you think that's all parents do?"

"Can't rightly say. I s'pose there's a few good 'uns here and there about. Can't say as I've met any of 'em in person." For a moment, his mind flashed to the contented smile upon Oliver Twist's face, and the genuine affection for the lad that seemed to be displayed by the older man who was seated next to him in the cab. Then he dismissed it, because for all he knew, behind closed doors the old man might thrash Oliver soundly whenever the mood was upon him. And besides, it wasn't as if they'd been introduced, even if the man was a candidate for sainthood. As if confirming it for himself, he said again, "No. Can't say as I have met 'em. So your mum, then . . ."

"No," said Drina, and she smiled as if she found the thought absurd. "My mother may be controlling . . . suffocating in her attention . . . but she has never taken a hand to me."

"What's the worry, then?" said Dodger. "Why scarper?" As he asked, he deftly removed the sausages from the pan just before they began to burn, and transferred them to a metal plate. He handed it to Drina and said, "Eat'cher fill; I'll have the rest."

"That's . . . very generous of you."

He shrugged as if it meant nothing, while praying that she didn't eat all of it but left him some, for it had been a score of hours since he had consumed anything save toast. As Drina set to eating the sausages, he poured out tea carefully. She regarded the water with raised eyebrow. "You . . . did not get that from a horse trough or some such, did you?"

"Certainly not."

"Then where—?"

"I made a stoup somewhere," said the Artful carelessly, smiling inwardly at a private jest. "You've not answered my interlocutory. What did your mother to you that'cha felt the need to flee?"

"It is not simply her," said Drina with a sigh. "It is my entire life. It is so . . . so melancholy, my upbringing. Growing up, even to this day, I've had no involvement with anyone my own age. My mother is so guarding of me that she even shares a bedroom with me. The lengths to which I had to go in order to slip out . . . you cannot even conceive, Dodger. To spend a life knowing nothing of the people of England. People who I would ru—" She caught herself, transformed the hesitation into a cough, and then continued, "—would . . . rue never having had the opportunity to know before I become . . . older."

"Well, I got the knowin' of them all too well," said Dodger, "and knowin' them can be a ruesome experience, I know that, sure as like."

"And what of you, Dodger?" said Drina, quickly trying to move the conversation away from herself. "You've spoken of your father. What of your mother?"

The Artful suddenly seemed far more interested in the fire. He prepared the tea meticulously and hunched his shoulders as if he were expecting a blow to land upon them. "I would rather, if it be all of the same never mind to you, not speak of her . . ."

"How now?" said Drina. "I have been nothing less than honest with you." And then she paused, for she knew that she had in fact not been entirely forthcoming, but Dodger was preoccupied and thus did not notice the telling expression on her face that hinted at her lack of candor. "I would appreciate your reciprocating."

Dodger frowned at the word and then said, "A gentleman never repricates in front of a lady, and I'm shocked that you'd even suggest that I'd consider such a thing."

"Reciprocating means . . ." She shook her head, deciding it was pointless to pursue it. "I am simply saying that I wish to hear what happened to your mother."

"The thing of it is—"

She did not allow him to finish. Instead, she said even more firmly, in as commanding a voice as Dodger had ever heard, "Tell me."

Dodger was surprised at the change in her tone, and more than that, he felt as if he could not help but do as she commanded, if for no other reason than that commanding seemed to come ever so naturally to her.

And so he told her thusly:

"We lived in this place from when I was small. This was my home from as far back as I can remember. Me mum, she was a drab, I admit it, no different from Mary and Sarah and their like. She made her livin' off the streets, doin' everything she could to make enough money to support us. Me, I tried to do my bit. I begged in the streets, 'cause it's not as if I had too much pride not to. We were a team, me mum an' me. And if I sound like I'm proud of what she did, sellin' her body and all, well I'm not. Not of what she did. But I'm proud of her, you can bet your soul on that. I'm proud of the woman she was, 'cause no matter what it was like for her out in the streets—and there was days she'd come home cold, or wet, or bloodied or bruised if some rotter had done her dirt—when she was at home, she had a smile for me, and a hug. I heard preachers and such in their pomp-o-city, railing against the likes of me mum and sayin' we're just soulless sinners, but I'm tellin' you right now, they don't know nothin' and they don't know her.

"And then there came a time where I was fierce sick. Had a fever and the ague. I lay there, right over there, right where I got that pile of blankets now—that's where my bed used t' be . . . I lay there shiverin' and feelin' like I was dying of thirst, and I lost track of night and day. Didn't know what was what. All I knew was that right then, I needed my mum.

"When my dad left us, he left some of his clothes behind, 'cause he went durin' the summer and didn't feel like takin' nothin' heavier. I was so cold, like I said, that I grabbed one of his old coats—this one right here"—and he indicated the one he was wearing—"and one of his hats—this one right here—and I went out lookin' for her 'cause I wanted to see her so bad. Even if it meant less money that day, that was all well with me, 'cause it weren't like I was all for eating much of anythin' anyway.

"I went out into the streets lookin' for her, knowin' her reg'lar haunts, her reg'lar places. She weren't there. And then I got to one alley, and I was startin' to get sore dizzy and could barely stand upright, and I heard a scream and thought I was gone, just dreamin' while I was awake, or maybe I was asleep and didn't even know it, but there it was, right in front of me. Me mum was halfway down the alley, and there was a man holdin' her tight, but there weren't no love in what he was doin' or even the daft fakery of love that substitutes for whatever it is men feels or thinks they feels when they're with workin' ladies. He was crouched over her, and she was screamin' and strugglin' and tryin' to shove him away.

"And here's my shame, my secret shame what I never told no one, and I'm not even sure why I'm tellin' you, but I am. My shame is that what I should have done was run right at him then, shoutin' and shakin' my fists and tryin' to hurt him and make him leave me mum be. Instead, I stood there, and my feet were like rocks and my head like lead, and I didn't move a muscle, just stood there and watched and trembled like I was in a livin' nightmare. I couldn't have been more'n five years old, but that ain't no excuse. There's no excuse, really; it just is what it is.

"And then he stepped back from her, just threw wide his arms and let her fall, and she thudded to the ground like an empty sack of clothin', because really, that's all she was at that moment. She lay there on the ground, starin' at me with eyes that wouldn't see nothin' ever again, and there was a gash in her neck. He'd stabbed her in the neck, although he must have done a rubbish job of it, because there weren't hardly no blood. But she was just as dead as dead could be anyway, I figure from the shock, prob'ly.

"And I still couldn't see much of him, because it was like he was part of the shadows. I couldn't see him, but I could tell he saw me, because he hissed like a huge snake, and it was like I unfroze all at once. I started runnin' then, because damn me, now it was me own neck on the block, and I couldn't do nothin' to help me mum but to save myself, like I had wings on my heels. I turned and I ran, ran as fast as I could, ran faster than I ever had, ran across the street, ran like my life depended on it.

"And that's when I ran into *him*. He was right in my path, and he grabbed me and crouched down to talk to me.

"'Here now, my dear, what's all this then?' he said to me. 'You're the fastest lad I ever did see, and I seen more than my share.'

"For a heartbeat, I thought he was the one what attacked me mum, but then I realized, even in my panic, I realized that couldn't be, 'cause that murderin' monster was way far behind me, and there was no way he could've gotten ahead of me unless he could fly over rooftops, so that's not likely. I blabbered at him, told him what'd happened, and he said, 'Let's go see, my dear, let's go see.' He was rail thin, he was, with fiery red hair and a villainous air, but at that moment I was as happy to see him as I would have been to come upon a police officer. Happier, in fact, because the coppers, they ain't exactly friends of me and mine, and are as likely to toss us in the dock in the good times as help us in the bad times.

"I led him back to where my mum had been, and he went to her and looked her over. I'll never forget the way he picked up her hand and then released it, letting it flop down, and he turned and said with great sorrow, 'Sorry, my dear. She's in the arms of her Lord, now.' And I started to sob then, great huge tears of grief, for I had not had much place in the world, and now I had none. And he came toward me, moving sideways, like a great crab or some such, and looked me up and down and said, 'You're sick, my dear. If your skin was any more waxy, I could be stickin' a wick in you and light my lodgings for a month.' I said, 'But my mum—I have to do somethin' about my mum.' I said that even as the whole world was startin' to go white around me. And he said, 'Don't worry; old Fagin will take care of everything.'

"And I'm sure the name is one what sounds chimes with you. When you think rotter, you think of Fagin."

For the first time, Drina interrupted his narrative. "Actually, no," she said. "I've heard nothing of him. News of such things doesn't reach me all that often." Sounding as if she did not wish to appear wholly ignorant of such vile pleasantries as typically entertained the riffraff, she said hopefully, "I've heard tell of

Spring-Heeled Jack, though. He's quite new, I understand, and supposedly very much the rogue. Leaping in front of women, terrifying them, rushing off. The police are all in a lather about it."

The Artful waved it off as if Spring-Heeled Jack were not worth the slightest mention. "I got no patience what for someone whose main claim to fame is raising boorishness to the level of art. When Spring-Heeled Jack starts robbin' people or murderin' 'em, then he's worth a fig. Till then, he ain't worth nobody's time, and the police can chase their tails in a circle lookin' for him, and it's fine with me 'cause it draws their attention away from more legit criminals."

"Such as yourself?" asked Drina.

"I ain't no criminal. Criminals break the law 'cause they enjoys it. I merely does what I gots to, to survive. If society wants me to stop takin' what I need to in order to be able to serve up loverly meals such as this one, then all it needs to be doin' is findin' me a way of not doin' what I'm doin'. Some way that don't involve transportin' or swingin', if ya catch my drift."

"It's very well and truly caught," said Drina. By that point, she had handed the remaining sausages—exactly half of what had originally been available—to Dodger, whose impulse was to eat them greedily all at once; but instead, he took his time and tried to appear as genteel as possible out of deference to his guest. He then took a deep gulp of the tea before continuing.

"Fagin, he was someone what got a bad name from a lot of people. And I'd be a liar if I didn't say that there were times when he was fierce with me. But he took me in when the only other place for me woulda been the workhouses, if even that. He nursed me back to health. He took care of gettin' me mum a decent burial. And he taught me a trade which a lot of people would say weren't no good at all, except you saw some of the tricks I learned from him on display this evenin', and they certainly worked to your con-vee-nee-ence, am I right?"

"I cannot deny that," she said. "Still . . . taking a small boy and bringing him into a life of crime . . . ."

"D'pends on what you take the meanin' of crime to be now, don't it?" said the Artful, sounding a touch defensive. He leaned forward and regarded Drina intently. "Who are the guardians of the law, after all? The magistrates and judges what swear an oath to be just to all, but never temper that justice with care or compassion? The fat councilmen who eat at one of their meals more food than a workhouse full of orphans sees in a week? The right bast—sorry, miss, blackguards would be the more politer term—what passed the poor laws what said that unmarried mothers are the ones what got to pay for raisin' the children while the fathers are off doin' whatever?"

"But Fagin . . . from what you've said, he took you in in order to teach you to be a criminal . . . ."

"Not just me. Lots of other lads."

"He preyed on you!"

"How is it preyin' when it's someone what's not got any other kind of prayer?"

"But . . . it's not right."

Looking as serious as the grave, the Artful Dodger said, "Live on our side of the road for a long time, Miss Drina, and you'll see the truth of it. Right, wrong—those are words thrown around by those what is in power in order to sit on the backs of those what ain't. The biggest evildoers in the world, the ones who do what's not right, are the ones who have all the power, and that's what makes it right. It's right not 'cause you say so, or I say, or even if the Lord on high says so. It's right 'cause them what's got the money and the power, they say it's right, and that makes it right even if it's dead wrong. Dead wrong. I seen stuff that all those pompous windbags who says what is right and wrong would nod and smile and say that justice is served and God's will be done, but they wouldn't know justice if it bit 'em and wouldn't know God if His words showed up in flaming letters thirty feet high on their walls. And sitting above it all, the royal family, looking down like gods from Mount Olympia, not caring about nothin' that matters to the everyday folk like you and me."

"Really." Her mood was turning frosty, not that the Artful Dodger noticed. "You think the royal family doesn't care?"

He gazed at her levelly. "Prove that they do."

She returned his gaze but then, as much to her surprise as his, lowered it and said softly, "I can't, actually."

Dodger bobbed his head in triumph, but then, for no reason that he could readily discern, he didn't feel as if he had won much of anything at all.

The two of them stared at their empty teacups for a brief time, and then the Artful Dodger said, "Seems to have stopped raining. Care to walk around a bit? See the sights?"

"With you as my guide?"

"None better."

"I would like that, Dodger," she said, and she hesitated for a moment and then reached over and placed her hand atop his. "I would like that very much."

The room suddenly seemed much warmer to the Artful than it had been only moments before.

SEVEN

In Which is Treated the Artful's Encounter
with the Second Person of Interest in This
Overwhelmingly Singular Evening

I t is indeed a remarkable night when you meet someone
who is going to have a significant impact upon your life,
and to meet two upon the same night admittedly strains
credulity, and yet coincidence does happen, and indeed
seems to do so with unusual frequency in the presence of the
Artful Dodger, if one considers—as a single example—that
the Artful, in the company of Charley Bates and Oliver Twist,
sought to liberate the pocketed contents of one Mr. Brownlow,
who turned out—through a staggeringly unlikely series of
circumstances—to hold a key piece to the puzzle of Oliver's
parentage. Dubious, and yet, in sum, the way that life is:
replete with odd happenstances that in works of fiction would
be dismissed as absurd. Indeed, fiction is a harsher, more
demanding mistress than fact.

So be kind and understand when you read of the following events and know that, when it comes to the caprices and
manipulations of the gods or God, whichever philosophy you
may embrace, we are all of us merely pawns in their games,
rather than players.

So it was that Artful and Drina emerged from Dodger's
home into a cool, crisp London evening, which was to say, a
typical London evening. Dodger thumped his chest several
times and declared, "The city is splendid after a rain."

"It is," she said. "The cobblestones glisten so nicely, and the drops hang just so from the rooftops."

"That and the stink is largely washed away."

"I had not noticed," said Drina, when in fact she had but was simply too refined to make note of it aloud.

Dodger had an entire plan for his random stroll that would take Drina through all the best parts of town, which was to say, the least odorous. He had had a rather successful week in terms of earning money, and if you do not believe that picking pockets clean of funds therein is hard work and therefore the dipper has earned his income, then we defy you to try it and see how well *you* do. So, being rather flush, Dodger had the wherewithal to genuinely purchase some niceties for Drina or perhaps even hire up a ride for them, a nice hansom cab that would emulate the sort of gentlemanly behavior to which the Artful aspired.

As they were heading out, however, Mary called from her corner, "'Oy! Dodger! Goin' somewheres with yer dollymop?'"

Drina looked at Dodger questioningly. Rather than inform her that Mary was referring to her as an amateur prostitute, Dodger shrugged as if he had no idea what Mary was talking about. Then he turned to Mary and called back, "Sing to someone else, me fine ladybird. I got no ears for you tonight."

"Well, yer lucky I have eyes for you, or better to say, eyes out for you! You owe me, Dodger, ya do."

"Owe you?" This comment puzzled him tremendously, for he had never sought to avail Mary of her services and so could not imagine what possible monetary transaction between them was outstanding. "What'cha talkin' about?"

"There was some lad lookin' fer ya. Some boy what swore that only the Artful Dodger could help 'im."

Drina and the Artful exchanged confused looks. It was Drina who said, "Why did he say that?"

"Said he was in trouble and could'na trust th' crushers," she said, her face screwing up as if talking to Drina was distasteful.

Now it was Drina's turn to look back at Dodger. "Crushers?"

"Rozzers," said the Artful, and when he saw the continued confusion on her face, he further explained, "Coppers."

"Oh. Policemen. You have a great many names for them."

"Keep comin' up with new ones so we can talk about 'em while they're near, and they don't know." Dodger turned back to Mary. "Did he say what kind of trouble?"

"Naw. Just said that he was askin' other lads where t'go to if he was in a fix and hadda stay lavendered in."

This time Dodger didn't even wait for Drina to ask. "Stay hidden from the law," he explained.

"Ah," she said. She looked around. "So . . . where is the boy, then?"

Mary smiled proudly. "Sent him off that way," she said and pointed west. "Told 'im ye'd most likely be at the common house up the King's Road."

"By Aldwych?" When she nodded, he laughed. "Good girl," said Dodger. "You're right, I do owe you."

"Wait, wait," said Drina, even more confused than she had been. "Your lodgings were in the other direction. Why send him that way?"

At that question, Mary rolled her eyes and said, "Don't'cher little midinette know nothin' at all, Artful?" With a great show of insincere patience, she said to Drina, "The boy was likely a nose, tryin' t' sniff out Dodger for the . . ."—she paused and then overpronounced with as arch a tone as she could—". . . po . . . lice . . . men."

"You mean you think he was a spy of some sort?"

"Oooo, she's a bright one, she is," said Mary sarcastically. "And the boys at the commons house there, the Broken Nail, they don't take well t' spies. Which is what he most likely is."

With a touch of pride, Dodger said, "We get at least one new nose pokin' around every few months. I got a bit of a reputation, ya know, and the coppers are always tryin' to send someone down here to see if they can get a sniff of the ol' Artful." He scratched his chin thoughtfully. "Never sent a young one before. Gettin' more cleverer, I'll give 'em that."

"But . . . you don't know of a certainty that he was a spy," said Drina. "He might well have been a child in genuine trouble."

"Not likely."

"All right, well,"—she gave a small shrug—"I suppose that you would be much more knowledgeable about these things than I would."

At first, Dodger nodded, pleased that she had wound up agreeing with him. But her voice had trailed off a bit at the end in a manner that raised his suspicions. "What d'ya mean by that?"

"Mean by it? Nothing, really."

"I know what'cher thinkin' ," he said after a moment. "You're figurin' that right now, even as we're here, there's some kid what needs my help and I'm just sittin' here laughin' at 'im. And that Mary's arranged even more problems for 'im, but here I am, not carin' ."

"Well . . . you're not," said Drina reasonably. "I mean, it's obvious you don't care."

"And you do."

"A bit, yes."

"Why do you care?" said Dodger. He knew it should have been irrelevant to him, but he couldn't help but ask.

"Why do you *not* care? How long ago was it that you were a young lad in trouble, and someone stepped in to help you when he didn't have to."

"You mean *preyin'* on me, don't'cher?"

"Whatever his reason was, he helped you. From what you've said, you'd be dead if it weren't for him."

"So what if that's the case?"

"So," she said, and she pointed in the direction the boy had been sent, "it could be argued—and because you brought it up, then obviously you're choosing to argue it—that you have a moral obligation to help him as you were helped by someone else."

"Get *her*! A moral obligation!" Mary howled with laughter over the prospect. "As if the Artful has anythin' t'do with morals of any kind!" She continued to howl with merriment at the prospect, and the Artful Dodger felt a burning in his cheeks, and when he saw the way that Drina was looking at him, the disappointment in her face, the silent chastening in her eyes, he felt something for the first time in the entirety of his existence.

He felt shame.

He turned back to Mary and said, "What did he look like?"

"What?"

"The boy. What did he look like?"

"Um . . . black coat, short pants. Square jaw, biggish nose, large forehead, shock of red hair . . . Dodger, you're not thinkin' of—"

Taking Drina's now gloved hand firmly, he said, "Let's go get him," and he started off at a rapid trot toward the Broken Nail.

Mary, appalled, shouted after him, "You're putting your neck in the noose, tryin' t' impress that Judy! You'll be dancing on air, Dodger, mark me! Mark me!"

The Artful Dodger did indeed mark her, and he was fully aware that there was every possibility that Mary was absolutely correct. But to his astonishment, he realized that he would rather face the possibility of dodging the law than the probability that Drina would give him another look of disappointment. He wasn't entirely sure why the opinion of someone he had known a relatively brief time was of any consequence to him, but it was. Perhaps it was because she carried herself with a quiet air of authority and importance that consequently lent weight to her estimation of his character. It was an unusual sensation for Dodger, caring what someone else thought of him. There was something about Drina that made him want to be better than he was. To aspire to something beyond being the most skilled tooler—that is, pickpocket—in the whole of London.

None of which he would admit to her, of course. There were some things that a gentleman simply did not discuss with a lady, and feelings were most definitely one of them. Ten of them, even.

"I'm . . . I'm having trouble keeping up!" Drina said, and he realized she was gasping for breath.

He felt a flash of anger despite everything, or perhaps because of everything. He wanted to tell her that if she was having problems, they were entirely of her own doing. Then, to make matters worse, he felt guilty over feeling angry. The girl was beginning to get on his nerves, twisting his emotions around the way she was, without even trying.

Suddenly he saw a hackney rolling their way from behind, empty of passengers. Without hesitation, he let go of her hand and waved his arms to flag it down. The driver made eye contact with him and, flicking his whip, prepared to send the horse-drawn cab barreling right past, clearly unimpressed by the youth who was endeavoring to catch his attention.

Drina looked from the Artful to the driver, and then she took in a breath and called out a single word, an order, in a voice that would not allow for even the slightest possibility of being ignored.

"Halt!"

Reflexively, automatically, the driver yanked hard on the reins, forcing the horse to a stop so abruptly that the animal let out a startled and irritated whinny of protest.

Without waiting for the driver to clamber down, Drina strode forward and yanked open the door. "Get in," she said to the Artful and then fixed an angry glare upon the driver. "Is that what you consider proper business conduct? Ignoring a customer who was endeavoring to engage your services?"

The driver looked taken aback. "Sorry, miss," he said. "Didn't mean nothing by it. Just meant to be a bit of a laugh."

Icily she said, "We are not amused."

They clambered in, and the Artful Dodger gave quick instructions. The driver sent the horse speeding down the King's Way while Dodger kept his eyes upon the road in front of them, scanning the walks, trying to catch a glimpse of the lad that he was certain they would overtake. He did take time, however, to glance toward Drina. The heat of the moment having passed, she seemed ever so slightly contrite. "I hope you're not upset," she said, "that I did that."

"You mean take charge?"

"Yes."

"No. No, you were brilliant," he said in wonderment. "I think . . . I think it's good you're strong." He looked away from her then and said softly, "I cared about two women in my life. My mum. And a girl named Nancy. Both of them were gentle souls. Both of them paid for it with their lives. World don't seem t' welcome gentle souls. You stay strong, you take charge, and you can meet the world on its own terms, which means maybe you won't go the way they did. That's fine with me."

"Mr. Dawkins," said Drina, "that may be the most sincere thing I've heard you say. I'm flattered. And . . . intrigued, to be honest. Are you insinuating that you care about—"

"*There!*" said the Artful Dodger abruptly. "Pull over! There!"

Just ahead of them, approaching the Broken Nail, was a boy who exactly matched the description that Mary had provided them. He was moving with quick, steady strides, his arms pumping furiously. It was remarkable how much distance those little legs could consume.

And then two men seemed to come out of nowhere and grabbed the boy by either arm. They were cloaked in brown Inverness capes that were ragged and tatty around the edges. The boy let out a startled yelp and tried to pull away, but they easily hoisted him off his feet and carried him off into the darkness of a nearby alley.

For half a heartbeat, the Artful was back in his young mind from years ago, and he saw his mother struggling in a similar dark alley. He remembered his cowardice, being frozen with indecision and fear, and doing nothing as she died.

"Not again," he snarled. "Not this time!" Without further hesitation, he vaulted out the side of the hansom cab as it rolled up, swinging his walking stick down and around at the head of the nearer of the two men.

"Dodger, be careful!" Drina cried out.

There was a sharp crack and Dodger landed on the sidewalk, looking up at the man whom he had bludgeoned with his cane . . . only to find the man was looking down at him without the slightest indication of any injury. A clang alerted Dodger to dart his eyes downward, where he saw the heavy metal head of the cane landed on the street, having snapped clean off.

"Let him go!" shouted the boy, struggling furiously in the hands of the man who was holding him. "Don't hurt anybody because of me!" His voice sounded odd, foreign. Clearly he was not English, and that crime alone was sufficient to prompt the Artful to wonder why he was bothering.

Both men had—there was no other way to say it—evil faces. They had distended brows; small, ferocious eyes; and scraggly black hair, coupled with a stench like the dead coming off them. One of them said to the boy, "Ya should have thought of that before ya run off!"

Meanwhile, the one who had shown no ill effects from Dodger's assault reached down and grabbed the Artful by the front of his shirt, yanking him off his feet as if he weighed nothing. "And yew, li'l mon," he said in a thick Scots brogue, bringing the Artful face to face with him, "yew'll pay fuh thot!" Indeed, his breath was so foul that the Artful Dodger thought he was already paying for it.

"*Release him! At once!*" Drina's voice thundered, but unlike the cab driver, the man who was holding Dodger was not overwhelmed by an urge to obey her. In fact, he rather seemed nothing but entertained . . . until he turned and looked at her as she leaned out of the side of the cab. Then his jaw dropped, his eyes widened, and he was clearly stunned by what he saw.

At that point, the Artful did the only thing he could think of doing: He pursed his lips, sucked in his cheeks, and then left fly a huge wad of spit directly in his assailant's face. The hope was that it would startle him sufficiently that he would lose his grip on the young thief, allowing Dodger to slip free.

Instead, it had a far more profound impact than Dodger could possibly have anticipated.

The moment the saliva struck his face, the man let out a screech like unto a howl of the damned. The liquid did not simply run down his face; instead it began to eat right into it with a sizzling and hissing, and the foul smell of the man's breath was obliterated by a brand new aroma: the stench of burning flesh.

He dropped the Artful as he staggered backward and then fell, clutching at his face, thrashing about like a fish just landed on a pier.

"*What the bleeding Christ did you do!*" shouted the other man, the one who was holding the boy roughly, and the truth was that Dodger had absolutely no idea, but he knew one thing and one thing only, and that was that something that had worked once might well work again. He wadded up and spat once more, although this did not strike as directly as the first one had. Instead, it grazed the other man's cheek, but it was sufficient to cause him extreme pain. The ruffian staggered, grabbing at his face and letting out a string of profanities, but he still clutched the boy. The Artful Dodger grabbed the man's hand and spat upon it, and it had the same effect as his spit had upon their faces, causing the skin on the back to sizzle. Now the man released the boy, grabbing at his own wrist, and Dodger seized the boy's hand and yanked him toward himself. In his other hand, he was still clutching the remains of his walking stick, and he ran toward the hansom cab, hauling the boy behind him. He as much as hurled the boy bodily into the cab even as he shouted, *"Go! Go!"*

The driver had observed everything that had happened with eyes the size of two half-crown coins. But the moment the Artful and the boy were in the cab, he snapped the reins and yelled, *"Yaaaah!"* at the top of his lungs. The horse wheeled around and started barreling down the King's Way.

"What happened back there?" asked Drina. She seemed out of breath, although that might well have been from the excitement of what she'd just witnessed. "Dodger, what happened?"

"I don't know. Honest to God, I have no idea."

"Dodger?" said the boy. "You're the Artful Dodger?"

"The same." Reflexively Dodger tipped his hat even as he felt his mind was whirling.

"What did you do to them?" Drina was still looking stunned.

"I spat on them. I spat on them and it just . . . it burned them somehow. How is that possible?"

"Pardon what may seem a ridiculous question," said the boy, "but you haven't been drinking holy water by any chance, have you?"

"Holy water?" said Drina before Dodger could answer. "That's ridiculous! Why would he be drinking holy water?"

Then her voice trailed off and she looked at him with suspicion. "Wait. The . . . the tea . . .?"

"The water was just sitting there in the stoup," he said defensively.

"You stole *water* from a *church*? To make *tea*?"

"It's not like I was impersonatin' a choker and goin' 'round and usin' it to baptize babies and chargin' a quid for it!"

"That's not the point, and . . . choker?"

"Priest," he said, motioning to his neck to indicate a collar. And before Drina could start up with her recriminations once more, he quickly turned his attentions back to the boy. "What dif'rence would it make what I was drinking?"

"It probably won't last for long—a few hours from now, your saliva will be back to normal—but for the moment there was enough residue in your spit to be effective against them," said the boy.

"Effective how?" said Drina. "I don't understand. Who were those villains?"

"Not who. *What.*" The boy said very darkly, with much drama and pronouncement, "Vampyres."

Drina and the Artful Dodger exchanged looks. Dodger didn't know whether to laugh or cry at the notion. "Vampyres," said Drina slowly. "You cannot be serious."

"Serious as the grave, miss," he said. "Those two took me prisoner . . . held me captive . . ."

"And that makes them vampyres?"

"No, the fact that they are undead, drink blood, and are burned by holy water makes them vampyres."

"But there's no such things!" said the Artful. "They're myths and stories and things that parents try to scare their children with!"

"There *are* such things," the boy said firmly. "And there's more of them than you'd think, and they are more highly placed and in positions of influence than you can imagine. Which is why we cannot trust anyone in authority."

"Well, I'm with you in that regard, at least," said Dodger. "Still, you can't think that—"

"Bloody hell!"

It was a startled exclamation from the driver above. Immediately, Dodger leaned out the side to look up and see what was happening, and then he gaped at what he saw.

The second blackguard, the one whom Dodger had slowed, but not badly injured, was running after the speeding carriage. Not just running; bounding, as if he were a great jungle cat.

And he was overtaking it.

Yet with all that before him—and all the boy had said—still the Artful Dodger was having trouble grasping the reality of what he was seeing, precisely because it all seemed so utterly unreal. But the threat presented seemed real enough, and Dodger shouted, "Faster! *Faster!*"

The horse needed no urging from its driver, for there was terror in the creature's eyes.

The carriage turned sharply onto Great Queen Street, losing a bit of speed in the turn but able to take advantage of the greater width of the road. Their pursuer drew closer, and his clawlike fingers almost reached the cab. Then the cab picked up speed and barreled down Great Queen, heading toward Long Acre Road. Their pursuer seemed to be falling back, and within moments Dodger was certain he would lose his taste for the chase.

Dodger sagged back in his seat, the hansom cab—not precisely designed for high speeds—swaying wildly back and forth as it sped down the road. "I think we've lost him," he said, and that was the moment that Drina let out a scream of alarm, because their pursuer was right there, right next to them, having picked up speed with apparently no effort whatsoever, and was now clinging to the side of the hansom cab. His arm was thrust into the cab, and he was clawing at Drina, trying to yank her bodily out of it. She cried out, trying to pull loose from his grip, but he was clearly too strong.

The Artful Dodger tried to wad up more spit, but his mouth was dry. He lunged forward, yanking at the villain's hands, trying to force them off, but they were like unto iron. The villain looked at him, and his appearance seemed to change as his fury mounted upon seeing Dodger. His eyes were blazing an unearthly red, and his lips were drawn back to reveal fangs that would have been more at home in the mouth of a snarling beast.

That was when Dodger saw that as Drina had endeavored to pull free of the villain who was trying to yank her from the cab, a jeweled necklace had slipped out from under her bodice. Dangling from a string of purple beads was an ornate cross.

Desperate in the face of the unreal, but remembering the ancient tales that he'd heard, Dodger grabbed the cross and yanked it free of the beads. It snapped off and he held the cross up directly before the intruder's eyes.

The fiery eyes widened and the creature hissed, reflexively drawing back, allowing just enough slack in his grasp for the Artful to yank Drina away from him. But there was not much room in the cab, and with a roar of fury, overcoming his initial revulsion to the cross, the monster yanked open the door, presenting the entirety of his body as he prepared to climb in and do the Lord only knew what to the passengers.

And it was at that moment that the boy, a youth still in his short pants, grabbed up Dodger's cane—or the remnants of the cane, which was now little more than a long wooden pole with a jagged point—and thrust forward with all the strength his small but determined body possessed. The villain clinging to the cab had only a moment's warning, and it was insufficient, as the lad drove the wooden shaft into the attacker's chest with surgical precision. One would have thought that such an effort would have required considerable power, perhaps even a hammer to drive it in with finality. Not so; it punched through the creature's chest as easily as through a wall of cheapest plaster and straight into the pathetic, shriveled thing that passed for his heart.

He let out a high-pitched shriek and there, before the eyes of the stunned youngsters in the coach—although in actuality only two sets of eyes were stunned, whereas the third set knew all too well what it was looking upon—the body began to desiccate as if a thousand years of existence were passing within a few scant seconds. His burning red eyes receded entirely into his head, leaving nothing but blackened sockets; his gums peeled back, and his fangs fell out; the flesh upon his head shriveled and revealed the skull beneath, and then that burned away as if being consumed from the inside out. With a final low, mournful howl, their pursuer fell away from the cab, hitting the ground as nothing more than a sack of clothing with some bones within.

The youngsters barely had time to adjust to what they had witnessed before the hansom cab jolted to a halt. They were thrown about, Dodger slamming into Drina and apologizing profusely for doing so. They jumped then, startled, crying out as another dark form appeared at the door, but this time it was the driver who was shouting, *"What the bloody hell 'ave you lot gotten me drug into!"*

"Here now! There's a lady present!" the Artful said. "No need for such language!"

The driver stared at them, stupefied, and then the young man who had stabbed Dodger's cane into their attacker said with supreme calm, "There shouldn't be any more attackers. At least, not for now. All will be well. But we'd be advised to gain some distance until we can plan our next move." He fixed a stare upon his companions. "Are you beginning to believe more in vampyres now?"

"It would seem problematic not to," admitted Drina. "But who *are* you?"

"Abraham. Abraham Van Helsing. My friends call me Bram. We need to find my father; he'll know what to do."

"Where is he?"

"I don't know," said Bram in obvious frustration. "We were staying in some inn somewhere, but I don't remember the town name."

"How can you not remember?" asked Drina.

A tad defensive, he said, "They all sound alike to me. Something ending in 'shire,' I think."

"Well, that narrows it down to a few dozen or a hundred, perhaps," said the Artful drily.

The driver was becoming increasingly impatient. "Look, you lot! Either give me a destination so I can be quit of you, or get the hell out of my cab!"

"We . . . we need to go to the police, or the magistrates, or someone—" began Drina.

Bram shook his head vigorously. "No. It's what I said before, what my father said: We can't trust anyone like that. We'll find ourselves right back in the hands of the vampyres if we do."

"Never did trust coppers," Dodger muttered. His mind racing, he said, "I know a place. I wound up there once, years ago. The women there took care of me."

"The women?" Drina inquired with an arched eyebrow.

Dodger was confused from the sound of her voice at first, but then he understood and would have laughed were the situation not so serious. "Nuns. It's an abbey. They're good women and true. I may not trust chokers farther'n I can toss 'em, but I'd stake my life to those nuns. It's a distance from here . . ."

"Distance is exactly what we need," said Bram.

"All right then." He turned to the driver. "We need to go to Purfleet."

"Purfleet? In Essex?"

"Unless they moved it to Liverpool, aye." The Artful removed his purse and jingled it, the coins within making an impressive noise. "It'll be worth your while."

The driver, embracing the notion to focus on more rational and natural pursuits such as making money, nodded, touched the brim of his hat, and climbed upon the coach to his seat. Moments later the hansom cab was in motion once more, although with far less of a mad headlong rush than before.

Drina looked as if her head were spinning. "You seem so . . . so calm, Bram," she said. "I can scarcely conceive of the reality of that which you take as a matter of course."

Bram shrugged and then, as if it meant nothing to him, turned to Dodger and said, "Are you sure this place you're taking us to will be secure?"

"Absolutely," said the Artful Dodger as the hansom cab headed toward the outskirts of London. "If there's one place that will never have nothin' to do with vampyres or any matter of monsters, it's Carfax Abbey."

EIGHT

IN WHICH IS PROVIDED AS MUCH BACKGROUND
ABOUT FAGIN AS IS REQUIRED TO UNDERSTAND
SUBSEQUENT EVENTS

L et us now shift our attention many decades and at least one century prior to the beginnings of our story, to an orphanage in central London, a place that was then—if it were even possible—a worse place to reside in than it was during the bulk of this narrative . . . and considering the level of wretchedness that we have been discussing thus far, you can certainly appreciate the degree of awfulness that was standard day-to-day existence for the poor, pathetic refugees therein.

The Black Plague, which had sent so many to a premature death, was itself in its death throes. One of the places that had been sorely decimated by the plague was a particular orphanage in one of the seedier London suburbs, and it is at that orphanage that we focus on two young men who wound up coming of age in that foul place.

One of them was named Joseph, and the other, Reuben. Joseph was the taller as well as the planner, the schemer, the individual with a sense of destiny that far exceeded his particular station in life. He was a muscular lad, was Joseph, and the other lads tended to steer clear of him after the several occasions when he had had the opportunity to display his considerable physical prowess. Indeed, Joseph had come to acquire the nickname of the Magistrate, for he was often asked to adjudicate over matters of dispute amongst the orphans—mostly because he had the strength of body and mind to enforce his rulings.

Reuben, by contrast, with red hair and furrowed brow, had no respect from anyone. He tended to think it was because he was a Jew and thus a pariah by definition, but truth to tell, even had he been the most devout of Christians, he still would have acquired the disdain of others in the same way that a pond acquires scum, because religion or race would not have altered his fundamental personality, which was more akin to that of a weasel than a man.

Yet none harassed him, for although he was not Joseph's brother by blood, he was nevertheless like unto a brother in every other way. They had arrived in the orphanage the very same day, many years earlier, and Reuben had been a small, scrawny boy that the others were drawn to abuse. Joseph had witnessed this behavior and found himself deeply and morally offended by it, and thus had taken a strong hand in Reuben's defense. Reuben had wound up returning the favor, for though he may have been pathetic at presenting any sort of physical challenge, he was second to none in his ability to spy upon others and overhear that which would have been better left unknown. Consequently, he had learned of a plot to retaliate against Joseph in his slumber and was thus able to warn his savior, enabling Joseph to thoroughly punish the miscreants and save himself some inconvenience and embarrassment. Thus had a bond been formed between the lads: one the stronger, the other his good right hand—or left hand, if you will, because there was always a touch of the sinister about him.

Neither of them knew anything of their parentage other than fleeting memories of mothers and fathers that, as they aged, were gradually beaten out of them through the miserable conditions of their personal circumstances. Eventually, they were of an age that they both sickened of the environment and so took it upon themselves to liberate themselves from their place of residence. Their departure aroused no reaction from anyone in any position of authority, save to make note of the fact that there would now be two less mouths to feed. The remaining boys, of whom there were quite a few, breathed a collective sigh of relief over the departure of the local enforcer of justice. Granted, there was some sorrow that their reviled whipping boy had likewise left the premises, because they would dearly have loved the opportunity to give him what-for had his protector ever had cause to leave him behind. But they settled for finding another youth to beat into submission and were content.

As Joseph and Reuben grew to manhood, they became adept at various schemes and such contrivances as were necessary for them to survive. Self-taught they were, and learned to be light fingered and quick footed. Thus did they wander the whole of Europe, developing unsavory skills and exploring unsavory lands.

It was during these wanderings that they also learned to appreciate each other's strengths and weaknesses. Joseph continued to be the stronger of the two, and Reuben continued to need his protection, so that suited the both of them perfectly.

And then they arrived in Romania, and matters took a decided turn for the worse.

By this point, they were both in their twenty-first year and had become—amongst other things—extraordinary thieves. Reuben had a remarkable knack for picking up languages, and during their time in the land of the Romany he had picked up a sufficient bit of their language to converse, albeit haltingly, with various of the villagers. Thus did they learn of a near-legendary castle, high upon a hill, set off by itself, that was reputed to be populated by "nothing save ghosts," as it was described to Reuben. And the castle was said to be rife with splendid artwork, artifacts, and valuables that had remained untouched all this time by the villagers, who were staggeringly superstitious. Joseph and Reuben, by contrast, were civilized men—or as civilized as homeless thieves could be—who knew better than to be at all concerned about such ridiculous notions as ghosts.

Consequently, they boldly entered the castle during the light of day, finding the great doors unlocked. They were amazed by the splendor they encountered therein, with such ornate furniture and objects ranging from the grand, such as centerpieces, to the small, such as candlesticks. And there was money in vast amounts, sitting in drawers or cabinets, ripe for the taking; money of various denominations, from countries that they recognized and many that they did not. Naturally they were purely interested in that which was easily transportable, but that did not deter them from taking in the whole of the castle, from top to bottom. Everywhere save for the cellar, the door to which was locked and inaccessible, but they did not care, for there was more than enough to interest them in the upper floors.

They spent the rest of the afternoon gathering all that they could, stuffing their pockets, the sacks that they had brought with them, even their hats.

And then, as the sun set, they prepared to take their leave, and they were walking past the door that led downstairs, when suddenly they heard a loud click that echoed violently through the vast cathedral of the main room. They froze in their tracks when they should have by rights scampered, but that was how startled they were, and they remained with their feet anchored much in the same way that prey is prompted to stand stock-still upon hearing the roar of a lion.

The door that led downstairs swung open, and a cadaverous man emerged from the depths of blackness.

"You have entered freely and of your own will," said he, "but you will not depart that way."

And then, with a speed and strength that would have seemed more suitable to a wolf than a man, he was across the room and upon Joseph in less time than is required to describe it. Reuben emitted a high-pitched shriek, and Joseph reached out to him, screaming for succor, for aid, but Reuben would have none of it. He dropped everything he had upon him that would have slowed him, and he bolted from the castle, Joseph's screams resounding in his ears.

Reuben ran, and kept running, and it seemed to him that he did not cease fleeing until near to the sun's rising, at which point he collapsed and fell into a stupor of sleep. He slept much of the day and then, once rested, he kept on going, stealing food where he could, snatching rest whenever possible, but in short determined to put as much distance between himself and that Godforsaken castle as humanly possible.

It was on the third day of his travels, late one night, that Joseph overtook him.

Reuben was moving through a thick forest, and suddenly there was a cracking of branches from overhead, and he thought at first that a great beast was descending upon him. As it so happened, he was right, but he had not expected it to be of the two-legged variety.

He gasped in shock as a dark form landed squarely in front of him and then slowly stood, uncoiling like a serpent. He saw red eyes glowering in the darkness and could scarcely conceive that they belonged to his erstwhile companion. "Joseph?" he whispered.

"Did you regret, even for a moment, abandoning me?" asked Joseph.

"A-a-abandoning you? Nay, you do me ill, my brother! I was . . . I was seeking help, yes, I was. Seeking help with which I would return so as to—"

Joseph grabbed him by the front of his coat and snarled in his face, "You dare lie to me? *To me?* Ingrate! Traitor! I should tear your miserable life from your throat!"

"Please, Joseph, no! You know that I have wanted nothing in my life save to be just like you! To emulate you in every way! If I had a moment of weakness, attribute it only to my human frailty, and condemn me not!"

"You wish to be like me, do you?" There was an awful smile upon Joseph's face when he said that, which, if Reuben had had more presence of mind, he would have noticed. "Just like me?"

"Yes! Just like you!"

And if, with his actions, Reuben had doomed himself, it was with his words that he provided his final condemnation. For Joseph sank his newly grown fangs deep into Reuben's throat, and Reuben let out a scream.

Thus did he join his brother in death and in the eternal life that followed it.

Now . . .

Here is what you must understand about vampyres.

It is believed by some that they are immortal, and by human standards, that is so. But they also continue to age, for nothing is forever, and the human body certainly no more exempt from that rule than anything else.

So it was that Joseph and Reuben did not remain perpetually men in their early twenties.

As the years passed, they aged. They did so far more slowly than if they had remained mortal, but older they did become. And over time, they aged into the individuals that we have come to know them as in this narrative, and we shall proceed to spell matters out in further detail.

NINE

In Which is Continued a Reluctant But Necessary Focus on Fagin

Having presented Fagin's sullied distant past, we now turn to a more recent past, and in short order his present, so that his future will become clear, and so we turn our attentions to Fagin's having been summarily shunted away from London at the behest of Mr. Fang, and to his current activities, as they will be extremely germane to the history that is being recounted in the pages of this volume.

Upon his departure, Fagin endeavored to convince himself that he was enthused about the prospects that were before him. That excitement dwindled in short order, however, for all that Fagin could dwell upon was the life that he was leaving behind, rather than anything that he might be accomplishing in the future. *What will become of my beauties?* he asked himself, for he was more of a father to the boys who thieved for him than any of their actual fathers had ever been, and thus felt righteous in his concern for them. He had not yet fully learned of the dismantling of his old gang, or perhaps learned and simply refused to believe it, which amounted to much the same thing.

Taking Mr. Fang's advice, which had been less advice than it was a direct order, Fagin had left London behind and sought his fortune in the outlying regions and later up into the wilds of Scotland. Ultimately, he had decided that the horse and carriage were too much trouble to maintain, plus they had a tendency to attract notice wherever he went, and Fagin was not one for attracting notice if it could be helped. So he sold both horse and carriage for a tidy sum and made his way on foot. He traveled exclusively at night, which was natural enough, considering his vampyric status, and was quite adept at finding somewhere to take refuge during the daylight hours.

Wherever he went, however, he found it difficult to set down roots, for every place that he encountered seemed nothing more than a pale reflection of London. Never did he feel comfortable, nor did the suspicion with which he was regarded help significantly.

He had known a life of thievery for so long that he actually endeavored to try more legitimate endeavors for a time. He had a knack for tailoring and stitching, born from so many years of meticulously removing monograms from snatched handkerchiefs. He would set up a makeshift shop in the midst of busy markets and attempt to garner business, but people would steer clear of him. It was difficult to blame them, really. The fact that he was a Jew was off-putting to some of the less enlightened, but it did not help that he was only open for business during daylight hours when the sky was overcast and forbidding, and even then he would tend to stick to the shadows. Dressed in black, with a broad-brimmed hat, and hunched over like a great vulture, his was not a figure that encouraged a great deal of patronage. Yet though we can see him from the outside looking in, Fagin did not discern the same viewpoint from the inside looking out, and so it was that as more time passed, the more foul and darksome his mood became. He did not attribute his poor business to logical reasons, but instead to such motives as unreasoning hatred for the circumstances of his birth.

For much of the time, it was directed toward the rest of the world, but that only aggravated his inability to earn a living. It really didn't matter what part of England he was in, or Scotland, because geography and topography and accents might vary from place to place, but no matter where he went, no one who was not a criminal desired to do business with a glowering, black-clad man in the shadows.

With the abject failure of any legal pursuits, Fagin drifted back toward more illegal ones. But slowly he discovered that he had lost the taste for it. He had become long accustomed to using children as his cat's paws and thus not having to risk his own neck, and as his own neck had already been stretched once, he wasn't entirely anxious to risk a second, and possibly less fortuitous, engagement with the hangman.

So when the opportunities to relieve others of their handkerchiefs, purses, and other valuables presented themselves, he was lackluster in his endeavors, so much so that on two occasions he was actually spotted in the attempt by passersby or onlookers, and had to flee the scene before the authorities could be summoned.

Thus did Fagin, over a period of many months, find himself slipping deeper and deeper into despair and frustration, for he could not leave behind the life he had once had, but could not conceive of a new life that he could embrace.

It happened, then, that one night, so long after the encounter with Sanguine Harry that it seemed a lifetime ago—an odd happenstance, really, considering the number of lifetimes he had led—Fagin found himself walking a road that he realized, if followed to its inevitable conclusion, would return him to London. He wondered if sufficient time had passed so that such a return would not result in his being arrested or fled from, considering that he was believed long dead. After some deliberation, he came to the decision that he really didn't care.

And that was when he came to the startling realization that he did not care about anything.

This sudden revelation would have come across to another almost as a burst of light behind the eyes, so forceful was it.

Because he was what he was, though, it was instead an explosion of blackness, albeit in the same locale.

He stopped dead in his tracks, next to a large tree, and the night waited to hear what he had to say.

"Is this what it has come to then, after so many years? Me, what's got no true life to propel me, after all. Willpower is what fuels me, and if I don't have the will to go on, then how do I do it? What's the point of it all? Of any of it?"

Overcome by a sense of blinding ennui, he sank to the ground and stared at London in the distance, a great silhouette against the night sky, simultaneously seeming to beckon him and urging him to keep away.

"I miss the sun," he said, beset with melancholy, "and tire of the shadow. There are so many who are given greatness even though they are not entitled to it. And me, what has dwelt at the bottom of society's dregs for so long that I can't rightly guess what the top would even look like . . . what's the bloody point of it all, is what I'm sayin'. Look at me: a creature of the night, and people fear the night, but nobody fears old Fagin. Despise me, yes. Hate me. Want to see me strung up they did, and I was, and they cheered to see a ripe old villain get what's comin' to him. But why can't I be doin' more than that? Why can't I—?"

How long his discourse might have continued unabated is unknown. Instead, he was interrupted by a loud, brusque voice that said, "All right, Jew! On your feet!"

For an instant, Fagin froze, naturally believing that officers of the law had fallen upon him. A thorough terror of how Mr. Fang would react upon a general discovery that Fagin was close to London, having ignored his banishment, hurtled through him. He put his hands over his head and slowly turned, and then puzzlement registered upon his face as he saw a curious figure facing him.

It was an extraordinarily sharply dressed man, attired in a most splendid suit, and he cut an extraordinary figure in it. He wore a riding cape of deepest purple, which was an extraordinary fashion decision for him to make, considering that he seemed most unlikely to have any claim to royalty. His extraordinary suit was similarly well turned out, and the one allowance made for his environment was that there was dirt on the rims of his boots. Even the boots were extraordinary, of fine black leather, and Fagin regarded him with a sideways cock of the head and arched eyebrow. Before he could stop himself, Fagin breathed, "Extraordinary."

"Indeed," the man said. He was holding a pistol on Fagin, but Fagin paid it no mind.

"Who might you be, my dear?" Fagin inquired.

"I," said the gunman, "am giving you the *extraordinary* honor of being robbed by none other than the renowned highwayman, Jack Sheppard. Now"—and he waved his pistol impatiently—"I'll be havin' your purse."

"Jack . . . Sheppard?" Fagin said the name slowly to make certain that he had heard it properly. "Jack Sheppard the highwayman died over a century ago. Executed for his crimes. You claim to be he?"

"I do. Now . . ."—he waved the pistol again—"I should hate to waste a shot on you, but I will if you continue to prolong this encounter."

Although the highwayman did not notice it, Fagin's nostrils flared as he took in the scent of the man facing him. The logical assumption to make was that this man, Sheppard, was a creature similar to Fagin, a vampyre. Or perhaps some other manner of ambulatory corpse, if such there was. But such creatures produce an aroma that is distinctive to others of the undead, for in truth, they are really nothing more than slowly rotting meat, and thus can be perceived as such by those with the peculiarly sharp olfactory senses that vampyres possess. Furthermore, human beings perspire, another scent that Fagin would easily be able to perceive and thus determine whether he was truly looking at one of his own kind.

He was quickly able to determine that he was not, for the highwayman produced the sort of aromas typical for humans, and none of those that the undead possessed.

"You are Jack Sheppard in name only," said Fagin. "You are not truly he."

For the first time, the highwayman's veneer of suavity seemed to slip a notch or two. "Are you feeble-minded? Of course, I'm not the *original*. But," he said with determination, "I have read of him, and know of him, and am keeping his legacy alive."

"His . . . *legacy*." It had never been a word that Fagin would have associated with those that practiced his particular calling, but it fascinated him. "A *legacy*. I never considered such a thing. Legacies . . . why, they're for those what are looking to see somethin' lastin' beyond their lifetimes, are they not?" He was talking more to himself than to the highwayman. "But that makes so much sense, does it not, now? When one is faced with endless nights, why, then it's just a matter of trying to get through every one of 'em. But if one sees the cutoff in the road, one thinks beyond one's own immediate needs. One seeks immortality in name, as body cannot provide it. But immortality in mind distracts from what the name can achieve."

"What in God's name are you blathering about?" The highwayman had completely lost his patience as well as his panache. "Right, then. I have had more than enough of this nonsense."

He approached Fagin quickly, assuming that Fagin could not possibly present any manner of threat. He grabbed Fagin by the throat and put the gun against the older man's skull, cocking the hammer. "I am going to count to three," he said.

"No need for that, my dear," said Fagin, and his hand moved so quickly that Jack Sheppard, or whatever his true name might have been, never saw it. All he knew was that one moment the gun was in his hand, and then it was in Fagin's. Had he been at all aware of what he was faced with, he would have backed off, backed away, and perhaps there would have been an outside chance that Fagin might have let him escape. Instead, he made a terrible mistake and lunged for the pistol that Fagin was holding securely. He grabbed the barrel, yanking upward, and the hammer slammed home. Its fatal lead discharged and lodged itself straightaway into Jack Sheppard's stomach.

He let out an alarmed shriek of pain and stumbled backward, banging into a crooked tree and sliding to the ground. His eyes were wide with horror, and he clutched at his gut, feeling the spreading warmth against it. "Am . . . am I killed?" he managed to say, and with all of his bravado gone, he sounded as if he were little more than a child.

"Aye, my dear, I'm afraid so," said Fagin, and his hands were clasping and unclasping rapidly. "And sad to say, because it's a shot to the stomach, you won't have a quick or easy time of it. A day, two, maybe three of slow agony, and there's nothing to be done." He licked his lips hungrily. "You know what a drunkard is, Jack, me boy?"

"What? I . . ." He shook his head, uncomprehending.

"A drunkard is him what can't help himself. What drinks too much for his own good. It's a sad, sad thing, being unable to control oneself. And the only way to stop being that way . . . is to stop being that way."

"Oh my God . . . oh my God, I'm shot . . . I . . . I'm going to die . . . ."

"Yes, yes, we've established that, my dear," said Fagin with an impressive attempt at sympathy that still fell well short of the genuine article. "But we're on to *my* problems now, and my problem . . . I was a drunkard of a sort, ya see. I had my own drink that I craved, and I didn't like what drinkin' it did to me, and what it did to others. You might believe an old criminal like me, that I'd have no conscience, but that's wrong thinkin', it is. Just wrong. I have a conscience, I does, and a heart, even if it is a withered and useless thing, and so I quit. I quit, even though every single night without it pained me. My kind, we don't need the drink to survive, not really. Just to thrive and be what nature—or unnature, I'm thinkin'—wants us to be.

"But if I'm goin' to leave a legacy, then I'm goin' to have to be so much more than I am, and I can't do that without your help, I'm afraid, Jack." His body was trembling with the need that he had long ago thought he could control. But the smell of the blood that was seeping from Jack's wound was simply irresistible. It pervaded his very being, became more than he could stand, and really, why should he have to stand it? Why turn away from what he was clearly meant to be? Certainly there was no answer to this question that presented itself to him, although admittedly he did not strive too greatly to discern it. He returned his attention to the catalyst of his epiphany. "But if it's of any consolation to you, why . . . in your helpin' me, I'm goin' to be able to help you as well."

"You . . . you will . . .?" His voice stirred with the slightest glimmer of hope that Fagin seemed to be presenting to him. "How . . . ?"

"By making your death quick."

Fagin's eyes turned a fiery red with bloodlust, and Jack Sheppard let out a scream of terror that accomplished nothing except to cause Fagin to leap forward like a great beast of the jungle. He landed upon Jack, who tried to bring up his arms to fend him off, but poor Jack had absolutely no chance. With a roar of boundless triumph, unleashing the creature that had been stymied within him through sheer willpower and what seemed an eternity of thwarted desire, Fagin sank his fangs into Jack's throat and drained him. The blood cascaded over Fagin's tongue and down his throat, and strength and power began to ripple through him. He drank and drank until there was not a drop of blood left in the highwayman's body. Fagin stood fully upright for what seemed the first time in decades, which it might well have been, as his natural posture tended toward the hunch or the crouch. His shoulders were square, his chin thrust forward proudly. He threw back his head and unleashed a noise that was a combination of a howl and a roar, and wolves who heard it miles away returned the salutation, whereas any domesticated dogs whimpered and hid, being thus reminded that they were mere shadows of the wild and truly terrifying creatures that still roamed the night.

"Why," whispered Fagin, once the echoes of his triumphant bellow had faded, "did I deprive myself of this . . . this feast? What madness possessed me?" He received no answer as there were none to provide it, nor would he have listened even if it had been given.

Feeling energized, he looked down at the body on the ground. A benefit of draining Jack so thoroughly was that it ceased the spreading of blood from the gut wound, and because it had been flowing quite slowly to begin with, the result was that although his shirt was quite ruined, the magnificent embroidered vest he had been wearing was largely unmolested, save for the small hole as a result of the pistol's discharge.

Fagin moved quickly, stripping the highwayman of his fine garments. He kept his own shirt, although resolving to find something far grander later, and within minutes had attired himself in the late Jack Sheppard's clothing.

He tossed his old clothes upon Jack's corpse, not bothering to dress him in them. When daylight reared its illuminated head once more, someone would come across his body and notify the locals, and it would be assumed that someone had accosted him, killed him, and stripped him of his clothes in search of valuables. Thus would the highwayman be buried in some deserved pauper's grave, or perhaps cremated, taking with him the last bit of Fagin that existed in the world.

Satisfied with the night's work, Fagin turned his back on the deceased and faced London, calling to it from the distance. "I hear you, my beauty," said he, "and will heed your call. And by all the gods below, I shall give them something to talk about and remember me by, yes, I will."

He started moving quickly down the road, but his enthusiasm was so overwhelming, and the youthful blood pounding within him so intoxicating, that in short order mere walking was insufficient to contain him. A walk became a trot and then a run, and soon even gravity could not contain him. He started leaping down the road, as graceful as a gazelle, covering many yards with each stride, as if the earth had only a passing claim upon him.

Thus did Fagin, a true bounder if ever there was, reach London, and waste no time in making a name for himself.

And so now do we bring our villain current with the events that have been otherwise transpiring, and we find ourselves in one chill night, focusing on a young actress named Celia Dugan who has just performed in a penny dreadful theatrical detailing—as coincidence would have it—the criminal career of Jack Sheppard, being the original, gone more than a century, and not the thoroughly unmemorable and unmourned version who had been dispatched truly by his own hand and thundering incompetence weeks ago.

Celia drew her shawl tightly around herself, for it was a chill night, and her purse was dangling from her wrist. She was passing a low building, and suddenly she heard a startling and chilling cackle, and she looked up and saw a darkened figure crouching atop the roof. For a moment, she was certain that she was about to witness a suicide, and she called out to him, "Wait! Do not! Matters cannot be as bad as all that!"

Matters indeed could be that bad, but for her, not the figure.

She shrieked as he leaped from the rooftop, cape fluttering around him, falling four stories, and landing directly in front of her. He, by all rights, should have been injured or perhaps even dead. Instead, he clutched at her and groped her, laughing dementedly the entire time, grabbing her purse and snatching her valuables before yanking her arm toward his mouth and starting to chew on it. His teeth punctured the skin, not too deeply, but enough that blood began to flow, and he licked at it eagerly.

"Stop! Get away!" shrieked Celia, and she pummeled at him with her small fists, which did nothing to dissuade him. Then he tore his lips away from her arm, and his mouth was smeared with blood, and his eyes were red and wild. Terrified, she tried to pull away.

"Jack thanksss you," he hissed, and then he released her. As she had been endeavoring to get clear of him, this resulted in her losing her balance and falling to the street. She watched in wide-eyed amazement as he turned from her and vaulted straight up to another rooftop, as if he were a marionette being yanked skyward by a great, unseen puppeteer. He landed upon the rooftop, an impossible leap completed with inhuman ease, tossed off a wave, and vanished into the darkness, taking his crazed laughter with him.

"Spring-Heeled Jack," whispered Celia. She was holding her gloved hand against the wound she had sustained, and the bleeding was already slowing and would soon stop. "My God, that was Spring-Heeled Jack. I thought he was a . . . a legend."

And even though he was already two rooftops away, Jack heard her, and inwardly danced with joy.

-᚛ ✳ ᚜-

He leaped from rooftop to rooftop, London spread out below him, his town, all his for the taking. He reveled in his strength, in his audacity, in his . . . dared he say it himself? Why not? "Legend," he said. "I am legend. I am—"

He never saw the arm that emerged from the shadows, straight and hard as a log, that caught him across the face. He had been moving so quickly that it knocked him completely off his feet, and he landed hard on the rooftop. The world spun around him for a moment and then righted itself.

A figure stepped out of the shadows and glared down at him.

"Fang," whispered Spring-Heeled Jack, and quickly he clambered to his feet. "I . . . that is to say . . . I didn't—"

"Shut up, Fagin," said Mr. Fang, and Fagin promptly did so. "Did you think I would not know it was you? Did you think I would not figure out that Spring-Heeled Jack, bounding around London with his flaming red hair and crimson eyes and snatching purses and handkerchiefs . . . did you think I would not figure out that it was you?" When Fagin did not respond immediately, Fang prompted, "*Well?*"

"You, ah . . . told me to shut up, so I wasn't rightly sure if respondin' was—"

"Never mind," said Fang impatiently. He folded his arms and looked Fagin up and down, like a scientist scrutinizing a disease under a microscope lens. "At least," he said finally, "you are doing something with your potential. I will admit that much. This business of not drinking blood . . . it was ridiculous."

"How did ye know I was not drinkin' blood?"

"My spies are everywhere, Fagin. There is nothing I don't know. Except, perhaps, what it was that you were trying to prove."

"Somethin'. But truly, my dear, I can't remember what it might have been. The foolishness is washed away by the cleansin' power of the crimson ichor that nourishes all our kind. "

And Fang actually smiled at that and, to Fagin's astonishment, threw wide his arms. "Embrace me, then, brother, as you have embraced your heritage, for both of us have been too far apart for too long."

Fagin stared at him, drawing his cape more tightly around him, like a burial shroud.

"How now?" said Fang. He continued to stand there with his arms spread wide, as if he were being crucified, an ironic similarity when one considers it. "You would reject my overture?"

"It is not the overture that concerns me, brother," said Fagin slowly, "but rather the main event. You want something of me."

"How can you say that?" said Fang, looking abashed.

"It is not that great a difficulty, my dear. My lips move; my tongue forms the sounds."

"I am shocked!"

"And I am waiting," Fagin rejoined. "Mistake me not for the thing I was. No longer Fagin or even Reuben am I, but Jack, Spring-Heeled Jack, and I am not a fool and will not be treated as such."

Mr. Fang's mood darkened then, and for perhaps the first time in their association, he perceived Fagin as something he never had before: a threat. He raised a cautioning finger then, and his voice dropped to its customary growl, bereft of anything approaching humanity. "Have a care, 'Jack.' Newly revitalized you may be, and that's all to the good. But my organization is not to be trifled with, and if you endeavor to come to a head with me or mine, it will not end well for you."

"Or perhaps the same might be said of you," said Fagin, but there was more barley than beef in his stew, for he knew that Mr. Fang was speaking truly of the breadth and depth of his influence and power. "But let this reunion not be a time of threats. Rather, tell me, brother, for old time's sake . . . what would you have of me?"

"Your assistance."

"In exchange for . . .?"

"My gratitude."

"Which is worth more to me than all the riches in London," said Fagin expansively, for that was the sort of mood that he was in. "Say on, then; I am listening."

Fang, his hands draped behind his back, began to walk in a slowly and gradually diminishing circle upon the rooftop. "We seek a pair of individuals," said he, "a young boy and a girl who shall be a woman ere long. The latter is of greater interest than the former."

"Meaning?"

"Meaning if you can only acquire one, she is the more important."

"Indeed. And who would they be?"

"The boy is Abraham Van Helsing."

"Van Helsing?" Fagin spat out the name. "Son of the hunter, I take it?"

"The very same."

Fagin growled in disgust. "If someone of such infamous name as Van Helsing is of lesser interest, who, I must wonder, is of greater?"

Mr. Fang paused, as if uncertain whether total candor were advisable under the circumstances, and then seemed to shrug and yielded to the inevitable. "Alexandrina Victoria."

"Named after the princess?" asked Fagin, not yet understanding. But then he saw the impatient look in Mr. Fang's face, and his eyes widened. "Ah."

"Yes."

"You wish to mount an assault on Buckingham?"

"That would be a pointless endeavor," said Mr. Fang, "as she is not there."

"Not there? How can that be? Her mother—"

"She is not there. If you trust nothing else I say, trust that."

"Then I do not see the problem."

"She is at a nun's haven called Carfax Abbey."

"I see the problem," said Fagin immediately.

"They fled there, in the company of a young thief. Harry was able to trace them there because he had the boy's scent, and there is no greater tracker than Sanguine Harry. But he reached the doors and was thwarted. The place," said Mr. Fang, his face twisting into a mask of disgust, "reeks of godliness. Crosses everywhere. A bastion of Christianity. Plus, naturally, he would have to be invited to enter, and that is not bound to happen anytime soon. But"—and he paused for dramatic emphasis— "of what consequence could the religious aspects possibly be to one of your . . . persuasion."

"My part in this becomes clear," said Fagin slowly.

Mr. Fang nodded, clearly pleased that Fagin comprehended. "You, who have never bowed to the cross . . . who have never taken communion . . . who have never, at any time, taken Jesus into your heart . . . you will be able to enter the abbey with no difficulty. Remove the crosses so that they do not repel us. Defile, deconsecrate it. Thus will we be able to enter and carry her off."

"One small problem," said Fagin. "Even I cannot go where I am not invited."

"Ah," said Fang, "and again, that is where you are uniquely suited to the task. You may say that you are Fagin no longer, but your old identity will serve you in good stead. All you need do is convince the young boy thief whom I mentioned to do you that particular service, and then you can enter and do as you please."

"Why should he feel inclined to do so?"

"Because," said Mr. Fang, "he will be overjoyed to see that his old teacher and mentor is, in fact, alive, having escaped the hangman's noose. By the time he questions, it will be too late."

"Of whom do you—?" And then, somehow, he intuited of whom Mr. Fang was speaking. "Not . . . the Artful?"

"His very same self," said Mr. Fang. "That will be a worthy reunion, do you not think so?"

"Yes," said Spring-Heeled Jack—previously Fagin, née Reuben—a small smile on his lips. "A very worthy one indeed. Very well then, brother: I shall now accept your embrace, if you still feel inclined to provide it."

"Absolutely, brother," replied Mr. Fang, and the two vampyres threw their arms around each other, patting one another on the back and both trying to figure out just how and when they could drive stakes into those respective backs.

TEN

In Which are Presented Drina's Confession,
the Artful's Terrible Mistake, and the Tragic
Outcome That Results

The Mother Abbess of Carfax Abbey studied the young woman seated in front of her, the young woman who had asked specifically for and received a private meeting with the abbess—just the two of them, bereft of both other nuns and the lads with whom she had arrived at the abbey; the abbess was clearly trying to determine whether the girl was out of her mind or engaged in some sort of bizarre jest, perhaps at the instigation of the lads who had accompanied her.

The abbess knew little of what the lad, Bram, was capable of, for he was new to her, but she remembered the redoubtable Mr. Dawkins from years back and knew that he was perfectly capable of putting the girl up to this absurdity for some reason known only to him. Some sort of elaborate confidence plan in which the good sisters were mere pawns.

The abbess sat back in her chair, her fingers steepled. "I still remember," she said, "when young Mr. Dawkins first arrived on our doorstep."

Drina looked slightly confused, because the Mother's words had absolutely nothing to do with what she had just told her. But she respected the wisdom of the older woman, and responded accordingly: "Do you?"

"I do indeed. He had been engaged in a spot of burglary. He had sustained a wound upon his upper arm when whoever's home he had been involved in stealing from arrived prematurely and used him for target practice as he escaped. The wound had become severely inflamed, and he was terrified he would lose the arm entirely, if not his life. The idea of going to a doctor was anathema to him, and he knew that we practiced healing arts here, so he arrived at the abbey in desperation, spouting some nonsense story about having been the victim of a hunting accident."

"He robbed houses?" said Drina, unable to keep the distaste from her voice.

"You knew him to be a thief already, did you not?"

Drina shifted uncomfortably in her chair. "Of handkerchiefs and such. A pickpocket. That somehow seems . . . I don't know . . . less severe than breaking into someone's home . . . ."

"Theft is theft, my dear. Unacceptable behavior knows no degrees," said the abbess primly. "We endeavored to impart that lesson upon young Mr. Dawkins during the time that we nursed him back to health, and hoped that when we sent him back out into the world, it would be as a penitent. That was some years ago, though, and now he shows up here with a young boy spouting stories about monsters, and you . . . ." She shook her head.

"You do not believe me?" Drina was surprised. The notion that the abbess would not accept her word had never occurred to her. "That I am who I say I am?"

"That you are the Princess Alexandrina Victoria?" She arched a graying eyebrow. "Which is the more likely? That you are the princess on a holiday with a thief and a demented boy? Or that you are either delusional or likewise a thief with some greater scheme in mind?"

Slowly Drina rose to her feet, and she reached into the folds of her coat. Something about her seemed to change; it was as if she were growing taller, her shoulders squaring, and her eyes hardening like unto steel. There were several round, thick pillar candles situated upon the desk, their flickering wicks providing the minimal illumination in the room. Drina leaned forward and blew out one of the candles. "What are you doing?" demanded the abbess.

From within her interior pockets, Drina produced a round wooden stamp. Fortunately, it was not so overly large that she had been unable to keep it concealed within the folds of her dress. The handle was ornate, meticulously carved and inlaid with gold, and with a firm downward thrust of her arm she brought the stamp down into the top of the extinguished candle. The candle jolted slightly from the force of it, and when Drina spoke once more, there was none of the sound of the timid girl about her. "I brought this with me just in case I found myself in this position, wherein I had to prove my verity. Look at it," she said firmly in a commanding voice that seemed to fill the room. "Look at it and tell me what you see."

The Mother Abbess was tempted to scold her for her presumptuous tone, but something prompted her to hold her tongue, possibly the tone Drina used, similar—if not grander—than the one she used with the hansom cab driver. So instead she did as instructed, and her eyes widened when she saw the imprint lodged in the candle.

"Do you know what that is?" asked Drina. When the abbess simply nodded, Drina persisted, "Tell me. Say it aloud."

"The royal seal of England," she whispered.

"To produce a fake would be treason. I venture to say not even the most dedicated counterfeiter would dare attempt it."

"I daresay."

"Which, then, is the more likely?" said Drina, invoking the abbess's own logic. "That a demented young girl has managed somehow to acquire the royal seal? Or that I am who I say I am?"

The abbess looked too stunned to reply. Wasting no time, for there was none to waste, Drina demanded that a paper, envelope, writing implements, and sealing wax be brought to her. This the abbess did, never taking her eyes from the princess the entire time. Drina wrote quickly, then inserted the paper in the envelope and, using the wax and her seal, imprinted her crest upon it. She extended the envelope to the abbess. "Have this sent by messenger immediately to the archbishop," she ordered. "If there is any man holy enough to weed out vampyric influence in the upper reaches of government, it is he."

"And you believe there to be such?"

"Bram does," she said. "And if he declares it to be so, I have little reason to disbelieve him. He appears to be rather expert in these matters. You will do as I have requested?"

"Yes, of course, your . . . your Highness." The abbess sounded hesitant, all of her confidence seeming to have departed her. "Is that the accepted way by which to address you?"

Drina allowed herself a small smile. Part of her regretted the necessity of having been honest with the abbess over the truth of her identity. But there had been simply nothing else for it. She needed to get word back to Buckingham Palace, and this seemed the only means by which to do so.

She noticed that the abbess was no longer looking her directly in the eyes. Instead, she was glancing down or to the side; anywhere, really, save directly at her. "Do not cease looking upon me, I beg you," Drina said. "It is really unnecessary."

"As you wish," said the abbess, but it was clearly an effort for her. "May I ask you a question?"

"Is it why am I here rather than at the palace?"

"It would seem the natural matter to be curious about."

Drina shrugged. "What answer would satisfy you?"

"The truth, I would suspect."

"There is no one truth," replied Drina. "There is the truth of a daughter who had one too many fights with her mother. There is the truth of a future ruler who knows nothing of the people over whom she is supposed to rule. There is the truth of just being bored and wanting more from life than lessons and endless meetings. Take your pick."

"Perhaps I am old-fashioned," said the abbess, "but I do not consider it my place to make choices over why royalty does what it does. Does Jack know?"

"Jack?" She was confused at first but then realized. "Oh. The Artful. No, he has no idea. Nor do I desire him to know."

"Whyever not?"

"Because," she said, smiling wanly, "it is my belief—whether accurate or not—that Dodger likes me. It is a new sensation for me—to be liked because of *who* I am rather than *what* I am. I am not inclined to toss it away so quickly."

"As you wish." She tapped the note that was upon her desk. "It is a trifle late to send someone out now, but first thing in the morning, this will be heading to the palace."

"Thank you."

"Do you remember the way back to your bedchamber? Considering your status, I regret we do not have something more grand with which to accommodate you."

"I assure you that I'm quite satisfied with all that you have provided me. Any other reaction would be far less than gracious."

"You are royalty. You do not have to be gracious."

Drina shook her head. "If not us, then who?"

⊰ ✳ ⊱

Bram had quickly fallen asleep the moment his head touched the pillow. The Artful could not say that he was surprised; God only knew the strains that the lad had been under in recent days. From what Bram had told him, this was the first time since he had been snatched from out of his father's protection that he could actually rest. They were in an abbey, after all. There were crosses and crucifixes everywhere. If Dodger were to believe the legends of the vampyres, then certainly the abbey's decorations should be providing them with all the protection they required.

Yet it was still difficult for Dodger to fully believe the truth of what Bram had told him. Vampyres? In modern London? The entire idea seemed preposterous. Yes, he had witnessed events with his own eyes that seemed to provide proof, but could there not have been other explanations?

Except none were readily coming to mind.

Indeed, if anything, it caused his thoughts to flash back to the death of his mother at the hands of that slaughterer. It had all happened so quickly, and the Artful Dodger had always assumed that the attacker had some manner of knife that he had used to gouge his mother's throat.

Except . . . no blood.

There had been no blood from the wound, as if the assailant had somehow drained it all. At the time, the idea had seemed preposterous to Dodger. His mother's passing had been so traumatic that he had not really given much thought at all to the absence of blood from her body. Indeed, why should he have given that any thought? Was not the tragedy of her murder sufficient to grieve over? He was neither constable nor detective. It was not up to him to dwell on such matters.

Yet he could not help but dwell upon them now.

He found himself frustrated over the lack of firsthand knowledge he possessed in the matter of his mother's passing. There was, of course, an adult who had been present, but his neck had long ago been stretched. It had been quite some time— indeed, possibly never—since the Artful Dodger had thought nostalgically of the man named Fagin, but now he realized he could not help himself.

"Ahhh, Fagin," he said in a low, wistful voice. "If only I could talk with you for five minutes. Just five minutes would be enough. Should'a talked to you about it while ye were still here, but there's no use for it now, I suppose. But if I had a wish at my service, it would be to look into your ugly mug once more."

With that, his gaze drifted over toward the window and his heart nearly stopped, for Fagin, the one and only, was staring in at him from the darkness.

He would have let out a yell of shock, and had he done so, matters would have turned out very differently. Because such a yell would have awakened Bram, and had the lad woken up, things would have proceeded in a wholly different manner. But instead, his reaction took him in a totally opposite direction; he lost his voice entirely. His throat completely closed up, and when the word "Fagin!" escaped his lips, there was no voice accompanying it. It was, at most, a whisper, and even then not much of one.

For his part, however, Fagin was perfectly vocal. "Let me in! Have me in there, old boy!" Fagin called out through the closed window that muffled his voice. "It's not too much trouble to invite an old mate in, is it?"

The Artful had no idea just how much trouble such an invitation would in fact present. But he had no way of knowing and consequently said and did that which he really should not have.

He spoke out of habit in a whisper, because that was customarily how he conversed with Fagin. Many was the time when they were speaking of matters that it was preferable to hide from others, and so did he speak in that manner now. "Of course!" he said and immediately worked to slide the window open. It remained frozen shut at first, as if it somehow knew the disaster that would befall should Dodger manage to open it.

But Dodger redoubled his efforts, grunting and straining until finally he managed to shove the window open.

"Excellent, my dear! Ever so excellent!" chortled Fagin. As he weighed next to nothing, it took him almost no time at all to slide his body through the opening.

The Artful Dodger stepped back to provide him room, and even as he did so, his mind was racing in confusion. "How are you not dead? They said you was dead!"

"And I was told that you were transported to Australia. Yet here we both are," Fagin said easily.

"But how did you know I was here?" said Dodger. "After all this time . . . ."

"Ah, but what is time to beings such as you and I?" Fagin said. "We moves through time at our own pace, and let the rest of the world keep up. That's the way I see it, at any rate. Do you see it that way? Course ya do! Give us a hug, then!" To Dodger's surprise and considerable lack of comfort, Fagin then threw his arms around him and drew the youth to him. Dodger did not fight the embrace, but some part of him felt he should. "Here now, let me take a look at ye! Bedad, but it's good to see you, boy! You've grown, I swear ye have!"

"Well, it has been a few years, and blokes my age tend to do that," Dodger said carefully. He wasn't entirely sure why he was being cautious. Perhaps his common sense was belatedly trying to get through to him. "But what are you doin' here?"

"Why, I come to see you, of course."

"And how did ya know I was goin' to be here?" he asked again.

"Got me sources, I do. Now," he said, glancing around the room, "where's the princess?"

"The who?"

"The young woman you've been accompanyin'. Don't'cha know who she is?"

The Artful stared at him uncomprehendingly. "I got no idea what you're talkin' about."

It was at that particularly ill-timed moment that Bram Van Helsing woke up from his slumber. It is hard to say precisely what awoke him: some random noise, perhaps, or maybe a sense that jeopardy had entered the room and was waiting for him.

Whatever the reason, awake he did. He did not do so gradually, but instead all at once, as if he had been jabbed with a needle. He immediately blinked the vestiges of sleep from his eyes, and his gaze settled upon the newly arrived individual who was standing next to Dodger. Sensing the boy's sudden wakefulness, Fagin turned and looked straight at him.

Bram took one look at him and let out a startled yelp. Before either Fagin or Dodger could respond, Bram backed up so quickly that he banged into the small bunk upon which he had been lying. Even as he fought to right himself, his hand sought the recesses of his pocket, and seconds later a crucifix was dangling on a chain from his hand.

Dodger gaped at him as if he were out of his mind. "What's this about, then?" was all he could think to say.

In response, Bram pointed straight at Fagin. "Are you allies with this vampyre? Have I misjudged you?"

"Vampyre? Where?" He actually had to turn and see that Bram was indicating Fagin. "Bram, Fagin may be many things— a Jew, a thief, any number of things that no reasonable person would want any part of—but a vampyre? Why would ya think that?"

"Yes, boy," said Fagin as he slowly approached Bram, his near toothless mouth spread into a wide smile. "Why in the world would you think such things of me? I admit I may not be much to look at, but a creature of myth and legend?"

"Stay where you are!" Bram was frantically and determinedly searching through his jacket pocket.

"Now, now," Fagin said soothingly. "Certainly we can come to terms on—"

And then to Dodger's astonishment, Fagin threw up his arms defensively and let out a roar combined with an infuriated hissing sound, as if someone had just stepped upon a snake. Dodger stepped back in confusion, trying to determine what had elicited so strident a reaction.

With a glance, he saw that a Mogen David, a Jewish star, was now in Bram's hand. Several other religious icons were there as well, all dangling from the same chain, but it was the star that was foremost. "A cross will have no impact on him," said Bram, never coming close to displaying any manner of passion. "But the Jewish star that he once worshipped is another matter entirely. Isn't that right?"

He advanced upon Fagin, and Fagin backed up, still snarling and spitting. Dodger looked on in utter astonishment. For the first few moments, it was too much shock for Dodger to process. It was understandable. He was already having trouble adjusting to the notion that Fagin was alive at all, and now to have his very humanity questioned . . . it was all too much.

And yet the evidence was clear in front of him. Van Helsing advanced on Fagin, and Fagin could do nothing but back up, helpless in the presence of the religious icon.

For a moment, Dodger's mind went out of his present situation. Instead, for no reason that he could at first discern, his thoughts flew back to a time that seemed an age ago: the death of his mother. Her demise at the hands of that strange creature of a man and the way that all the blood had been drained from her body and, most significantly at that moment, the manner in which Fagin *just so happened* to be there at the moment of her demise.

He had always simply accepted that as the way things were. Fagin's presence had been a simple coincidence, nothing more. But if Bram was correct, if Fagin was indeed a creature of the night . . . .

The Artful stepped backward, his legs trembling. Fagin quickly pulled himself together, having backed far enough from the Mogen David to remove the impact it was having on him. "Dodger," he said, "my lovely boy . . . what is this youngster goin' on about? A vampyre? Certainly you cannot . . . ."

"Keep back!" Dodger shouted. He continued backward, distancing himself from Fagin until he was standing next to Bram. "It all makes sense! My senseless life finally makes sense! You were involved with me mum's death!"

"My dear boy . . ."

"Stop calling me that! I'm right! I know I'm right!"

Fagin appeared inclined to continue to defend his innocence, but then something within him seemed to change. It was as if he had suddenly decided that pretending to be human was simply a game that he was no longer interested in playing. He smiled and his fangs appeared, seeming to lengthen. "Your mother," he said simply, "was killed by me brother. Not an actual brother, ya understand, but one who was as close to me as any true brother of blood could hope to have been. He wanted you as well, ye know. But I stopped him. I did that for you because I saw the possibilities within you. So perhaps you might consider lookin' at me with something other than revulsion and bein' aware of just which side your bread is buttered on. Savvy?"

"Are you saying I should be . . . what? Grateful to you?"

"You might want to be considerin' it, aye."

"You were 'sponsible for me mum's death, and I'm supposed to be *grateful*?"

"Not responsible! Lord God, boy, could ye overstate things in any greater of a nature?" He gave an impatient wave. "Ya know what? I see no reason to keep discussin' this. I have concerns of a more immediate nature."

With that abrupt comment, Fagin simply turned away from Dodger, his greatcoat swirling around him, and headed out of the room.

Dodger and Bram exchanged confused looks, and then Bram cried out, "After him!"

Dodger was momentarily paralyzed by the events and revelations that had just been handed him. But Bram was already out the door, so he physically shook it off and sprinted after Fagin.

Fagin was striding down the hallway, his arms swinging back and forth casually as if he were on a stroll down the middle of a London street. From behind him, Dodger shouted, "Stop, you monster!"

"Cannot. Have things to do."

"I said *stop!*" The Artful grabbed his arm in a pointless endeavor to try and turn Fagin around to face him.

Fagin raised his arm, hauling the struggling Dodger off his feet. "You are becoming something of a pain, boy. And I have neither the time nor the patience for it."

With that comment, he swept his arm with ease, causing the Artful to lose his grip and fly through the air, crashing into a far wall and crumpling to the ground.

Just as that happened, the Mother Abbess stepped into view. She virtually shook with outrage when she saw the manner in which Fagin had just disposed of Dodger. "What is happening here!" she demanded. "How dare you! Leave here at once!"

Fagin paused, seemingly considering it. "There would have been a time," he said finally, "when I would have traded words with ye. But I'm on a schedule and that time has long passed."

He took two quick steps forward, grabbed the Mother Abbess by the head, and quickly twisted. Dodger cried out as he heard the snap of her neck from where he was seated. Fagin did not bother to drain her blood, but simply released her, allowing her lifeless body to fall to the ground.

The Artful sat there, stunned at what he had just witnessed. It was as if the world were spinning out of control. Fagin, apparently having forgotten what he had just done, kept on walking. As he disappeared around the far end of the hallway, Bram suddenly appeared, seemingly out of nowhere, at Dodger's shoulder. "We have to go. Now," he said firmly.

"No. We have to stop Fagin . . ."

"We can't. He's almost to the front door, and there can be only one reason for that."

"He's leaving?"

"No. He's going to invite other vampyres in. And once he does, they're going to tear through here, and anything living won't be when they're done."

The Artful managed to process this, and then he said, "Drina! We have to find Drina. Where did they put her?"

"We'll find her. Come along."

Fagin, meantime, had arrived at the great front door of the abbey. Along the way, he had made a point of pulling down any religious iconography from the walls, breaking those artifacts effortlessly. There was a large but simple lock barring the entrance, but Fagin removed the block of wood from its place with ease, tossing it aside to let it clatter to the floor. He yanked the doors both open, and they swung wide on their hinges. The creaking was like a rifle shot in the stillness.

"Come in," he called out into the darkness. "All within sound of my voice—I invite you in."

There were small glowing orbs in the darkness, and then they came forward as one. They were the eyes of the vampyres, glowing yellow or red, depending upon the vampyre's particular persuasion. There was audible snickering and guffawing from them as they approached, and moments later the front hallway was crowded with undead bodies looking around in curiosity. There was a large cross upon the wall that Fagin had missed, and several of the vampyres flinched back, hissing angrily.

"Ignore 'em," said Fagin, and reaching up, he grabbed the cross firmly and pulled it from the wall. With an indifferent heave, he tossed it aside. "These aren't the rays of the sun that burns us whether we like it or not. These are purely the subjects of our heads, is what they are. They hurt you only if you give them the ability to do so. Now"—and his voice dropped to low amusement—"find the girl. If you see the boys, capture or dispose of them. Either way. Do what ye will—it makes no difference to me."

The Artful and Bram were quickly making their way down the seemingly endless hallway that they had come upon. Several of the sisters were emerging from their cells, wearing their nightclothes. It struck Dodger that at that moment, they didn't seem like nuns at all. That indeed they were nothing more than scared and confused women. They demanded explanations from the two lads as to what was transpiring, but Bram's explanation—"We are under attack by vampyres"—hardly did anything to assuage their concerns or even answer their questions. Instead, they did what you would likely do: They expressed immediate disbelief and demanded that the boys stop playing games with them.

"This is no game," said Dodger. "A monster has already slain the Mother Abbess and I have no doubt the rest of you are—"

At that moment, one of the nuns cried out in alarm. The boys whirled and saw a cluster of vampyres at the far end of the hallway. Their eyes blazed red, and when they drew back their lips, their fangs were quite easy to see.

The nuns let out a collective shriek. The boys were mixed in with the group, and thus the vampyres did not initially see them. So it was that the boys sprinted away from the crowd of women, continuing down the corridor, their arms pumping furiously. Behind them, the terrified screams were transformed into agonies of pain, and the boys could actually hear the flesh being rent from their throats as the vampyres descended upon them en masse.

We're abandoning them. We're leaving them to the non-mercies of the vampyres. The truth of this reality hammered through Dodger, and all he could think of was his helplessness in the face of his mother's death so long ago. He had sworn when he grew up that he would never turn away from a woman being killed again, and yet now he was doing exactly that. Guilt rather than sweat seeped through his pores, but even as it did, he knew he had no choice. There were dozens of vampyres and only one of him (two, counting Bram). If he went back to fight on the nuns' behalf, he would assuredly die, and Drina would wind up dead as well. He had no choice but to run, and yet the lack of choice choked him.

The boys kept running, shouting Drina's name. There was no response. She might well have been on a different floor, and so they started up the nearest steps. They sprinted quickly and reached the upper floor.

Two vampyres were waiting for them.

Not "waiting," per se. It wasn't as if they were standing there prepared for the boys to show up. They were simply there, with blood-streaked lips, and their red eyes widened when they saw Dodger and Bram.

Bram immediately held up his crucifix and his Mogen David, playing it safe. The vampyres flinched back, but then one of them stubbornly moved forward as if fighting through the power that the cross wielded upon him. With a roar, he grabbed Dodger by the front of his shirt and started pulling the lad toward him.

The Artful fought back desperately. Bram shouted his name, and the vampyre and boy struggled back and forth, each striving for leverage—and the vampyre was winning. Dodger cried out, feeling himself being drawn toward the bloody fangs of the monster before him, and he had all but given up hope when suddenly Bram was there at Dodger's side. He jammed the crucifix directly into the vampyre's face, against his skin. There was a loud burning sound and a hissing, and the vampyre let out an agonized shriek. The stench of his breath washed over Dodger, and it was all the lad could do not to pass out. He needn't have worried about that, though, because the vampyre turned and flung Dodger as hard as he could.

The Artful braced himself, prepared to slam up against a wall. In this he was disappointed. There was no wall; instead, there was a wide window that overlooked nothing. Darkness yawned before him, and he cried out, arms waving frantically, as he plummeted.

He was fully prepared to hit ground and was thus rather astounded when he hit a tree instead. The branches seemed to reach out to him and grab him as if the tree were filled with living thought, which was, of course, just an imagining of his fevered brain. He crashed into the branches that, rather than support him, snapped rapidly at the impact. He continued to fall but was thrown about considerably, which served to lessen his velocity, so that was a help. Moments later he struck the ground, shaking every bone in his body. He lay there, gasping heavily, scarcely able to catch his breath.

It was then that he truly thought he'd pass out.

That was, until he heard afresh screams and shrieks from within the abbey. "Drina," he whispered, for that was his greatest concern, but he was also worried about the nuns. They had never done anything save support him and give him a place to live, and so naturally he was anxious for their welfare. But he knew in his heart that there was nothing left for him to worry about. There was no doubt in his mind that they were dead or dying. There were too many vampyres for anyone to deter. They were unleashing their bloodlust upon the helpless women, and there was nothing he could do about it.

He wanted to get up. He wanted to rush into the fray and battle back against them. In his mind's eye, he was a fully capable warrior, rising to the challenge, throwing himself into the war against them and triumphing over them, even though they outnumbered him at least twenty to one.

Whatever his dream, though, that was all it was.

In the reality in which he was anchored, Dodger allowed terror to wash over him. He drew his legs up, wrapped his arms around them, and lay there at the base of the tree, shaking uncontrollably. He heard every scream and simply lay there, helpless, overwhelmed by what he had learned and the evil that had been part of his life for so long, all without him knowing.

Fagin, the man who had been a substitute father to him—a teacher, a mentor—was part of some evil cadre of mythic characters and was partly responsible for the death of Dodger's mother. It was almost more than the boy could reasonably process. Not surprising, really. How would you fare, dear reader, after learning and seeing such things? As easy as it is to sit in harsh judgment upon Dodger's less than heroic actions, it seems fairly safe to say that you yourself would scarcely have done better.

Eventually the incessant screaming dwindled off. The nuns were dead. All of them. It was remotely possible that a few or perhaps only one or two of them might have found somewhere to hide that was beyond the vampyres' ability to find. The Artful doubted it, however. To his mind, they were all dead. All of them. Even Bram and Drina, for certainly they had been seeking her in order to kill her. Why else?

Why else?

He realized there had to be something else. Fagin had wanted Drina. But why? What was it about her that made her of particular interest? There had to be something, some reason. Fagin had said something about a princess . . . .

It was at that moment that Dodger heard something.

Footsteps approaching him, tentatively but firmly.

The Artful had no idea to whom they belonged, but he was hardly about to take a chance. He sat up, somewhat surprised that he was able to do so. He had not eliminated the possibility that he had broken something severe on the way down and was in fact paralyzed. But this was obviously not the case. He was banged up, scratched up, but otherwise he was in fine shape— the only paralysis had been that of spirit. He was able to marshal his strength, and he scrambled to hide amongst some nearby bushes. There he crouched, waiting, trying to ignore the fact that his legs were trembling. For all he knew, this was going to be his last moment on earth. The approaching feet would belong to a vampyre who would, in turn, be led right to him, courtesy of his sharp nostrils or some other advantage.

It took seemingly forever, and then a small, slight form emerged into the darkness, looking around desperately. "Dodger!" came a familiar voice.

"Bram!" Dodger could scarcely believe it. Immediately he emerged from the bush and, sure enough, there was Abraham Van Helsing, looking none the worse for wear.

Despite the seriousness of the situation and his general distaste for touching other people unless it entailed depriving them of their wallets, Dodger crossed quickly to Bram and embraced him. "I thought you were dead! There's no way you should not be dead!" Then he pushed the boy back several feet and regarded him suspiciously. "Are you dead? Did they transform you into—?" He could not bring himself to finish the sentence.

Bram shook his head and, despite the dire situation in which they found themselves, still could not help but smile. "I assure you I'm quite fit. They'd never have been able to change me that quickly."

"But how did you escape?"

"I retraced my steps, with the vampyres following but staying back because of the crucifix," he said. "I went back down the stairs and found an entrance into a wine cellar and availed myself of it before they could catch up with me. And there was an exit out from there into the fresh air."

"Why didn't they pursue you, though? I can't believe they just gave up . . . ."

"They didn't follow because they got what they wanted."

"What did they—?" Then the realization set in upon him, and his face went ashen. "Drina. They got Drina."

"Yes," said Bram grimly. "I was hiding in the shadows and saw Fagin drag her out, followed by his vampyric brethren."

"And did they—?" The Artful was unable even to finish the sentence, unwilling to put to voice his fear for what they had done to her.

At first, Bram didn't quite understand Dodger's hesitancy, but then he did. "Oh. No, no, they didn't slay her, if that's what you're worried about."

"They're vampyres. What else would I be worried about?"

"I think there's plenty to worry about, starting with what they are doing to her, whatever that is." He frowned. "It was strange, the way they referred to her, though."

"Referred to her?" Dodger didn't understand. "How did they refer to her?"

"They kept calling her 'your Highness.' They did it mockingly, of course. They were making fun of her. But still: 'Right this way, your Highness. Best not struggle, your Highness.' They kept saying things like that to her. I mean . . ." He shook his head, clearly bewildered. "I don't pretend to know royalty in various countries. There's no way I could keep track of them. But there's no way she's a queen, is there?"

"We don't have a queen," said Dodger. "I mean, all right, yes, we do. I guess. We have the Princess Victoria, and she has a daughter who will be the queen when she's eighteen. Right now she's—I don't know—sixteen or seventeen."

"What's the princess's name? The young princess."

"Also Victoria. Alexandrina Victor—"

His voice trailed off, and for a long moment silence hung like a shroud between them.

"Bugger all," said Dodger in a low, trembling voice. "You don't think that she's . . . I mean, it's not possible, is it . . .?"

"Maybe not," said Bram, "but the vampyres definitely think so. They think they've got their hands on the next ruler of England."

The Artful was having extreme trouble processing it. For a moment, he was actually having difficulty standing, but that could be based on the fact that he had but recently descended from the abbey by way of being thrown out a window. "What do we do? What can we do?"

"We go after her," said Bram. "Just as we would if she were just some ordinary girl. Princess or no, we do what any decent and God-fearing person would do. We track them down and rescue her and show the vampyres that they aren't allowed to do this kind of thing."

"You're insane," Dodger said incredulously. "You saw what they are, what they can do. They can do whatever they want to whomever they want. Who are you and me to tell them otherwise, eh?"

"We are the forces for right. And if we don't, no one else will."

There were so many things that Dodger wanted to say in response to that. He wanted to question the boy's sanity. He wanted to tell Bram to sod off. He wanted to start walking and never look back. He wanted to distance himself from all this insanity as fast and as far as he possibly could.

All this and much more went through his mind.

Then he adjusted his hat and said, "Let's go find her, then."

ELEVEN

In Which the Baker Street Irregulars are
Pressed Into Service Along With an Old Friend

M r. Brownlow had never been the most imaginative of men, and so it was that when he went to sleep that night, he had never in his remotest dreams come up with the notion that something would disturb him and roust him from his slumber, and so it was that when he was in fact thrown from his slumbers by the pounding at his front door, it was a severely disconcerting sensation and one that he had no desire to repeat at any time in the near or even far future.

The sharp, disturbing, and urgent pounding at the door of the estate was more than enough to roust the people residing within. Mr. Brownlow was heading down the stairs, but the butler, performing his customary job duties, reached the door first. "I'll attend to it, sir," he said, still rubbing sleep from his eyes. "It's the middle of the night; you've no business being awake."

"When someone deems it acceptable to come pounding at one's doors at all hours of the morning, it seems my business cannot be helped," said Brownlow. However, he remained where he was upon the stairs that led down to the main hall, waiting to see who was calling at such an hour.

The butler shuffled to the door. He was an elderly gentleman, having been in Mr. Brownlow's employ to such a ripe age that one would think he was, by this point, entitled to the services of a butler himself. Yet he served because that was what he had been trained to do, and so he did.

He pulled open the door, and for just a moment fear flitted through his still groggy brain. He had not bothered to ask who was there; it might be some criminal who was intending to perform some manner of dire harm to whomever answered their summons. Yet it was one of those moments where he was already in motion and could not restrain himself from opening the door so as to see who was there.

It was most definitely two presences that he was not expecting. One was a teen boy with a tall hat set jauntily on his head. The other was a child with the most serious mien he had ever seen on a young man.

The older boy was all business. "We're here to see Oliver," he said. "He still lives here? You didn't just throw him out, did you?"

"What?" The butler stared in confusion and then turned to Mr. Brownlow. "What?" he said again.

"What is your interest in Oliver?" asked Mr. Brownlow. Still standing perched at the top of the steps, he descended several in order to convey the idea that, at the very least, his interest was engaged.

"We need his help."

"How did you know he was here?"

The older boy made a dismissive noise. "I keep up on the whereabouts of all me former associates. Just the way I operate."

"Wait a moment," said Mr. Brownlow. He advanced more steps so that he was now merely a full man's height taller than his visitors. "I know you. I've seen you in court some years back."

"You have quite the memory, sir."

"I remember the clothes. You were a young man wearing men's clothing that was far too big on you. You are wearing the same outfit. You just seem to have grown into it somewhat."

"An eye for fashion you have, and good on you for that. But much as I'd love to discuss this with you at great length, we're in a bit of a hurry."

"What's your name?"

The boy seemed to hesitate, and then bowed and said, "Jack Dawkins, at your service, sir."

Mr. Brownlow assumed that to be a false name since the boy had hesitated before saying it, causing Brownlow to conclude that he had a real name he wished to keep to himself. That was acceptable to Brownlow; it did not matter to him what the lad's true name was, so long as he departed the premises with all due speed. Indeed, he briefly considered simply closing the door in the boy's face and being done with him, but quickly he dismissed the notion for two reasons. The first is that the boy would doubtless just start pounding again. And second, it wasn't exactly polite. "What can I do for you, Mr. Dawkins?"

"I'm here t'speak to Oliver, if you'd be so kind."

"I think I would rather not be so kind," replied Brownlow. "He does not need to be disturbed by random boys at such an ungodly hour as this."

"Random boys!" said Dawkins, his voice quivering with indignity. "Thanks to this random boy, you met Oliver in the first place. If it weren't for me, you'd never have seen him, never brought him to this fine mansion out in the—"

"Wait a moment," said Brownlow. "I met Oliver when I mistakenly thought he picked my pocket. Are you saying *you* were the actual thief?"

Dawkins started to respond readily but then stopped. Different expressions warred upon his face before he finally settled for an abashed grin. "I obviously didn't plan this through too well . . . ."

"You're fortunate I don't have you arrested!"

Before Dawkins could reply, the youngster with him stepped forward. "Sir, none of this matters," a statement that, coming from a child, seemed impossibly serious—and yet, Brownlow found himself intrigued. The boy continued, "We are here because we need a fast ride back to London. That is literally all we require. The Artful . . . Mister Dawkins here,"—and he gestured toward the older lad—"he recalled that you had a house in these parts and thought you might be able to aid us in this matter."

"And why would I do that? Why would I do anything other than have my man see you back into the streets where you belong?"

"Because," said the young man, "vampyres have kidnapped the future queen of England. We discerned from things they said that they were returning to London, but we have no idea where they have taken her and are hoping that we can catch up with them, find her, and save your nation's future."

Unsurprisingly, Brownlow had no ready answer for that. "What?" He looked to Dawkins, who simply nodded, although he rolled his eyes as he did so. It was evident that he was unenthused about the young man's reply but did not consider it his place to gainsay him. "Is he serious?"

"Completely," said Dawkins. "We were hoping that Oliver might be able t'arrange transit for us back to London."

For a long moment, he stared at them silently. Then in a loud, firm voice, he said, "Frost."

Frost, who happened to be the butler, turned and looked at his master. "Yes, sir?"

"Awaken Quinn. Have him ready the carriage and bring these two lads wherever they need to go."

Frost's eyes widened in surprise. "Excuse me, sir?"

"You are excused, but I am reasonably certain you heard me."

"Sir, are you sure? This . . ." He paused, gesturing toward the two lads. "This tale they're spinning—it's utter nonsense."

"Yes, it is. But what if it is truth?"

"Truth?"

"If it is true, and the young Princess Victoria is indeed in trouble, and these lads can attend to it, then they should be allowed to do so. And what citizens of England would we be if we stood in their way or impeded them?"

The butler had no ready answer for that—aloud, that is. His face spoke volumes, though, and it wasn't hard to translate his expression to answer his master's question with "Bloody sane ones, sir."

Even the older boy, Dawkins, seemed surprised. "I don't know what to say, sir."

"I believe the customary reply is 'Thank you.' But I need a promise from you before I lend you my services."

"Anything, sir."

"You," he said firmly, "are never again to approach Oliver for any service, under any circumstance. Ever. Is that clear?"

"Crystal, sir," said Dawkins, and he even gave a slight bow.

"See to it, Frost." That was clearly Brownlow's last comment on the topic, but as he headed back up the stairs, apparently young Mr. Dawkins could not restrain himself.

"Mr. Brownlow?"

Brownlow turned on the stairs and stared down at him, waiting for the next words to come from the teenager's mouth. It appeared at first that Dawkins was having difficulty thinking of those next words, but finally he spoke them. "Why? Why did you believe? I mean, I had an entire fake story to tell you. Wasn't expectin' this one," he said, gesturing toward the younger lad, "to opt to be so damned honest. And yet he tells you the entire truth, and you believe it, as unlikely as it sounds . . . ."

"I don't believe it," said Brownlow. "It is completely preposterous. I am ninety-nine percent certain that this is some pure feat of imagination. On the other hand, however, that leaves the faint one percent to allow for the possibility that you are speaking the truth. And if that is the case, then a gentleman cannot ignore it. Quinn is quite the skilled driver, and he will come with you to serve your needs during the 'emergency', which is likely not happening at all. If it is, however, then do give the young princess my regards when you see her. I had the occasion to meet her once when she was about ten. She was polite but sad, which is unfortunately about all that could be expected under her personal situation. You will see to that, will you not?"

The boys both nodded.

"Off with you, then," said Brownlow, and he continued upstairs.

As he walked down the hallway, a bedroom door opened. A young man was standing there, rubbing his eyes. "What is the matter, sir?"

"Nothing you need worry yourself over, Oliver. Go back to sleep."

"But—"

Brownlow rested an affectionate hand on his shoulder. "Oliver, we moved out here because I wanted to get you out of London and into a fresh, new environment."

"I know." The boy was staring at him with a distinct lack of comprehension. "What does that have to do with everyone being up so early?"

For a long moment, Brownlow stood there, all the possible responses warring within his head. Then he gave the small smile that Oliver knew so well. "Not a blessed thing. Return to bed. I know I'm going to."

"All right," said Oliver Twist, uncertain of what had just transpired, but knowing that if Mr. Brownlow was confident with the situation, then everything must be all right.

Oliver returned to his bedroom and lay down. There he remained for long minutes, his mind awhirl. There had been someone at the front door, of that he was quite certain. One of the voices had even sounded faintly familiar, but he could not be sure of the individual's identity. And it was obvious that, whoever it was, Mr. Brownlow didn't want him to have anything to do with him.

Who could it have been, though?

At that moment, he heard the sound of hoof beats. Whoever it was, that person was moving quite quickly.

Immediately Oliver was out of bed, his bedclothes swirling around his legs. He went to the window just in time to see Mr. Brownlow's horse and carriage go charging by. He had no idea who was in it, however. Mr. Brownlow it was not, though. He had told Oliver he was returning to sleep, and never in their relationship had Mr. Brownlow had cause to lie to him, so Oliver fully expected that now was not the time that he was going to start. But that left the question of who was in the coach?

He started to turn and head for the door but then stopped. Brownlow obviously knew who it was, and as he hadn't mentioned it to Oliver, he obviously did not want the lad to know. If that was the case, well . . . that was that. For Oliver did not have the sort of disposition that led him to challenge those who were above him. Indeed, the last time he had, daring to ask for more food, it had sent all manner of living hell into motion. He did not expect Brownlow to subject him to a similar punishment, but nevertheless it would be fair to say that he had learned his lesson.

Oliver returned to bed.

❧ ✳ ❧

Quinn was not what Dodger had expected. He didn't seem inclined to speak about his background, but he came across as being a former member of the army. Or perhaps a pirate, although Dodger had to admit he was being rather fanciful in that imagining . . . although he further had to admit that tonight had been more fanciful than any he had experienced previously. Regardless, Quinn was square built, with thick grayish muttonchops, and when he spoke, which was infrequent, he did so with a low and slightly impatient growl. He acted deferentially to Dodger and Bram because he had been told to do so, but apparently he had also been told of the specifics of their mission and so regarded them with a healthy dose of doubt.

And who could blame him? The Artful certainly could not.

"Where are we going again?" said Bram as the coach rattled around them. It was not the fanciest means of transportation existent, but at least it was going to get them where they needed to be, wherever that was. "You don't know where Drina is, do you?"

"No," said Dodger grimly. "But I'll wager the vampyres do."

"And where are we going to find them? Do you have any idea where they're hiding?"

"None." The Artful's mouth grew tight. "However, I have an idea who can help us in that matter."

"Who?"

"Wiggins."

"Who's Wiggins?"

"It changes," said Dodger. "'Wiggins' is what they call whoever's in charge. Face keeps changin'. This is the second one I know of."

"Should I be worried that I have no idea what you're talking about?"

"We're goin' to Baker Street," said Dodger. "There's a gang there what always fancied itself up against Fagin's group . . ." His voice trailed off. It had been the first time he'd said Fagin's name aloud since the slaughter at the Abbey. He hated to think of the bodies of the women strewn about on the floor, but there was nothing he could do about it. If he alerted the authorities, like as not they'd arrest him on suspicion. Perhaps they would even try to blame him for the entire mess. He simply had to take confidence that sooner or later someone would come by and discover the horrible crime that had befallen the helpless women. Then they would be given last rites and attended to properly.

He realized that his voice had trailed off, and he hadn't quite answered the question. "They call themselves the Baker Street Irregulars. I crossed with 'em now and again."

"If they were opposed to Fagin's group, shouldn't they be opposed to you?"

"Nonsense. No one's opposed to me," said Dodger with a cheer in his voice that he did not truly feel.

The coach pounded along the road, and Dodger drifted in and out of slumber. He had not slept the entire night, after all, and exhaustion was clawing at him eagerly. As his eyes closed, he never took his gaze off Bram, and was surprised to see that the younger lad was not looking the least bit tired. The last thought he had before he fell dead asleep was *I wonder if he's actually alive or really dead?*

Dreams fell upon him with terrifying speed. He was exactly where he feared: in the halls of the Abbey, watching the nuns being slaughtered. Except in this instance the vampyres were not satisfied with simply killing all the women. Instead, the vampyres were having the nuns drink their own blood, transforming them into vampyres themselves. The Artful watched in silent horror, unable to say or do anything except gaze upon the scene in complete helplessness.

Then the vampyre nuns turned almost as one and started to advance on Dodger. The youngster cried out, his arms flailing about, but he was helpless to move as they surrounded him. He begged for mercy—promised he would behave himself—but none of his pleas did him the least bit of good. Within moments, they were all around, and he even imagined he could smell their foul breath rolling out of their mouths.

Suddenly, one of them shook his shoulder. The Artful started awake and blinked furiously against the sunlight in his eyes. "What—?" he managed to say.

It was Bram who had awakened him. "Are you all right?"

"What? Oh . . . yes. Yes, I'm . . . I'm fine. Did you sleep?"

"Yes," said Bram so matter-of-factly that Dodger was convinced Bram was lying to him. "The coach stopped."

It clearly had. The Artful stuck his head out and called, "Why aren't we moving?"

"Because I've taken you where you wanted to go," said Quinn, scowling down at them. "We're on Baker Street."

A quick look around verified for Dodger that they had indeed arrived at their desired destination. "Awright," he said and emerged from the coach. A handful of pedestrians were strolling around, and although some of them glanced their way, most of them were far too preoccupied with going on about their own business.

"Wait here," Dodger said to Quinn.

Quinn tossed off a salute that was redolent with sarcasm. "Aye aye, sir. I'll be right here waiting for ye."

The Artful ignored his attitude. In truth, he couldn't really blame him for it. The man had been ordered to work for two youths involved in a quest that any rational adult would dismiss as the pastime of madmen—all at an hour that decent people were in their beds. It made perfect sense for him to be irritated. Fortunately enough, Dodger was preoccupied with too many other things to be annoyed by it.

"Come on," he said to Bram, and they started walking.

"Where are we going?"

"To find the Irregulars."

"Do they have a headquarters or some such meeting place?"

"If they did, they didn't tell me nothin'. But that's all right. We'll just fix it for them to find us."

"How?"

The Artful leaned against a corner. "First," he said, "we pick a place to stand. Right here seems fine."

"All right. Why are we standing here?"

"To be seen. We'll wait here about half an hour or so. That should be enough time."

Bram clearly didn't understand what Dodger was up to, but he did not question. Indeed, his implicit faith in Dodger's plans somewhat gladdened the heart of the young thief. That sort of trust did not always come easily, and he felt gratified that Bram Van Helsing clearly had no problems with leaving matters up to Dodger to plan.

The Artful simply wished that he felt worthy of it. Even as they waited, and even as the sun crawled dimly through the foggy sky, he felt a growing sense of helplessness. The vampyre conspiracy was something entirely beyond human ken, and contemplating it for even a few minutes was enough to give Dodger pause in his thoughts. Now that he was aware of the vampyre's existence, the world seemed even more foreboding and difficult than ever. For one such as Dodger, always brimming with a confidence that belied his stature—both in height and standing in society—to have his beliefs shaken so was a blow that had felled greater men before. That gave him pause, though: *Greater than I?* The thought almost made him smile.

It matters not how it seems. All that matters is what is, and I will simply have to deal with whatever that happens to be.

And that, as they say, was that.

Some small talk passed between the boys during the intervening half-hour. Surprisingly, considering the circumstances, they spoke about nothing that had any moment. Bram spoke idly of someplace where his father and he had eaten before Bram had been stolen. The Artful talked of how he had first met Drina. He had not yet fully processed that she would one day be the queen of England, and was still working on seeing the hidden meaning in what had previously been purely idle comments to which he had attached no importance.

Eventually, however, he nodded and said, "All right. Time to go to work. They've had enough time to see us."

Bram looked around, feeling vaguely apprehensive over the thought that someone was watching them without actually acknowledging their presence. "And . . . what now?"

"Now we bring them to us," said Dodger.

He watched carefully, looking for a proper target. He finally found one: a rather heavyset man with an ill-fitting topcoat and a conspicuous bulge in his jacket pocket. "Wait here," said Dodger, and he fell into step behind the larger man. The man didn't even come close to noticing him, which was exactly what Dodger anticipated.

The man walked as briskly as his large frame allowed him. He stopped briefly at a corner, and that was all the hesitation that Dodger required. He stepped up to him, and his practiced figures dipped into the man's oversized pocket. Within a moment, he was holding the oversized change purse in his hand.

"*Hey!*"

The Artful did not even have to bother to look in the direction of the outraged shout. He knew who it was. Instead, he cleared his throat and said, "'S'cuse me, sir!"

The man turned, his face the color of umber, sniffing in indignation over having his doubtlessly deep thoughts disrupted by the intervention of a young man. "What?" he said crossly.

"I noticed this fell out of your pocket. Couldn't help but pick it up and alert ya to it."

Clearly suspecting some manner of trick, the man's hand promptly slapped against his pocket. When he discovered it empty, he gasped in shock. Without a word, Dodger tossed the purse to him with an underhanded gesture. "Should be more careful," he advised.

"Yes . . . yes, I . . . ." Apparently feeling that the moment called for some tangible display of appreciation, he started to reach into it to remove a coin.

The Artful didn't permit it. He put up his hands and said, "No tip necessary, sir. Just doin' what I know is right an' honorable. Good day to ye." And he even bowed slightly and made a show of tipping his hat.

The heavyset man seemed confused, but tipped his hat back and then went on his way. The Artful wasn't giving him any more thought; instead, he had already turned to face the scowling young man who had previously shouted at him. This man had two youngsters with him, and they were all staring at Dodger suspiciously.

"Wiggins," said Dodger, tossing in a slight bow for show's sake.

"Dodger," replied Wiggins. He and the other two lads regarded Dodger with outright suspicion. "What just happened here?"

"Wanted to get'cher attention, I did," said Dodger.

"Well, you've managed that well enough," said Wiggins. "Don't quite understand the why of it, though."

"Bram," called Dodger. Answering the summons, Bram was immediately at his side. "This is Wiggins. Head of the Baker Street Irregulars. Wiggins, this is Bram, head of nothin' in particular."

Bram bobbed his head slightly in greeting. The Artful then waited for Wiggins to introduce the two lads who were standing with him, but he disdained to do so. Instead, he simply stared impatiently at Dodger and Bram. "What's goin' on? What's this all about?"

"We have need of some of the Irregulars' brand of magic."

"Do ye now?"

"We do."

"And we should provide this why, exactly?"

"Because we're out to stop a vampyre conspiracy," Bram said before Dodger could speak up.

Wiggins stared at him, and Dodger waited for Wiggins to burst into laughter as any right-thinking Londoner would be wont to do.

Instead, Wiggins simply stared at him. "Vampyre conspiracy?" he said after a long moment of thought.

"That's right."

"And who is involved in this conspiracy?"

"Princess Alexandrina Victoria. They've captured her, and we need help tracking her down," Bram said matter-of-factly.

Wiggins was a scruffy lad with unkempt hair. The two lads with him were similarly styled. They could easily have been members of Fagin's gang back in the day. Wiggins stroked slowly at his chin as if he had a beard and then said the last thing that Dodger could possibly have expected.

"So someone else knows about that. We thought we were the only ones."

Bram looked with quiet triumph at Dodger, who was clearly dumbfounded. "You knew about it?" Dodger said in utter shock.

"Of course we did. We're the Baker Street Irregulars. There's no dirty dealin' goin' on in London that we're not twigged to in some way, shape or form." He took a step toward Dodger, and his eyes narrowed. "But how did you get caught up in this, Dodger? Helpin' queen and country ain't somethin' that you're typically part of."

"I met the princess without knowin' who she was."

"How could you not know?"

"How was I s'posed to?" Dodger said defensively. "It's not like she had a glow or somethin' about her. There's no way I could've known."

"If you'd paid attention, ye would've."

"If you're so very much fixed with payin' attention," Dodger said tartly, "then impress me. Give me some inf'mation that could lead me to her."

"I have no idea where she is. Gents?" Wiggins had turned to the two lads standing next to him, and they both shook their heads.

"Devil take your not knowin'!" said Dodger. "You're the bloody Baker Street Irregulars. You said it yourself—there's not nothin' goin' on that you don't have some angle on."

"Are you callin' me a liar?" said Wiggins.

Dodger took a few steps from him so that he was only a couple of paces away. He was doing everything he could to keep himself together, but his voice was unmistakably quavering as he spoke. "I ain't callin' you a liar, Wiggins . . . I just . . . we need your help. I know ye don't think much of me. And I know what you thought of Fagin . . . an opinion that, just let me say, turns out to be more on spot than anything I could have guessed. But the bottom line is that I'm afraid for Drina's safety, and by the way, you should be as well. That is, if you're an Englishman. Which I know you to be."

Wiggins glanced right and left, and then in a low voice he said, "Wait here." That was all. Then he turned away from Dodger and Bram and headed off.

Bram looked up at Oliver questioningly. "Now what?"

Dodger shrugged. "Now we wait here."

They had no other option. So they remained where they were.

The Artful worried the entire time that this was some sort of strange prank on Wiggins's part. It was certainly possible. There was no love lost between the two of them, and Wiggins required no excuse whatsoever to take advantage of Dodger's desperation and just leave him standing there forever.

Yet it was only an hour later when Dodger looked up and saw that Wiggins was approaching him again. This time he was on his own. "Where are your comrades?" asked Dodger.

In a low voice, all business, Wiggins said, "They're outside the Bazaar."

"The Bazaar? The Baker Street Bazaar?"

Wiggins nodded.

"The museum?"

"Aye."

Immediately Dodger felt as if something was crawling up his back very slowly. He detested the Bazaar. The museum there consisted of wax images, set up a few years earlier by some French woman. She had come to London to make her fortune and now charged six shillings a visitor to come and visit her chambers dedicated to memorializing the French Revolution, not to mention her chamber of horrors. The Artful had visited it when it first opened, seeing it as a likely place to do some pickpocketing business. But he had found the entire place so appalling that he had decided very quickly he was never going to set foot there again. He had faithfully kept that promise to himself all these years later.

"Why are they at the Bazaar?"

"To make sure he doesn't leave." Wiggins glanced skyward. "Not terribly likely. It's broad daylight, after all. Still, it's always wiser not to underestimate what vampyres are capable of doing."

"Make sure *who* doesn't leave?"

Wiggins once more glanced right and left, as if concerned that someone might be eavesdropping. Then he lowered his voice and said softly, "One of me boys thinks there may be an actual vampyre in the chamber of horrors. He says a body showed up there the other day outta nowhere."

"Couldn't it just be another waxwork?"

"My boy doesn't think so. He's pretty sure he saw it breathin'. Or doin' whatever it is they do that passes for breathin'."

"Sounds like a hell of a long shot to me," said Dodger, who was hardly convinced that this was what they were searching for.

"You have a better idea?"

The Artful started to fire off a reply but then stopped. The truth was that he had no better idea, and not only was he aware of it, but so was Wiggins, who smiled grimly. "All right then," said Wiggins. "Off you go. You know where it is?" The Artful nodded, trying not to show his distaste. "Fine." He reached into his pocket and pulled out some change. "Here."

"What's this?"

"Twelve shillings so that you two can get in. I don't want you to have to pick someone's pocket in order to gain entrance."

"Damned decent of you," said the Artful.

"Just trying to keep my street clear of . . . well, people like you, truth to tell."

Dodger nodded in acknowledgment of the sentiment, and they then parted ways.

It was a short walk to the Bazaar, and Dodger dreaded it the entire way. But he knew he had absolutely no choice. The fact that the Irregulars had been of any help at all was nothing short of miraculous; he and Bram simply did not have the option of asking more than they already had.

A few people were filing in at the open double doors of the Bazaar. They were chattering eagerly amongst themselves. Dodger could discern from what they were saying that all of them were out-of-town travelers; no return guests in his particular outing. He was not certain why, but he took some degree of comfort in that.

The first room to engage the tourists when they entered was the exhibit of the French Revolution. It could take quite some time to see it, and that suited Dodger just fine. "This way," he murmured to Bram, and the two lads headed straight for the signs that pointed them to the chamber of horrors. Even as he passed through, the Artful Dodger became more and more concerned. They were not heading into this situation with anything resembling a plan, and lack of planning was a good way to get oneself nicked at the very least. But the fact was that they simply did not have time to plan. Everything had to be done as expeditiously as possible, and so there was nothing for it but to throw themselves directly into matters and pray that it all worked out to their advantage.

Quickly the two lads sidled into the chamber of horrors. Dodger had been braced for it but it was nevertheless, at least initially, bordering on the overwhelming. He was faced with an assortment of creatures spat up from the most hideous and unfortunate aspects of human imagination. They were surrounded by wax vampyres, werewolves, and creatures climbing up out of the depths, with every intention of lunging straight at anyone who happened to be nearby. The interior of the place had been properly done up, giving the lads the impression that they had somehow wandered into a haunted forest somewhere in eastern Europe. It was disturbingly simple to forget that they were in the heart of London. They might well have been on the native ground of these monstrosities, face to face with them with no hope of survival.

Artful felt his heartbeat speeding up rapidly, and he had to do everything within his abilities to slow himself down to something more manageable. He took slow, steady breaths in an attempt to keep calm. He reminded himself that just last night he had been face to face with the actual monstrosities that were merely being represented here, and he had managed to survive. If he had accomplished that much, then this should be no problem for him at all.

A hand suddenly touched his arm, and he jumped involuntarily, letting out a cry of fright. It took a moment for his scattered brain to process the fact that it was merely Bram making contact. Bram, for his part, appeared completely at ease. The Artful Dodger was beginning to think that there was nothing in the world capable of throwing Abraham Van Helsing for a loop. He did not know whether to feel reassured by that. He was, after all, accustomed to thinking rather highly of himself and his capacity for adjusting to unusual situations. Yet here, with the vampyres, he had been slow to do so whereas Bram had had no difficulties whatsoever in rolling with whatever machinations the vampyres had engaged in. To acknowledge Bram's skill in adjustments was to acknowledge where he was coming up short. He didn't feel quite ready for that.

"Over there," said Bram, and he pointed toward the far end of the chamber of horrors. "Everything else is out and open to inspection. But over there is sheltered."

"Yes, it is," said Dodger. He could see exactly what Bram was pointing at: It was a coffin that read, "Final Resting Place of Dracula."

"Who's Dracula?" asked Artful.

"A former Romanian prince," replied Bram. "Supposedly several hundred years old. When he was alive, he was known as Vlad the Impaler for his habit of beheading his opponents and putting their heads on pikes."

"How lovely." He paused. "I suspect you don't believe that Dracula is within there."

"Dracula is somewhere in the world," replied Bram. "In Romania, I should think. But he is most definitely not in there, no."

"Then let's see who or what is."

Artful glanced around, and his eyes widened. There was a "vampyre" off to the right who was leaning on a skull-headed walking stick. The Artful had been sorely missing his own ever since it had been shattered in action, and he saw this as a genuine opportunity to retrieve something. Plus he would be able to put it to immediate use.

He crossed quickly to the vampyre, stepping over the rope that was hanging to keep the public at bay. It might serve fine for ordinary museumgoers, but that was certainly not an accurate description of the Artful Dodger. Carefully, so as not to damage the figure, he extracted the cane from it. He wielded it back and forth and smiled. Yes. This would do extremely nicely.

Immediately, he strode back across the room and went to the coffin. "Get ready," he said. Bram nodded and extracted quite possibly the largest cross that Dodger had ever seen from within the folds of his coat. The Artful could not quite believe that Bram had managed to keep that secreted on his person all this time, but he supposed he shouldn't have been surprised. Indeed, at this point there was nothing that Bram could say or do that would wind up surprising the Artful.

The Artful shoved the end of the cane into the separation just under the lid and levered it. The lid resisted at first, and it took Dodger several attempts to manage to get it moving. Finally, though, he accomplished it, and he began prying the lid open. Bram, shoving the cross into his belt, lent a hand and began to pull with far greater strength than Dodger would have credited him to possess. The Artful then stepped in and added his own strength to the endeavor, and within moments, they had managed to shove the lid open.

Part of the Artful had suspected that this was all for naught—that they would either find the coffin empty or else it would have a wax figure of the imagined Count Dracula.

Instead, there was a body in there. It was not doing anything except lying there. Its face, however, was badly scarred.

Dodger recognized it immediately. It was the vampyre that had attacked them on the hansom cab. The one at whom he had spat and whose skin he had wound up sizzling because he had been drinking tea made with holy water.

"I'll be damned," he whispered.

Bram recognized him as well. "I wager he would recognize you quite easily."

"I would take that wager. He's sound asleep, though. How do we wake him up?"

"I'm not sure," said Bram. "I know that a vampyre sleeps very deeply. When he is asleep, I'm not sure there is any way to awaken him. He will likely be unconscious for—"

At that moment, the vampyre's eyes snapped open. He took one look at the boys staring down at him and let out a shriek of anger and terror mixed together.

"You sure about that?" said Dodger, unable to keep the sarcasm from his voice.

The vampyre, with a roar, leaped up and out of the coffin, which rattled around him as he moved. He vaulted through the air, landed, turned, and spun to face the two lads. His lips were drawn back in fury, and his fangs protruded from them.

Bram pulled his crucifix from his belt and held it up.

If God was at all interested in what was happening, then perhaps this was evidence of that, because the vampyre shrank back, bringing his hands up defensively and gasping out a startled and angry hiss. He snarled several extremely unfortunate and ungentlemanly words, none of which Dodger or Bram would ever care to repeat.

Then, to their astonishment, he turned and ran.

The boys did not hesitate: They ran directly after him.

He dashed from the chamber of horrors directly into the French Revolution display. Various visitors gasped in confusion upon his entrance, and two women fainted at the sight of his heavily scarred face. He looked right and left for some manner of escape. Momentarily, he turned, perhaps toying with the idea of returning the way he'd come, but he saw the two lads in pursuit, with Bram waving the extremely large cross. The only remaining means of escape appeared to be the great front doors of the room.

He did not hesitate but made straight for them. He burst through the doors, but in the quest to leave the boys behind and make good his escape, he had apparently completely lost track of the time. As a result, when he threw open the doors, he was hit with a massive blast of sunlight.

The vampyre let out a high, ululating scream. Instinctively, he tried to do the only thing he could and retreat to within the wax museum, but that option was not open to him. The Artful Dodger plowed into him from behind, thrusting him forward. The vampyre fought back with everything he could, but at that moment he had no idea which way to focus his attentions: Should he concern himself with the scrappy, top-hatted young man, or the younger fellow wielding a cross, or the blazing heat of the sun? For once the perpetually foggy air of London had actually given way to the sun's rays, and so he was experiencing the unfortunate sensation of literally being burned alive.

Quinn, standing next to the coach several feet away, reacted with widened eyes. "What's all this, then?" he demanded.

"The door! Throw open the door!" Dodger shouted, and Quinn—who had spent a lifetime obeying orders—did not fail in that capacity. Instantly, he yanked open the door to the coach, and the Artful shoved the burning vampyre toward it. Unable to comprehend why the boys appeared to be saving his

life, but hardly in a position to question it, the vampyre allowed himself to be pushed in to salvation. Bram had run around the other side and was waiting at the far door, cross at the ready. The vampyre lay there gasping for several long moments, clutching at his skin. There were several patches of redness from where the sun had scored him, but otherwise he did not seem particularly the worse for wear. Finally, he managed to gather himself sufficiently to look at Dodger, who was leaning over him with his cane firmly in his hand, looking prepared to assail his victim with a series of blows.

"What'll ye have of me?" demanded the vampyre. His voice was hoarse, and he was gasping for breath, which Dodger found curious considering that the vampyre had long since parted from the necessity of breathing. Doubtless, it was a lifelong habit that the simple act of dying was insufficient to dispose of.

"The girl your ilk captured," Dodger said intently. "Where is she?"

"I've no idea what yer speaking of."

"Really?" Though that was exactly what Dodger had expected of him. The vampyre was evil incarnate, after all. He was unlikely to be honest first crack of the cricket bat. "Okay, then. We've no further need of ye."

He nodded toward Bram and Bram, with a look of quiet determination, thrust the large crucifix through the window. He shoved it against the vampyre's face, and the creature let out a scream so ear-splitting that it was all Dodger could do not to cover his ears. He refrained from doing so, however, for he was certain that such a move would make him appear weak.

"Wait! Wait!" the vampyre howled as he clawed at the cross. Bram withdrew it but kept it nearby, prepared at any moment to shove it forward again. The vampyre rubbed at his face and let out an irritated hiss. Then he dropped his voice and whispered, "You can't help her."

"Leave that to us," said Dodger. "Now where is she?"

"And how do you know?" added Bram.

The vampyre looked disdainfully at Bram. "I know because I know, boy. We always know each other's business. We're joined in blood. You humans have no ken of that."

"Not 'specially sure I want any ken of it," said Dodger. "So out with it. Where is she?"

"I'm telling ye, she's beyond ye," the vampyre repeated. "All of this is beyond ye. Ye'd be well advised to get back to the shadows what spat ye out—"

Bram had clearly had enough. Yet again he shoved the cross forward, and once more the vampyre let out a high scream. This time Bram kept it pressed against his skin far longer. The vampyre shook and writhed on the bench, and it was all Dodger could do to hold him in place.

Some part of Dodger actually felt sorry for the creature. Once upon a time, this had been a normal, God-fearing human being. The Artful knew nothing of the circumstances under which he had been transformed into this vampyric thing. There was every likelihood that he had been as much a victim as anyone else. Yet here they were treating him as if he had never been a human being at all. As if he had always been an inhuman monster who could be treated as little more than an animal. But then he realized that there was simply no way around it nor anything that could be done. Whatever he might have been in the past no longer mattered. The only relevant thing was his current status as an undead creature of the night, and it was clear that Bram van Helsing was perfectly willing to treat him in that capacity. That being the case, the Artful had no choice but to follow his lead.

Finally, after what seemed forever, Bram withdrew the cross. Dodger saw a large blackened crisscross upon the left side of the creature's face. He clawed at it as if intending to rip the skin right off his own face. When Bram threatened to bring the cross down again, the vampyre threw his hands up and screamed, *"No! No! I'll tell all!"*

"Do so," said Dodger, fighting to keep his voice flat and even and to maintain his own revulsion deep within and out of sight.

"They're hidden her away right enough," said the vampyre. "She's in Bethlem Hospital."

"Bethlehem?" said Bram, not understanding.

"Nay! Bethlem! Didn't ye hear me right?"

"I heard you," said Dodger. He nodded toward Bram. "He's new in town. He doesn't know what's what or what's where."

"Bethlem?" Bram repeated.

"That's its official name," Dodger said grimly. He was already understanding what the vampyre was talking about when he was saying that they were going to have difficulty. "The unofficial name is Bedlam. It's a madhouse."

"Aye, and what better place for 'er?" said the vampyre. "After all, if she rattles around in her cell claiming that she's the future queen, who's gonna believe her, eh? There's blokes in there claiming that they're all people from history."

"The future queen in that place." The Artful trembled inside just contemplating it. He had never been inside Bedlam. He might have had many quirks to his personality, but no one had ever thought to deem him insane. "From what I've heard of it, you can go into that place sane as anything and go mad while you're there just from the surroundings."

"That won't happen to her," said Bram firmly. "She is much too strong."

The Artful Dodger very much wanted to believe that. He had never so strenuously wished that someone else was correct about something. Then he turned his attention back to the vampyre. "How do we get into Bedlam?"

The vampyre shook his head strenuously. "I've no idea, and that's the God's honest truth, I swear to ye."

"As if something like you has any knowledge of God," Bram said.

"I did!" the vampyre protested. "I was once no different than ye! It ain't my fault that God's turned His face from me! I swear!"

Bram did not appear convinced. He started to bring the cross down once more, and this time the vampyre did not even try to shrink from it. "Do it! Burn me face off! Ye can sear every bit of skin from me body, and it won't change the fact that I told ye everything I know! Now give me a cloak, and let me go!"

For a long moment, nothing was said. Then Dodger reached back onto the chair and grabbed a seat cover off it. He tossed it to the vampyre. "Get out of here," he said tersely.

"Thank ye!" said the vampyre. "Bless ye!" He drew the cover over his upper body, shielding himself from the sun. The Artful tossed open the opposite door, and the vampyre slid out through it.

Quinn was waiting for him. "Here now! That's mine!" He grabbed the seat cover off the vampyre's back before the unfortunate creature could do anything to prevent it.

"No, wait!" shouted Dodger, but it was too late. With the full light of the sun upon him, the vampyre fell to his knees and screamed in agony. But there was nowhere for him to go because passersby were blocking his path back into the Bazaar and were standing there in confusion, staring at the man who was writhing for no reason.

"What the hell?" said Quinn, and it was fitting that was the last thing the vampyre heard as the sunlight immolated him, sending him to the hell Quinn had just questioned. The vampyre burst into flames, causing confused screams and shrieks from the passersby, who had no comprehension of what they were looking at. He twisted about on the ground, beating furiously at himself even as he screamed in agony, but it was too late for him to do anything except burn. His skin erupted in flame, and then his clothing caught. Having no moisture in his body, he was one large tinderbox ready to flame out, and that was precisely what he did. People scrambled to a nearby horse trough to try and get water to extinguish him, but it was too late. In less time than it takes to read of it now, the vampyre was reduced to nothing but ashes.

Quinn stood there, stunned, staring uncomprehendingly at the covering that he had removed from the vampyre, which had sent him into a ball of flame. "Quickly," the Artful said into his ear. "Get us out of here. Now. *Now!*" Responding to the boy's urging, Quinn scrambled up onto his seat, and moments later, even as the police came running up in response to the crowd's screams of confusion, the coach rolled away into the London streets. It left behind an assortment of bewildered citizens and a small bit of ash that was blowing away in a convenient breeze.

TWELVE

In Which the Advantage of It Being Tuesday is Made Clear to Our Heroes

There were many places that the Artful Dodger might have been given to visit on any particular day, but he was quite sure that St. George's Fields in Southwark was not remotely one of those locations and thus until today had never really registered on his consciousness or awareness of the world around him, and yet that was now precisely and exactly where Quinn was driving him.

It had not been an easy endeavor. Quinn had hied the carriage out of the immediate area of the Bazaar, but once he had put some distance between them and the place of the vampyre's death, he pulled the carriage over to a side street and came down from his seat. He stepped over to the side of the carriage and threw the door open. His face was purpling with rage. Curiously, Dodger could see no fear in it. *"What in the world have ye gotten me into?"* he thundered.

"We told you already," said Bram, the picture of calm.

"But ye didn't tell me men would be bursting into flame! What the hell was that thing?"

"A vampyre. You were told there were vampyres involved in this."

"Aye, but I didn't believe it!"

"Well," said Bram, being utterly reasonable, "I don't see how that's our problem. Your problem, perhaps . . . ."

"I dinna understand how these things are possible!"

"There is far more," said Bram, "on heaven and earth than is dreamt of in your philosophy. The question is, now that you know, what are you going to do about it?"

"I don't know. I . . ." His voice tapered off and he scratched his head, letting his outright confusion show.

"You have a choice," Dodger spoke up. "Either you can help us try t'save the Princess Alexandrina Victoria from the hands of the right bastards who have taken her. Or you can stand aside, return to Mr. Brownlow, without havin' done what you were s'posed to do. It's up to you."

"Fine. Get out," said Quinn.

That was not the response that either of the lads expected, but they obediently clambered out of the coach as Quinn jumped up to his seat and snapped the reins.

The boys remained where they were as the carriage started to roll away down the dusty road. It got about fifty feet, and then Quinn yanked the horse to a halt. The animal appeared mildly confused but otherwise was not especially put out.

"What is he doing?" asked Bram in a low voice.

"He's figuring it out," Dodger replied.

For about ten seconds, nothing was said. Then Quinn stepped down from his place atop the coach and landed once more in the dirt road. He strode toward the two lads and folded his arms. "I was in the army, ye know. Wasn't much older than you. Lied about me age."

"Very brave of you," said Dodger.

"Weren't nothing to do with brave. Just didn't have any other job. And I served. And then I was mustered out. I used to ride horses into battle. Now I ride them around town."

"And now you ride them to save royalty," Dodger told him. "That seems like a step up to me."

"Aye, it is." Quinn was as straightforward as possible about that. "You sure this is the princess we're talking about? You wouldn't be making that up, would ye?"

"Swear on me mum's name," said Dodger. It was a harmless swear, with his mother being long dead. But Quinn had no idea of her demise. Nor did it occur to him to ask. "So are ya with us or not? I'd really like t'know."

Quinn slowly nodded. "Bethlem, eh?"

"Yes. Assuming," said Dodger with a touch of dread, "we can figure out how to get in."

"Shouldn't be an issue. It's Tuesday, after all."

The Artful and Bram exchanged confused looks. "Why should that be making any dif'rence?" asked Dodger.

"Because Tuesday is visitin' day."

"Visitin' day?"

"Aye. It's a regular fund-raising activity. Me uncle used to be a resident there, and some days I'd go to see him, so that's how I know. Bedlam is open to the public on Tuesdays. Anyone with half a crown to spend can walk around inside, and see what's what. Used to be that they were open every day, but they cut back on that because . . ." He shrugged. He really didn't have any idea why. That was simply the way it was, and Quinn wasn't much for questioning the way things were.

"So all we each need is half a crown and we can just stroll in!"

"Exactly right."

"Um . . ." The Artful scratched his pockets as if he had an itch there. "Do ye by any chance happen t'have a crown or two on ya?"

Quinn made an impatient face. "Do ye have any money on ye at all?"

"Not enough to do us any good. Not really in the habit of carrying a lot on me."

"Why not?"

"There's thieves everywhere. Don't fancy makin' meself a target."

Quinn stared at him, his jaw dropping open and just hanging there for a long moment. Then he let out a roar of laughter that startled Bram. The Artful, however, didn't react in the slightest other than to scratch his nose for a moment.

"All right, then," said Quinn, shaking his head at Dodger's audacity. "Get back in the coach. Off to Bedlam then."

Feeling the need to ask, Dodger inquired, "Um . . . what happened with your uncle?"

"Killed 'imself. Happens a lot to people there."

"Ah. Well . . . sorry."

"Don't be. He was a bit of a git."

Moments later they were barreling down the road. It had been awhile since the boys had eaten anything. Bram reached into his pocket and withdrew a few apples that he and Dodger quickly devoured. "Where did you get these?" Dodger asked.

"Mr. Brownlow's kitchen."

"You stole 'em?"

"I don't like to think of it that way, but yes, I suppose I did."

In spite of himself, Dodger smiled at that. "So it seems there's hope for you after all."

"I hope not," Bram replied.

The Artful wasn't sure how to respond to that comment, and wisely let it pass.

Instead, he turned his attention to the sun. The fog had settled back in and was partly covering it, but he was still able to discern its rays as it crept across the sky. It was odd to him; he had never previously had any strong feelings about the sun at all. Why would he? It was just a glowing orb in the sky.

Now, though, he saw it very differently. He saw it as an ally against the forces that waited for the dark in order to launch their various schemes. It wasn't a knowing ally, of course. It was inanimate. Except, for all Dodger knew, perhaps it wasn't. Perhaps the sun was alive in a way that a simple London street lad could never understand. Perhaps it comprehended that it was the greatest warrior existent in an ongoing battle against creatures that had lurked in shadow since the days that humanity was cowering within caves and staring out at the darkness in fear.

(At least, we think he was thinking this. Perhaps he was not, because it is a rather deep consideration for a street urchin. But let us allow for the possibility that he was so that we can then examine it.)

What was the most disconcerting to Dodger was the sun's progress. As it made its way across the sky, it was signaling the amount of time he had left before the vampyres would again be able to wander out and begin committing their crimes. They would be able to inflict their horrors upon Drina, not to mention anyone else. The notion was inwardly terrifying to Dodger, and it was everything he could do to keep his fears repressed. It was not an easy endeavor. Part of Dodger desperately wanted to leap out of the coach that was taking them to Bedlam, to vault clear of it even though it was moving. To take his chances upon escaping the moving vehicle and run in the other direction, leaving Bram to deal with this entire mess. And why not? This was Bram's business, after all. This was something he was raised to fight. His father had taught him how. There was really no reason for Dodger to have been pulled into this madness at all. Even the fact that he now knew Drina's true identity didn't make all that much of a difference. Since when did the royals give the slightest of damns about people like Mr. Jack Dawkins? She was the head of a way of life that would have been perfectly happy to ship Dodger off to Australia if he hadn't been able to escape.

Stay, he found himself mentally pleading with the sun. *Don't leave. Stay where you are, and keep bathing the world in your rays so that the vampyres will always be trapped within their coffins or wherever they rest during the day. Don't abandon us. Stay . . . .*

But he knew that he was wasting his time. The sun could not be stilled in its movements, even though he found himself wishing that he had some sort of biblical ability to halt it by blowing a trumpet or some such.

"You have a lot on your mind," said Bram. The Artful had lost track of how much time he had been silent.

"How can you tell?"

"You seem lost in thought."

"Can you blame me?" He shifted uncomfortably in his seat, trying to adjust to the constant swaying as the carriage made its way down the road. "We have to get into Bedlam, find the future queen, and rescue her. What are we doing here, Bram? Why can't we just turn this over to the authorities and bow out like right gen'lemen?"

"Is that what you really want to do?"

The Artful thought about it for a moment and was surprised at how quickly the answer came:

"No. They took Drina from us. It's our responsibility to get 'er back. Hell, the authorities would probably think we're nutters. This is our job and no one else's. Besides," he added grimly, "I still want to dish out some personal payback for what they did to the nuns."

"I'm glad to hear that," said Bram. "I was starting to get a bit worried there for a minute. You're the hero of this adventure, Dodger. I hope you understand that."

"Bloody right, I do. So let's get it done."

Dodger allowed his head to slump back. This time when sleep came pounding for him, he did nothing to resist it. Despite the bumping and swaying of the coach, he was unconscious in a matter of seconds.

The next thing he knew, Bram was shaking his shoulder, and Dodger realized that the coach had ceased its forward motion. "We're here," said Bram in a low tone, his eyes narrowed as if he were concerned that a vampyre might somehow sneak up on them during broad daylight.

Except the daylight was not, in fact, as broad as it had been. It was not quite sundown, but nevertheless the sun was most definitely approaching the horizon line. This fact alone was enough to put a sense of dread into Dodger's awareness, but he quickly shoved this fact out of his brain as hurriedly as he could. He could simply not allow for any distraction.

He twisted the handle of the door and swung it open, clambering out of the coach, with Bram right behind him. Quinn had been in the process of climbing down from his perch. "We're here," he told them, as if they were unaware.

The Artful didn't let Quinn know that the fact he was standing on the ground was indication that such a pronouncement was unnecessary. He simply offered a brief nod.

The large building popularly referred to as Bedlam stretched out in front of them. It was a vast, two-story brick structure with windows dotting the exterior; Dodger could not help but notice they were barred. That did not bode well for endeavoring to undertake an escape attempt.

"All right," Bram said briskly. "If this is where she's being kept, then in we go."

The Artful looked to Quinn. "Lend a lad a crown?" he said with a tone crossed between genuine hope and mild sarcasm.

With an unamused grunt, Quinn reached into his pocket and carefully pulled out a change purse. Opening it, he fished around for a moment or two before extracting a gleaming crown. "Should I assume I'm never going to get this back?"

"I wouldn't make that assumption," said Dodger. "Life is full of twists and turns that—"

"Am I getting it back?" demanded Quinn.

"Not bloody likely, no."

Quinn grunted once more and then flipped it to Dodger, who caught it easily enough. "Well, at least ye were honest about it."

Without another word, Dodger and Bram headed toward the large entrance to Bethlem Hospital. As they approached, Artful imagined that he could hear distant screams emanating from within . . . .

No. You're not imagining it.

From within the halls of Bedlam, he could indeed hear the mournful cries of residents. England's sickest and most depraved people had been herded into one spot, and there they were being kept clustered together like rabid and depraved animals.

"Dodger . . . ?"

The Artful wondered why Bram sounded puzzled, and then realized that he, Dodger, had stopped walking. He had been so overwhelmed by the depressed howling coming from within that it had halted his progress completely.

"Dodger," Bram said again, plucking at the sleeve of his coat. "Are you coming?"

The Artful stared at him. "How do you do it?" he said, and only when he spoke did he realize his voice was just above a whisper. "How do you just deal with everything? There's nothing what throws you for a loop. How is that possible?"

"You keep asking me things like that. Haven't I given you an answer you can accept?"

"No."

Bram stared at him for a long moment and then said, "My father didn't give me any other choice. Do you think I wanted this? That I wanted to be this way? I didn't get to be a boy, Dodger. My father made sure of that. I just want to go to school, to be with other children, to be normal. Instead, I hunt monsters and, right now, try to save England. That's not a life—that's just existence. But it's all I've got, so that's the way things are. And you can waste both our times asking me about it, or you can buckle down and do what needs to be done. All right?"

The Artful nodded because frankly he couldn't think of anything else to say or do. If this little boy could walk into the fire, then shame alone would keep Dodger moving. "Fine then. Let's go rescue a princess."

"Let's," agreed Bram.

They headed for the doors. The closer they drew, the more clearly they could hear the cries echoing from within. Even with Bram's example, it was everything Dodger could do to keep moving, but he kept his feet going with an inward determination. Drina needed them, and Dodger was determined not to let her down, even though the distant screaming—drawing closer by the moment—was extremely disturbing.

They reached the large front doors, and there was a guard standing there with bushy eyebrows and a nose that was thick and veined with the results of a lifetime imbibing more drink than was healthy. He scowled down at them and immediately said, "You boys best be moving along. This place ain't for the likes of you."

"I don't think it's for you t'judge," said Dodger. He held up the crown. "We have the means to pay right enough."

"Most of the day's gone," said the guard. "Come back next Tuesday when you can stay longer."

"We know what we want." The Artful was more insistent in thrusting the crown forward. "We wants t'go in now."

The guard's face twisted in an annoyed sneer. "Get out of here, the both of ye."

Bram stepped forward. "Can we speak to your superior, please?"

"Me what?"

"Your boss. We wish to tell him that he has an employee who thinks he gets to judge who's allowed to come and go in Bedlam."

Bram had spoken with complete calm. It was as if the guard weren't even really there, and he was already speaking directly to the guard's superior.

Drina does that, too, Dodger couldn't help but think. *If I could talk like that, there'd be nothing I couldn't steal.* The thought made him perk up a bit.

The guard was clearly struggling between his impulse to send the boys on their way and a vague apprehension that somehow this young boy might actually be able to make life difficult for him.

Finally, with an annoyed grunt, he stuck out a hand. The Artful promptly placed the crown in it and then the guard gestured with a thumb behind him. "Go on in before I change me mind."

"Right then," said Dodger, and he and Bram quickly entered the halls of Bedlam.

The very first thing that hit them was the smell. The stench of waste wafted through the air, so much so that Dodger actually staggered and clapped his hand over his nose. Bram was even more profoundly affected, retching audibly and doing everything he could not to actually throw up. For some reason, the fact that Bram wasn't, in fact, unaffected by everything made Dodger feel better.

In a low voice, Dodger muttered, "I feel like I walked into a corpse."

"Well, well! What have we here!"

The voice was loud and booming and disproportionately in a good mood, considering their surroundings. The Artful and Bram turned toward the origin that happened to be, quite clearly, a gentleman of some sort. He was wearing a gray suit and had a long, bristling beard. "Are you lads tourists?" he inquired as if he were greeting them outside of the palace.

"Aye, we are, sir," Dodger said immediately. He removed his hat and held it in what he fancied was an appropriate manner for a young gentleman inside a posh establishment. "We thought we'd take a look around. Who might you be?"

"Doctor Huddleston," said the bearded man. He bowed slightly, which, for some reason, made Dodger feel good. "Would you like me to show you lads around?"

The answer, of course, was, *Not really.* The boys were on a rescue mission, and Dodger very much suspected that having the doctor along would impede their efforts. But there didn't seem to be any way around it. A brusque refusal or any manner of brush-off might engender suspicion, and that was not what they needed right then. So Dodger said the only thing he could: "Ab-so-loot-ly."

Doctor Huddleston smiled and gestured for them to follow. They did so, falling into step behind him. The Artful whistled as he walked, doing his best to seem as casual as he could. Bram, feeling under no compulsion to feign being at ease, looked steadily left and right as they walked.

"We don't get a lot of lads your age in here," said Huddleston conversationally. "What spurs your interest?"

"Oh, we're int'rested in everything that happens everywhere in the city," said Dodger as if being curious about the confines of an asylum were the most natural thing in the world.

"How much do you know about the Hospital of St. Mary of Bethlehem?"

"Pardon?"

"Here," said Huddleston, looking a bit confused.

"About Bedlam? A little."

Huddleston stopped and made a face of irritation. "I have to say, Mister . . ."

"Dawkins."

"Mister Dawkins, I do not especially appreciate the nickname 'Bedlam.' It has garnered many negative connotations, and I find St. Mary to be a far more appropriate and, frankly, less disparaging term."

"Very well," said Dodger, bowing slightly. "I know very little about St. Mary's."

"Well," said the doctor, and he rubbed his hands together as if about to dig into a particularly attractive dessert. "It has a most intriguing history."

He proceeded to tell it, and we will not bore you with it because there are many places you could go to read about it if it is of any true interest to you. We will save time by simply saying that Bethlem had a long and frankly somewhat depressing history and had moved several times before finally setting up shop in its current location.

The Artful and Bram had no choice but to listen or at least pretend to listen. It was not an easy endeavor, though, because there was much to steal their attention: namely, the patients.

They passed a series of closed doors, but there were decent sized windows in each of them so that it was easily possible to observe the people within. What they saw was extremely distressing. People were in there—presumably patients, but they were not patients in any sense in which the boys were experienced with the word. There was nothing done to be making them better, to help them recover their senses.

Some were wandering free. They would move about the room, or perhaps simply sit in one place and stare off into space, their eyes far too disinterested in the world around them to react. A couple of them made eye contact with Dodger but seemed to be looking right through him. It was as if there were someone residing in their heads who was actively endeavoring to keep them from interacting with the world around them.

Those were the ones who were free. Far more disturbing were those who were anything but free. They were chained up, manacled in place. Some were at least able to move around, with their chain allowing them a few feet of latitude in any direction. Others were being kept right where they were. They struggled against their restraints; they screamed at the top of their lungs. The Artful was sure that he would never be able to cleanse those agonized screams from his mind. It was as if they cut right into the base of his brain.

Doctor Huddleston noticed the reaction on Dodger's face. Bram was once again his impassive self, but Dodger was having difficulty hiding his revulsion. "Are you all right, lad?" the doctor asked.

Realizing that he was leaving himself open to possibly being ushered out, Artful waved it off as if it were nothing. "I'm fine. I'm all right. I was just wondering about, you know . . . the necessities."

"Necessities?"

"How you decide who to chain up and who not to."

"Ah." Huddleston appeared to warm to the topic. "That is based entirely on interviews with each of the patients. If we are convinced that they will be harmless to themselves and others, then of course they are permitted to walk about unimpeded. If, on the other hand, they seem as if they are going to present a hazard, then naturally we have to take additional steps."

"Yes, yes, of course. That makes sense."

They continued to move past room after room. It quickly became depressingly monotonous. That did not distract, however, from Dodger's determination to study the face of everyone he was watching.

Men were kept in rooms with men, and women with women. Dodger assumed that there was no mingling of the genders for obvious reasons. He did his best to maintain full interest no matter which sex was occupying the room, yet nevertheless, he could not help but pay far closer attention to any room with females. He hadn't worked out exactly what they would do when they spotted Drina, but he wasn't all that concerned. He had outsmarted all manner of individuals in his life, and he was certain that Doctor Huddleston would prove no exception.

"Now this fellow," said Huddleston, "is a would-be murderer. At least, he says so. We've no evidence of anyone that he's actually killed, but naturally we're disinclined to take any chances."

Dodger looked through the window. The resident within was wearing only slacks and no shirt, and he was barefoot. The wall was spotted with the remains of food that he had apparently thrown against it in fits of rage. Chunks of his hair had been ripped out, presumably by the man himself. He glowered from beneath furrowed eyebrows at the boys. He shook the chains briefly and noisily.

"You have all types here, eh?" said Dodger.

"Oh yes. All the best and worst that humanity has to offer reside herein. Well, this is as far as we go."

They had halted in front of a large set of double doors. The Artful tilted his head in that direction. "What about there? What's through there?"

"Ah. That's the east wing. That's closed to the public, I'm afraid."

"Why?"

Huddleston looked saddened. "I'm afraid that there are some individuals who are simply too ill to be subjected to public view. We keep them secluded and sedated so that they present no threats to anyone, including themselves."

"That's prob'ly very wise," said Dodger, "but we'd still like to have a look-see, if you don't mind."

"Unfortunately, that simply isn't possible. But you've seen two floors of the hospital. Certainly, you must feel satisfied with what I have shown you."

Before Dodger could say anything, Bram spoke up. "I have a question. You said that that fellow in there believes himself to be a murderer."

"Aye, he does."

"Do you have other patients who likewise believe themselves to be something they're not?"

"Oh, my, yes. We have one fellow, for instance, who thinks—"

Bram did not bother to let him finish. "What about vampyres? Are there any who are convinced that they are vampyres?"

Huddleston seemed surprised by the question. "You mean fictional creatures of the night?"

"That's exactly what I mean, yes."

"Not that I'm aware of," said Doctor Huddleston, "but for all I know, perhaps someone does indeed believe that he or she is a monster."

"Would you keep any of those in the east wing?"

"Young man," said Doctor Huddleston, and his patience was clearly beginning to fade. "You are asking some very odd questions."

"It's an odd world," said Bram. "We need to go to the east wing," he said, more to Dodger than the doctor.

Huddleston looked from Bram to Dodger. "I'm afraid that's not possible," he said, his voice firm.

"We need you to make it possible."

"And why would that be?" He smiled thinly.

To Dodger's utter shock, Bram said, "Because we need to know where you are hiding the princess."

Huddleston's gaze flickered, and then something in his voice changed. It was as if he suddenly perceived the boys as some manner of enemy.

"Right. That's it," he said.

He brought his hands up to either side of his mouth, and it was quite clear that he was about to call for help. It was at that point that Dodger realized they were out of time. So he did the only thing he could think to do.

He swung his cane around as fast and as hard as he could manage.

It struck Doctor Huddleston on the side of his head, sending him to his knees. "What . . . what?" he managed to say. The Artful gave him no opportunity to say anything else. He struck again, this time on the back of the head, and Doctor Huddleston went down without another word.

Quickly, Dodger went through the insensate doctor's pockets and came up with exactly what he was looking for: a couple of large keys hanging on a ring. "Skeleton keys," said Dodger with satisfaction. "These should give us the run of the place."

"For as long as we don't get noticed."

Choosing one of the larger keys, Dodger struck it right, first crack out of the box: He opened the lock to the door that led into the cell of the nameless killer. Seeing the door open wide, the man stood exactly where he'd been, waiting with curiosity to see what would happen next.

It required the strength of both Dodger and Bram to drag Huddleston's unconscious body into the cell. Upon seeing the doctor lying there, helpless, the killer wasted no time and lunged for him. The chain, however, did its job, snapping tight so that the killer was brought up short by a couple of feet. He pulled at the chain furiously, shaking it with all of his might, but for all the effort he put into the endeavor, he was unable to snap the chain that was restraining him. He let out a deafening roar, and it was all that Dodger could do to ignore him. It was becoming easier for him, although he was loath to admit it.

"Here now, lads," whispered the killer. His fingers were twitching desperately as he tried to get the doctor within range. "We haven't met, but I feel good about asking you boys for a little favor."

"We can't free you."

"Of course not. Heavens no. Just bring him a little closer, would you? I'd be ever so grateful and couldn't wait to show you my gratitude."

"And how would you do that?" the Artful asked.

"Why, by killing you quickly 'stead of slowly."

"That's very kind of ya, mate, but I think we'll leave him where he is. But good luck to you with that." He gestured to Bram. "Let's go."

They headed out fast, taking care to shut the door behind them. Straightaway discerning which key opened it, Dodger opened the door to the east wing, and they headed through.

The smell of the place was even more pronounced, and it was all that Dodger could do not to vomit up the minimal amount of food he had in his stomach. They moved down the row of cells, looking into each and every one.

Most of the cell occupants didn't seem to pay them any mind. They were far too wrapped up in their own respective worlds. Some, however, did give them notice. Seeing unfamiliar faces, they cried out, "Get us out of here! Let us go!" In some instances, Dodger actually considered doing so. Why should he leave them clapped in irons in the heart of Bedlam? But without even asking, he knew the reason: because they truly could be insane. And if that were the case, then it was possible that they might try to do damage to Dodger and Bram. He simply couldn't take the chance of their adventure ending prematurely because he was trying to be of benefit to someone.

Besides, this whole helping others thing was a bit new to Dodger, so he figured it best to focus on the task at hand.

Then he passed one cell and stopped dead.

There was a young girl in it. She didn't appear to be more than ten years old. Her face was wan and exhausted, and her black hair hung limply around the sides of her face. She wasn't chained up, which seemed to bode well. "Help me," she called to him when he stared in at her. "I'm not supposed to be here. Please."

The Artful couldn't stand the notion of leaving the girl behind. He had no idea how he would manage to extricate her from this place, but he knew he had to do something.

As he brought the key up, however, Bram placed a hand on his. "No," said Bram. "Leave her be. We don't know what her situation is."

"I don't care," said Dodger. "I'm not just going to—"

"Hey! You two!"

From the hall behind him, two men were rapidly approaching. They were dressed very simply in white clothing. Clearly, they were workers here at Bedlam, burly fellows doubtless charged with keeping order amongst the inmates. And seeing two young lads wandering around on their own did not keep with their view of how the world was supposed to function.

"Stop where ya are! Right now!" They advanced on Dodger and Bram.

Dodger did the only thing he could think of. He shoved the key into the door lock and turned it as quickly as he could. He yanked the door open, and the ten-year-old girl bounded out on all fours.

That's unusual, thought Dodger even as he said to the girl, "Get out of here! Quickly!"

But the youngster showed no interest in departing. Instead, her eyes widened as she saw the guards and then she let out the most hellacious screech that had ever reached Dodger's ears. He actually clapped his hands to the side of his head to mute the sound. The guards, for their part, skidded to a halt, and there was fear in their eyes.

And just before Dodger could wonder why in the world the guards were looking concerned, the girl charged them. Still on all fours, she looked like an animal, a wolf of some kind. She moved, however, with incredible alacrity, and with a howl of fury she leaped upon the larger of the two guards and sank her teeth into the base of his throat.

She was not a vampyre; that much was certain. That, however, did not make the slightest difference in terms of the damage that she was doing. She yanked her head back and a chunk of the guard's skin came out with her. She spat it out, and it landed on the floor with a disgusting, moist sound. Blood seeped from the point where she had torn the skin loose, and the guard shrieked as he fell to his knees.

The second guard did the only thing he could: He grabbed her and endeavored to yank her clear. All it prompted her to do was turn her attentions to the attempts of the rescuer to inter-vene. She twisted in his grasp, pulled away, and dropped to the ground. The moment she was there, she bit into the man's calf. He shrieked and tried to pull her off, but it did no good. With her teeth sunk into his skin, she wasn't about to let herself be pulled away.

The Artful watched the entire encounter with wide eyes. He was so stunned he forgot to breathe. He jumped slightly as something grabbed his arm, but it was just Bram. "Let's go," he said briskly. "Before she remembers that we're standing here."

The Artful saw the wisdom in those words. There was no reason to assume that the girl would not turn her attentions to the two lads once she was done assaulting the guards. Plus they heard footsteps coming from farther down the hallway; the ruckus was obviously drawing attention. Which was ideal for them. If the berserk girl was occupying everyone here, then the boys could go elsewhere without being disturbed.

The girl did not notice they were departing. She was far too occupied trying to chew on anyone or anything that was getting within range of her. *Poor creature,* thought Dodger but then gave her no more thought beyond that. He had other things that he had to attend to, and if the girl's actions made them simpler, then so much the better.

They sprinted down the main corridor of the east wing. Aside from the fact that the stench was even more pronounced, it seemed reasonably similar to the rest of the facility. They went from door to door, looking in as quickly as they could. They encountered various staffers, but they seemed mostly interested in going about their jobs and did nothing to challenge the lads. Dodger was grateful for this; at least, finally, something was going their way.

Reaching the end of the corridor, they sprinted up the stairs. But as they raced along, they heard a distant voice behind them. It was male and thundering and angry, and it was saying, "Did you see them? Where are they?"

The boys cast a quick, nervous glance between each other. It sounded as if the easy time they were having of it so far— minus having to knock out the doctor and siccing a feral child on two hapless workers, of course—was going to be ending fairly quickly. Someone was in pursuit of them, and it might be mere minutes before that person caught up with them.

They emerged onto the second floor and were running as quickly as they could. These doors were different from the others. There were no windows for them to peer in. Instead, there were simply narrow slot bars set into them that could be pulled aside so one could gaze through. Also, the doors seemed heavier and more secure. Dodger was definitely not liking the looks of this, and worse, there was simply no time for them to pull aside every single slot bar. It was time for him to take a desperate chance. Bracketing his mouth with his hands, he shouted, "Drina! It's us! Where are you?"

It was nothing short of a desperation move, and honestly, by this point he wasn't really expecting it to work. So he was astounded when a voice called out from behind one of the doors, "Dodger?" It was faint and weak, but it was most definitely she.

"He told the truth," said Bram, sounding utterly astounded. "The vampyre told the truth. I'll be."

"Now I'm almost sorry he's dead," said Dodger, who actually was not, but he felt as if he should say something.

At that point, it was simply a matter of finding which door she was behind. This was not as easy as it sounded, because the moment Drina called out, so did a number of other patients. The cacophony of noise made it difficult for the boys to locate her; they ran from one door to the next, to the next, pressing their ears against each one and desperately trying to locate the voice's source.

Fortunately, it only took less than thirty seconds. It seemed like far longer, but it was most definitely not.

"Dodger!" came her familiar voice from the other side of one door toward the far end of the corridor.

"Here! I'm here! Hold on!" He rummaged quickly through the keys and found the one that had opened the door down on the first floor. He prayed that it was indeed a skeleton key that gained him access to all the rooms on the floor. Perhaps because God was feeling generous, his prayer was answered. The lock on the door clicked satisfyingly open, and Dodger threw wide the door. He took a step in and gulped.

Drina was inside, all right. She was completely naked, deprived of even the slightest vestige of clothing.

"Oh dear," said Bram. For the first time since they had joined forces, Bram actually seemed thrown off by something other than strong smells. Monsters crawling out of the woodwork to try and destroy him—that did not deter him in the slightest. But a naked young woman he clearly had no idea how to handle. Something on the ceiling drew his attention, and he focused his eyes on that.

The Artful was likewise curious about the state of the floor, wall, and ceiling, but he shook off the discomfiture much faster than Bram did. He stepped toward her quickly. Her hair was down and disheveled, hanging in her face. That worked out well, because she was so ashamed of her condition that she could not bring herself to look Dodger in the eye. She was seated on the floor with her legs curled up tightly against her bosom. Her hands wandered aimlessly over her body as she tried to cover herself and clearly was not sure where to place them. "I . . . I . . .," she started to stammer.

"Don't worry about it," said Dodger. He was quickly sliding off his overlong coat, and he draped it over her trembling shoulders. Her arms were fortunately not manacled; the chain was wrapped around her right ankle. Quickly she slid her arms in and drew the coat tightly around her. "Just hold tight, and we'll get you out of here, Highness."

Her head snapped around and she looked up at him, startled. "You know?" she said, her voice dropping to a whisper.

He nodded. "Hope that's all right with ye."

"Of course it's all right. It . . ." Her voice trailed off for a moment and then in an even lower voice, she said, "I'm sorry. I should have told you. I was being selfish."

"Ya were being a girl, and that's what gets ya that," Dodger said. He was going through the keys as quickly as he could, eliminating one after the other as he tried to unlock the lock that fastened her. "Just hold on."

Bram was glancing out the door. "Hurry up," he said. "I think we're about to have company."

"Telling me to hurry doesn't make me hurry any faster than I'm already hurryin'," said Dodger in irritation. He turned up the last key and looked at it nervously. If it didn't open the lock, then he didn't have the faintest idea what the hell he was going to do.

Closing his eyes, he slid the key in and turned.

At first, nothing happened, and a great sense of tragedy swept through him. But suddenly the lock turned. Apparently there was some rust in the lock that was impeding the turn, but that only lasted for a few seconds. When he applied more force, the rust gave way and the key turned. The lock snapped open with a click that seemed to reverberate through the room.

"Did it!" said Dodger, crying out in joy. He promptly yanked the lock off and unthreaded the chain from the manacle.

Drina drew herself to her feet and immediately fell over again. "Muscles . . . my muscles aren't working," she managed to say.

"Take it easy, Highness. One step at a time." He stepped in close to her, draping her arm over his shoulders, and helped her to stand.

"Dodger . . . would you please go back to calling me Drina. I don't feel much like a Highness right now."

"Whatever you say, Drina." Inwardly it tickled him slightly that he was on a first-name basis with a princess. Him! Jack Dawkins, the Artful Dodger, a street scum who picked pockets for a living, trading first names with a princess of the realm. What had the world come to, to have reached such a strange point in time?

To be fair, the world *had* come to apparently be filled with vampyres, so . . .

Having regained her feet, this time Drina seemed a bit more sure. He helped her forward a few steps, and in moments she was walking on her own. "There. That's . . . that's much better," she said.

"Good. Now let's get the hell out of here."

He guided her toward the door, and just as they got there, two large men were blocking their way. It was two more orderlies, and it was instantly clear who they were looking for.

"'Ere ya are! And where do ye think yer goin'?" said the larger one of them.

The Artful tried the only thing he could think of. "You," he said as sharply as he could, "will get out of the way of a princess of the realm, or know the consterquences of your inaction!"

"A what now?" The two larger men exchanged amused looks.

"This girl is the Princess Alexandrina Victoria!" Bram was now speaking. "And I can promise you she'll run a whole investigation into whoever is running this place and thought that locking her up was somehow acceptable!"

The two men were not the slightest bit convinced. "Right. That's it," said the larger, and he grabbed Drina by the wrist.

To their surprise—"their" being both the man and Drina—she pulled away from him. In fact, she yanked her arm clear of his as if he were not holding on to her at all. The Artful did not hesitate, but instead brought his cane around quickly and slugged the man on the side of his head. The man did not, however, go down. He staggered, clutched at his head, and let out an angry roar. When Dodger attacked again, this time the orderly managed to catch the walking stick in his hand and yank it from Dodger's grasp. He tossed it aside angrily and shouted, "Right! That's enough out of you!"

Drina leaped forward, her arm cocked back, and she threw a vicious punch. It caught the bigger man on his chin. His head snapped around, his eyes rolled up, and with nothing but a loud sigh he sank unconscious to the floor.

His associate looked on in shock and then turned to flee the room. He only got two feet, though, because Bram had thrown himself forward to block him, and the man tripped over the lad. He went down hard, and Bram grabbed the fallen cane, leaped onto his back, and started pounding away with the stick. He delivered several resounding shots to the back of his head before he threw Bram off. Before the man could get up, though, Drina was upon him . . . and pounding on him. Her small fists were flying with remarkable speed and strength. The Artful and Bram watched in astonishment as Drina drove the man into unconsciousness. And even then, she was not done. She grabbed up the fallen chain and swung it, prepared to slam him in the head with the heavy iron. Quickly, Dodger ran forward and grabbed her hands. "What're you doing?" he cried out.

She turned and looked at him and for a moment he didn't recognize her. Her face was twisted into an expression of pure primal fury. He called her name once, twice, and it was only on the third time of him calling out to her that she appeared to respond. Her breathing was rapid but shallow, and her pupils were dilated. Her hair was still hanging in her face, and she was straining to see him through random strands. "Dodger?" she finally managed to say.

"Are ya all right?" He was gripping her by the shoulders and looking with confusion into her face. "Drina? Are ya all right?"

She seemed irritated by the question. "Yes. Yes, of course I'm all right." She was reacting as if insinuating that there was anything wrong with her was somehow thickheaded on his part. "No thanks to them. They've kept me trapped here. You've seen what they did to me. They should die. They should all die. I should just . . . just kill them all."

"No one's killing anyone," Dodger said firmly. He buttoned the coat around her to prevent it from swinging open and exposing her nudity. She seemed less concerned about her state of undress now, and that bothered him. "Come. Let's get out of here." Bram snatched up his fallen walking stick and handed it to him.

Hastily, they withdrew from the room, but once they were in the hallway, they saw their larger problem.

Someone had apparently freed Doctor Huddleston. His eyes wide with fury, he was at the far end of the hall, and there were at least four guards surging behind him. Huddleston's jacket and shirt were torn, and on his face bite marks were bleeding. Apparently, one of his patients had worked him over before he'd been rescued.

"There! There they are!" he howled, and the group sprinted directly toward the youngsters.

The Artful was about to turn and run, and naturally assumed that his companions were going to follow him.

Instead, Drina turned to face the hospital workers. Her lips drew back into a snarl, her eyes went wide, and she let out a loud and infuriated hiss. It was so vicious, so animalistic, that the people charging toward them skidded to a halt. Huddleston even took several steps backward, looking thoroughly intimidated.

Seizing the opportunity of this momentary pause in the pursuit, Dodger grabbed Drina's arm. "Drina, come on! Come on!"

To his astonishment, Bram then said the last thing the Artful could have expected: "Leave her."

"What? Are you insane?"

"Dodger . . ." Bram began to speak.

The Artful wasn't interested in anything he had to say. "Drina! I said come on! Now!"

Reality appeared to sink in upon her, and she turned and nodded. They sprinted down the hallway, a reluctant Bram taking up the rear. Shaken from their momentary paralysis, their pursuers sprinted after them.

They got to the large door at the far end, and fortunately it was not locked. The Artful threw it open and ushered Drina and Bram through it. There was a stairway leading up, and they immediately started climbing it. The Artful hesitated long enough to slam the door, shove in the key, and twirl it. The lock within the door snapped closed with a satisfyingly loud clack. "That should hold them for a few minutes," said Dodger, hoping that one of their pursuers didn't have a set of keys on him.

They sprinted up the stairs, Dodger taking them two at a time. There was a door at the top of the stairs, and Drina banged into it first, shoving it open. The Artful heard a crack and realized that the door had been locked. Drina had simply struck the door so hard that she had broken it open. *How did she do that?* the Artful wondered, but something within him already knew the answer to that. He simply didn't want to face it.

He followed Drina, and they found themselves on the roof. The sun had already dropped below the horizon line; some distant orange streaks in the sky were the only remains of the sunlight. The group of them wandered the roof quickly, desperately looking for a way down. Nothing, though, seemed to be presenting itself.

A distance away, Dodger saw the coach in which they had arrived. Quinn was standing outside it, leaning against it and staring at the building with what seemed to be extreme boredom. The Artful shouted his name repeatedly. Quinn heard it immediately but initially could not determine whence it came. Eventually, though, he caught a glimpse of Dodger frantically waving his arms. Immediately, he ran to his horse, yanked the oat bag off the horse's face, and then clambered up into his seat. He shouted at the horse, snapping the reins, and the coach trotted toward the youngsters and their position on the roof.

Unfortunately, they were still standing on the roof, and the ground was a two-floor drop. Furthermore, there was banging from the door below. Bereft of keys, their pursuers had apparently decided simply to knock the door off its hinges.

"We seem to have a problem," said Dodger with no trace of sarcasm. He truly did not have the faintest idea how they were supposed to get safely down to the ground. "Bram, any thoughts?"

"None that are especially positive," said Bram.

Suddenly, Drina grabbed Dodger around the waist. He started to ask her what she was doing, but she silenced him with a loud "shush." Then she turned to Bram and simply said, "Come along. Now. Grab on."

Bram did as instructed without hesitation. He ran to her and as she knelt slightly, he threw his arms around her neck, hanging from her back.

"What are you doing?" cried out Dodger. Drina did not bother to respond. Instead, hauling Dodger along as if he weighed nothing, she sprinted straight toward the edge of the roof.

And leaped off.

The Artful cried out in alarm and closed his eyes, which was the only action he could take against the impending impact. Bram remained silent, as if none of this were remotely surprising to him.

A second later, they hit the ground. Drina absorbed all the impact with her legs but still lost her grip on Dodger. He rolled out from her grasp and hit the ground, and then bounded to his feet. "What just happened?" he cried out. "How are we not dead?"

Before Drina could reply, the carriage rolled up. Bram was not wasting any time. He dropped off Drina's back, ran to the door, and threw it open. "We leave now or we don't leave at all," he said.

Putting aside his confusion for the moment, Dodger ran for the carriage. Drina was ahead of him, and she climbed in. Dodger got in right behind her, and Bram clambered in after them. "Where to?" called down Quinn.

"Anywhere but here!" Dodger shouted back.

That was more than enough for Quinn. He snapped his whip and shouted for the horse to get moving as quickly as possible. This time the horse did not trot; instead it took off at a near gallop, hauling the coach behind it so quickly that it momentarily tilted on its wheels and Dodger thought it might actually fall over. Then the coach settled itself, and it was riding evenly as it barreled down the road.

"What happened back there?" said Dodger. "How are we still alive? How did you—?"

"Don't you know, Dodger? How could you not know?" said Bram. His face was paler than it had been, and he was clearly speaking with great effort. He was doing everything he could to keep his voice steady. "They've made her into one of them."

"That's right rubbish!" Dodger told him immediately. "That's—"

But then he saw the look in her eyes, the grimness in her face. He drew back from her on the seat and stared at her in horror. "No. No, it's . . . it's not . . . you're not . . . your neck! There's no mark on your neck . . .!"

Bram abruptly grabbed her right arm and shoved it upward. The sleeve of the coat slid down the arm and sure enough, there in the crook of her elbow, twin fang marks were easily visible. Naturally, they could have been noticed when she was naked, but Dodger had been busy making a point of looking every-where but right at her during that time.

Drina immediately yanked her arm away, allowing the sleeve to slide down back over it. "Don't touch me. Don't ever touch me," she said softly, her voice barely sounding like her own.

Bram completely ignored her. Instead, he thrust himself toward her, clambering on her so quickly that it was completely unexpected. She cried out but the determined young man ignored her, shoving his fingers up into her mouth, peeling back the upper lip.

The points of her fangs peeped out at them.

Dodger cried out in alarm even as Drina shoved Bram away as hard as she could. He slammed across the interior of the cramped coach, banging up against Dodger, who did a piss-poor job of halting his flight. Bram didn't appear to care. He was too preoccupied shouting, "See! See! I told you!"

"Drina," whispered Dodger. He stared at her but felt as if he wasn't really seeing her. "Drina, how . . .? When . . .?" His voice dropped. "Who?"

She looked at him defiantly for a moment, and then she dropped her gaze. The future queen of England was not able to stare into the shocked eyes of a young street urchin. "I don't know," she said softly. "I was blindfolded. I was . . . I was bitten. They drained my blood . . . so much . . . and someone . . . he had a deep voice. Polished. He dripped blood onto my mouth. I tried to spit it out, but there was too much . . . too much . . . then they locked me away. And I started to . . . to . . . ."

"Change," said Bram tonelessly.

Drina managed a nod and touched her fangs. "Then these came in. And I . . . I don't . . . I feel so much . . ." She raised her eyes, and there was desperation in them. Hard desperation, her eyebrows knitting. "Hunger. I'm so hungry. It's all I can think about. It's all I want. What am I going to do?"

Dodger had no idea. He turned to Bram and said desperately, "Is there a cure? Bram, is there a cure?"

"She hasn't killed yet," said Bram. "As long as she hasn't killed yet, there is still a chance."

"A chance? How much of one?"

"Not a great one," Bram admitted. "We have until midnight. We need to slay the vampyre who did this to her. If we are able to do that before midnight, then the change will reverse itself." Surprisingly, he hesitated for a moment—something Dodger had not expected to ever see from the young boy. Finally, Bram said, "At least, that's the theory."

"*The theory?*"

"It's the story I've heard. The tale of vampyre origins. I've never actually seen it happen, so for all I know, it's not true. But I think it is."

"And what if we can't? Is there some other—?"

Bram shook his head. "None that I know of. The only alternative then is to kill her. Maybe we should just do it now."

That was precisely and exactly the worst thing he could have said.

Drina's eyes opened wide. "What? What did you say?"

"He said nothin'!" Dodger told her, but he was hardly convincing.

Nor was he helped by Bram, who simply repeated, "Maybe we should just kill you now. The odds of our being able to help you are so slim that—"

Drina didn't wait for him to finish the sentence. Instead, she shoved Dodger out of the way and lunged for the door.

"Drina, wait!" shouted Dodger, but she was hardly of a mind to wait. Instead, she pushed him back with startling strength, although in retrospect it really should not have been all that startling anymore. She punched the door open. The ground was passing by quickly, but the speed of its passing didn't seem to deter her. With a furious roar, she leaped out of the speeding coach. She hit the ground and rolled immediately out of Dodger's sight.

Quinn, seeing that someone had fallen out of the coach, yanked the speeding horse to a halt. *"What the bloody hell—?"* he shouted.

Drina wasn't waiting. Instead, barefooted, she sped past the coach, running down the road as quickly as she could. Quinn watched with shocked eyes, unable to believe that this relative slip of a girl was moving so quickly.

The Artful hung out the door and shouted, "After her! Get after her!"

Quinn wanted to fire off questions about what was going on, but instead he simply followed orders. He snapped the reins, and the horse immediately bolted forward in pursuit.

"Faster! Faster!" Dodger howled. He did not want Drina to escape. If she got away, he had no idea what they were going to do.

She sped ahead of them, staying on the road, for which he was grateful. There was a thick grove of trees ahead, some swampy area, and the road curved off to the right. His view was blocked by another grove. Drina sped around the road curve and vanished from sight. That did not concern Dodger, though. She would only be out of his field of view for seconds; certainly they would be able to catch up.

The coach swept around the curve, and Dodger couldn't believe it.

Drina was gone.

Seeing what Dodger was seeing, or more correctly not seeing, Quinn hauled back on the reins, bringing the animal to a skidding halt. Dodger, who had been hanging out the door, leaped out and hit the ground. He strode ahead of the horse, trying to get a better view. When he continued to see no sign of Drina, he looked toward the trees and even behind them to see if she had slipped to the rear somehow. There was no point to his doing so. He saw no sign of her. Drina had disappeared into the evening air.

In frustration, Dodger slammed his fist against the coach. "I don't believe it! I don't bloody believe it!"

"Where did she get to?" said Quinn.

"I don't know! If I knew, I would tell you to bring us there straightaway, now wouldn't I?" He turned and saw that Bram had emerged from the coach. Furious, he pointed a trembling finger at the younger boy. "This is all your fault! You told her we should kill her! How could you expect her t'be stayin' with us when you say things like that!"

"It didn't matter if I said it or not," said Bram. "She was going to realize it sooner or later."

His impassive, calmly logical voice infuriated Dodger. The Artful grabbed Bram by the shirtfront, lifted him off his feet, and slammed him against the coach. The coach rocked from the impact. Bram gasped, his eyes widening—not in fear, but in surprise.

"*Stop that!*" shouted Quinn. He had leaped off his seat, and now the man was shoving his way between Dodger and Bram. With a grunt, he wedged his arms in between the boys and pushed Dodger back. Dodger stumbled and fell, hitting the ground hard. When he got back to his feet, he did it slowly and with a low, pained grunt. "We won't be havin' none of that!" Quinn said. "Do ye hear me?"

Dodger didn't respond. He knew his sleeves were dirty from the ground, but he couldn't bring himself to dust himself off. It was like admitting some sort of weakness.

"I said, do ye *hear* me?" Quinn demanded in a louder voice.

"I hear ya, all right?" The Artful folded his arms and glared at Bram. "But it's still your fault that she took off. How are we supposed to kill the vampyre what did 'er? We have no bloody idea who it is!"

"It was the vampyre in charge," said Bram.

"How the hell do ya know that?"

"Because I know how the hierarchy works. I know who does what. That was the future queen of England."

"Her?" said a stunned Quinn.

Bram ignored him. "She's way high up on the human food chain. Very high up. When someone makes you into a vampyre, the newly made vampyre winds up having to answer to whoever made him or her. That gives the maker a good deal of control over that vampyre. If you're making an English princess into a vampyre, that's going to be the job of whoever's in charge. All the vampyres would understand that, and no one would dare step in and take her for himself. That could cost him his life. No vampyre would take the risk. So it definitely had to be the head vampyre in London."

"And who would that be?" asked Dodger.

Bram ran his fingers through his hair, frowning. "There was one that my father talked about. Not to me. He rarely spoke to me about such things. But he spoke to some other chaps about this top vampyre. It was a code name."

"What was the code name?"

"Mr. Fang," said Bram.

Dodger stared at him. "Are you jesting with me?"

"No. Why?"

"Why do you say it was a code name?"

"Well, it's kind of obvious, isn't it? I mean, a vampyre wouldn't really go by the name of Mr. Fang, would he?"

"He would if that's his *name*."

"What?"

"I *know* Mr. Fang. I even know where he is."

Bram immediately stood straight up. "Are you sure?"

"Quite sure. Everyone in my line of work knows Mr. Fang. A magistrate, he is. Rules on the fates of hundreds like me. And he's a vampyre, eh?"

"My father seemed pretty sure, and he's rarely wrong in such instances."

"Makes sense," the Artful said, more to himself than Bram. He looked at the boy and Quinn. "Then we go after him."

"How do we find him?"

The Artful smiled grimly. "I told you: I know where he is. That won't be a problem at all, gettin' in t'see 'im. Gettin' out is what's gonna be the problem."

THIRTEEN

In Which Drina Briefly Returns to Old Haunts and Wrestles with Temptations

D rina had no idea when she ceased running; all she knew was that she had fled the coach that had been transporting her and that she had kept running, and it should be noted that running in this case was an utterly new experience for her because, as the princess, she had never been expected to run anywhere for anything and in fact had been discouraged from doing so on the rare instances that she had felt the need to move with any sort of alacrity, as it was deemed that such a desire for speed was inappropriate for a future ruler.

She had never fled so far, so fast, and so quickly. Yet her barefooted legs seemed to eat up the distance as if it were nothing. It was so subjective to her that it literally seemed thus: One moment, she was in the midst of the swamp where the hospital was situated; the next moment, the streets of London, miles away from where she had been, had claimed her.

She did the only thing she could think of: She continued to run. She dashed through the streets, ignoring the puzzled and confused looks of people she sprinted past. She darted left, then right, then left, and then down an alleyway purely at random. Moments later she found herself at a dead end, where a building several stories high stretched upward, defying her forward egress.

"'Ere now!" It was a voice from the far end of the alleyway. She spun and saw that a puzzled policeman was standing there, staring at her in confusion. He had his black club out and was gently tapping it against his palm. "Young lady! C'mon out here, please!"

Alexandrina Victoria hadn't the slightest interest in presenting herself to the police officer. She looked up the side of the building, saw the lacing of uneven brick, and a pipe that could provide additional purchase. It was all the handholds that she required. She took a few steps back and then bolted for the building. She leaped upward, and that spring alone took her ten feet into the air. She heard the police officer cry out in alarm and startlement, and it gave her a brief sensation of triumph. She landed on the drainpipe that ran upward and sank her fingers into it. For half a second, her grip was uncertain, but then she solidified the hold she had and held firm. She started to scramble up the side of the building, ignoring the pleas of the police officer to return to the ground.

She was aware of the faint, rapid beating of her heart. She wondered how that was possible. Was she not already dead? Obviously not. But she was also far more than human. What was she then?

What am I?

The words ran through her head, and once upon a time they would have been terrifying to her. Now, however, there was no fear in her thoughts at all. Instead, she found that she was excited about dwelling upon the prospects of her new state of being. That alone was enough to sound a distant trill of warning deep within her mind, but she did not dwell upon it.

Her experience with Dodger was rapidly fading from her mind. Bram was already forgotten. All that was mattering to her were the new and endless possibilities that lay before her. The night was calling to her, and she could think of nothing but answering it with a resounding and glorious howl.

Running, she reached the end of the roof, but that did not begin to deter her. She vaulted from it, sailed a short distance through the night air, and landed on another. She kept going, faster and faster. She had felt slight hesitation at that first leap, but much less on the second and nothing on the third. From then on, she was effortlessly leaping from roof to roof. Never had she felt so alive as she was at that moment.

This continued for an uncertain time, and then she skidded to a halt. She realized that she was in a very familiar neighborhood: the one that Dodger resided in. The one where she'd had the confrontation with . . . .

Yes. Yes, there she was.

Standing right there on the corner that Drina had unknowingly been standing upon, the street slut named Sarah was plying her trade. At the moment, she was trying to strike up a conversation with a gentleman. He seemed to have a slightly passing interest in her, but clearly he was going to require some convincing.

Drina thought about the manner in which the rude woman had treated her. A slow anger began to bubble within her. She had been a newcomer. More, she had been royalty, choosing to take up her valuable time and even likely upset her mother by taking off on her own into the streets of London. And this woman, this slattern, this nothing, had dared to treat her in such an upbraiding, deliberately insulting manner?

She took a few steps back and then ran once more. This time she gave no thought to the distance she was traversing, even though it was much farther than before. Ultimately, it did not matter; she landed on the rooftop with ease. She gripped tight to the drainpipe and scrambled down it as Sarah continued to try and engage the young gentleman before her.

The gentleman was facing the building when Drina reached the bottom and landed lightly on the street. He stepped back, startled, his eyes wide and confused. "What in the—?"

Drina had no patience for him. "Go," she said and pointed with her right arm. She was so excited to feel the power coursing through her that her arm actually wanted to tremble. It was no small effort for her to keep it steady and pointing. "Now," she added for emphasis.

The gentleman needed no further prodding. His interest in Sarah had been lukewarm at best, and this new arrival was all he needed as an excuse to vacate the area.

Sarah had not yet spotted the intruder, so it was that when she turned and looked behind herself, it was in confusion. And as she saw the barefoot, young girl there, attired in a coat that seemed familiar to her, it took her a few moments to put it together, but she eventually figured it out. "You! Dodger's girl!"

"I'm no one's girl save my own," said Drina. Slowly, she started walking toward Sarah. It was an exaggerated, provocative walk, one foot carefully placed in front of the other to give her an almost catlike approach.

"Ye got some nerve! Scaring off a customer, ya did! And this time"—she made an over-dramatized point of looking around—"I see ya don't have Dodger to step in and save ye from a beating ye so richly deserve!"

"And you're the one to give it to me, are you?" Drina smiled, taking care to keep her fangs tucked in, wanting to save them for a surprise, wanting to drag this out. "Here I am then. Let's see what you're capable of."

Sarah didn't hesitate. She strode briskly toward Drina, and drawing her arm back, let fly with a vicious slap. It cracked across Drina's cheek with a resounding noise, and Drina's face snapped with it. She barely felt it. She remained with her face staring away for a long moment and then slowly shifted her gaze back to Sarah. "That's it?"

Enraged, Sarah launched her full attack. Repeatedly she slapped Drina's face, both sides, as hard and as fast as she could.

Her eyes widened in concern as Drina stopped moving her head in time with the slaps. Instead, she simply continued to stare deeply into Sarah's face, and she was wearing a wide smile that seemed disinclined to acknowledge she was being attacked at all.

"What the hell?" muttered Sarah, and this time she swung her purse. Drina did not allow it to strike her. Instead, she caught it in mid-swing, yanked it from Sarah's hand, and tossed it aside. Sarah gasped in confusion and then drove a full punch toward Drina's mouth.

Drina snagged her wrist, stopping the punch short. Sarah tried to pull away from her but was unsuccessful. Drina just stood there, allowing Sarah to expend her best efforts to loosen her grip. It did Sarah no good; Drina was holding on far too tightly.

"Leggo!" shouted Sarah.

Drina did far more than that. She twisted her hand very quickly, and an audible snap was heard from the area of Sarah's wrist. Sarah let out an alarmed cry and sank to her knees as pain ripped through her entire right arm.

All of her arrogance and superiority vanished. "Please!" she cried out, and there was no command in her voice, but instead pleading. "Please, let go! Whatever you want, I swear . . .!"

"You couldn't possibly understand what I want," said Drina. Now she was moving, heading toward a nearby alley as she yanked Sarah off her feet. Sarah fell but her full weight did nothing to slow down Drina. She hauled Sarah as if the woman weighed nothing, dragging her into the alley and then pulling her to her feet once they were out of sight of any passersby.

She slammed Sarah up against the wall. Sarah looked into her eyes and let out a terrified shriek, for Drina's eyes were crimson red, and they were focused on the pulsing vein at Sarah's throat.

"No . . . no," Sarah managed to get out and then Drina did not hold back anymore. She drew back her lips, exposing her fangs. Sarah let out a terrified shriek, and then it was too much for her as she fainted dead away. That was fine with Drina, who enjoyed the relative peace and quiet of the now unconscious girl.

Her fangs descended toward Sarah's throat. Within seconds, they would tear into the pulsing jugular vein and drink every drop of blood from her very first victim.

She froze that way. The fangs were less than half an inch above their target and that was where they remained.

Stop! Stop! Don't do it! Don't!

It was her own mind screaming at her. She tried to ignore it, tried to set it aside, tried to tell herself that that wasn't her anymore. And yet she was still in denial and confusion, unsure of what to think and what to do.

She realized her entire body was trembling. She did everything she could to try and shove her fangs home, but something within her continued to prevent her from doing this. With a frustrated howl, she threw Sarah down. The girl's body thumped to the floor of the alley and lay there unmoving.

Drina stared at her trembling hands as if they belonged to someone else. "What is wrong with me?" she said aloud, but inwardly she knew. The Alexandrina she had been was still in force in some small segment of her brain, preventing her from taking the next normal step in her development. She was helpless to do anything to force herself forward. She let out a scream of frustration and looked down at the prostitute's sprawled body . . . .

Still, there was no reason she couldn't derive some benefit from the current situation. A smile formed on Drina's lips.

It took only a matter of minutes to strip Sarah's clothes from her. As she lay there naked, once more Drina felt the desire to drain her of her life's blood. But she was only able to take a few steps forward before something once again snapped her head back so that she was unable to proceed. She cried out a loud invective then at her helplessness, and that managed to relieve some of her frustration. Not much, but some.

Sarah's clothing was a bit too large for Drina. It hung loosely upon her, but at least it enabled her to cover herself. Taking Dodger's coat, she tossed it on Sarah's naked body. No reason she couldn't provide the girl some minimal cover, even if it was more than she would have done for Drina.

Suddenly, something split her head. It was as if someone were driving a wedge straight into her skull. She staggered, gasping, unable to understand what in the world was happening to her. She looked left and right frantically and then did the only thing she could think of: She leaped straight upward. She didn't require the drainpipe to scale up this time. The velocity of her jump propelled her vertically, and she landed atop the nearby roof in a crouch. The long dress swirled around her ankles as she staggered, trying to reorient herself.

Here, said a voice in her head. As opposed to a few moments before, when the voice speaking to her had been her own, this was someone else. She had no idea how she was hearing it, and was not even sure that she actually was. It was, however, guiding her. That much she knew.

For a moment, she considered going in the opposite direction from where the voice was calling her. She could do that—that tiny voice that was preventing her from feasting seemed to want to scream at her to do just that. She could simply flee into the abyss of London rather than meekly obey the summons of whoever was calling her. That desire, though, lasted for almost as short a time as it took her to think of it. Then her body continued to move east across the rooftops. It was operating completely on its own. She had no conscious awareness of where she was heading. All she knew was that she had to go in a particular direction because she was being commanded to.

She vaulted from one roof to the next. She was covering distance so quickly that anyone who happened to look up in her direction would not even see her. At most, they would spot a quick glimpse of something, the details of which they would not be able to discern.

Finally, ahead of her, she saw an upright form waiting for her. He was standing there, stock still, his coat blowing around him, his hat nestled securely on his head. She leaped the remaining distance and landed in front of him. It took her a few moments to gather herself, and then slowly she stood. "Who are you?" she demanded.

"You know the answer to that," he said quietly. "I am the one who made you."

She wanted to leap upon him. She wanted to bear him to the ground and tear into his throat. She wanted to kill him right then and there and, as a result, gain some peace for herself. Instead, all she was able to do was stand there and wait for him to speak.

"Bow to me," he said.

"No," she immediately replied. She was royalty. People bowed to her, not the other way around. Yet even as she said she would not, she felt her knees giving way. She dropped to one knee, lowering her head. She wanted to spit at him, but she was unable even to gather saliva to accomplish that.

He stared down at her. "Very good. You are properly obedient."

"And now what?" she snarled at him, showing he was not quite accurate in his assessment of the situation. "Now what are you going to do?"

He tsked, as if she were simply a child that still had things to learn. "Why, I'm going to do the only possible thing: I'm going to take you back home."

"I have no desire to go to your home," she said, the revulsion she was feeling warring with the compulsion in her head to simply go with him.

"You mishear me, your Highness. Not *my* home. *Your* home."

"What?" She couldn't quite believe she was hearing him properly.

"That's right. I'm taking you home to your mother. She must be dreadfully worried about you by now. Returning you is certainly the only option remaining."

"You can't," she said, shaking her head so violently that it threatened to topple off her neck. "She mustn't see me like this."

"I would not worry about that," he assured her. "She will have far greater problems than that before she knows it. All right, Victoria. Let us away. Now," he added when she seemed slow to respond.

Immediately, she was on her feet, and without another word she followed her lord and master off into the darkness.

⊰ ✳ ⊱

Mr. Fang stood upon the roof, looking at the spires of Buckingham Palace in the near distance. Drina stood next to him. She was trembling, her lower lip distended. "I can't go back there," she said for what seemed like the hundredth time. "They'll see me like this . . . ."

"Like what? In clothing you took off a street whore? I will tell them of the mishap you underwent that brought you to this situation," he assured her. "All will be well. And you, of course, will make certain of that."

"How?"

"Why, by making me your honored guest," Mr. Fang said. "And why would you not? I was responsible, after all, for saving you from your difficulties."

"Saving me? You helped place me squarely in them!"

"You will not tell them that," he told her. "You understand that, do you not? Not a word will you speak of our encounter. You ran off from the palace, you were assaulted by street individuals, and I found you in your desperate situation. You remember almost nothing beyond that. Is that clear, Victoria?"

Her face warred with what seemed a dozen different responses, but all she did was nod. "Yes, I understand."

"Good. That's very good . . ."

His voice trailed off. Something had caught his attention. He looked away from Drina, toward a nearby rooftop, and then called out, "I see you there. No use in hiding."

A form moved from the darkness. It was a form that Drina recognized all too readily. Despite the change in her physical position and shift in status, she nevertheless felt chilled to the bone when she set eyes upon him.

"What's he doing here?" she asked, her voice barely above a whisper.

"That's a good question," said Mr. Fang. "What, may I ask, are you doing here, Fagin?"

"Ah, and where else would I be?" Fagin sauntered forward, his head tucked down, his back slumped. He seemed indifferent to their surroundings. "May I ask what yer doing 'ere?"

"Simply followin' the plan," said Mr. Fang. "The plan that you were instrumental in aidin' with."

"Aye, that I was." Now the narrow division between the roofs was all that separated them. Fagin hesitated not at all and vaulted over the division. He landed several feet away from them and continued his slow approach. "B'cause you ordered me to, so ye did. And now I'd be int'rested t'know what is the rest of the plan."

"Why in the world should I tell you?"

Fagin actually seemed taken aback by the question. "We go back a long ways, don't we, brother? Long ways, we do. And nice would it be not t'feel as if I'm bein' left behind."

Mr. Fang stared at him silently for a long moment. "You know, Fagin, there is so much I could say right now. So much I could tell you."

"Then pray, go ahead."

Fagin had continued to approach him so that he was merely a foot or two away. Drina had taken refuge behind Mr. Fang. She couldn't even bear to look Fagin in the eye.

"Very well," said Fang, and suddenly his hand was around Fagin's throat. He lifted Fagin into the air. Fagin grabbed at the hand, his legs kicking in the air. He tried to speak, but he was unable to.

"You know I have always had little tolerance for you, Fagin," continued Mr. Fang. "But our joint history has kept us together for far longer than I think either of us were planning. Now, though, thanks to Victoria here, my life is about to enter a new position of power. And it is not a position that you can readily share. I'm sorry about that, but that's just the way things go. Right here, right now, I could rip your head off your shoulders. Vampyric powers or not, you won't be surviving that anytime soon. Yes. Yes, I think that would definitely be the best way to go."

His grip began to tighten even more on Fagin's neck, and we would very much delight in telling you that that was the end of Fagin right then and there, because thus far he has done nothing to enamor us of his continued presence.

But Fagin's place in our tale was not destined to be concluded quite that quickly. So it was that Fagin wound up doing the only thing he could think of to do. His fangs snapped out and he sank them firmly into Mr. Fang's hand. Upon doing so, he bit down as ferociously as he was able to.

Mr. Fang let out a startled gasp as blood flowed from his hand. It was not the typically red human blood, but rather a thick, black substance that moved much more slowly. Apparently, and oddly, it had not occurred to Mr. Fang that Fagin would be inclined to fight for his life. So startled was he that he lost his grip on Fagin's throat. Fagin dropped to the rooftop and did not hesitate. Rubbing his throat as he moved, he sprinted for the edge of the roof and then leaped off it. He made no attempt to cover the distance to the adjoining roof. Instead, he allowed gravity to take command of the situation and fell straight down to the street below. He landed in a crouch, looking up toward the angry face of Mr. Fang, which peered down at him from the rooftop above.

"As you wish," called Mr. Fang. "We have been together far too long, Fagin. Our business is done. If you are fortunate, this will be the last time you look upon me. Do we understand each other?"

"Far too well, me love," said Fagin. Curiously, under the circumstances he did not sound the least bit upset. Curious indeed, considering what Mr. Fang had just both done and attempted to do, but there is no discerning the thought process of such a creature as Fagin, even if he were human—which he most certainly was not.

Mr. Fang didn't seem overly concerned by any of that, and ignoring his former brother on the street, he turned his attention to Victoria. He extended a hand. "Let us get you home, Princess. And let us introduce me to your mother."

"That sounds wonderful," said Drina. Ironically, to her at that point it did sound wonderful. Mr. Fang had just disposed of the vampyre whom she feared more than any other. The one who had invaded the abbey and taken her out of safe environs to her new master. Granted, she felt her adoration for her new master growing by the moment, but even if Fagin was responsible for that union, she still sorely resented him. Seeing him disposed of in such an offhand fashion naturally elevated her spirits somewhat.

Thus it was that she and Mr. Fang descended from the rooftop, secure in Fagin's having departed the area, and headed for Alexandrina Victoria's former home.

FOURTEEN

IN WHICH THE ARTFUL DODGER IS ARRESTED, BUT BY DESIGN

The Artful Dodger knew every square foot of London town, which is to say that he knew the areas that were bountiful with police officers; the areas where police officers were rarely, if ever, to be seen; and every other area, particularly in how it related to the population of the police, which one has to admit makes a great deal of sense, considering the various and assorted unlawful activities that tended to occupy the Dodger's time.

Normally, he restrained his activities to the areas less populated by police. His reasoning was simple: Anyone who was stupid enough to wander around in such unpatrolled areas—and there were quite a few anyones—deserved whatever happened to him or her.

And if there was one thing that Dodger had learned quite early on, it was to give a wide berth to Mutton Hill.

He still remembered vividly when he had endeavored to pick some gent's pocket in that particular neighborhood. Oliver Twist had been in tow, and Dodger's actions had been spotted and immediately called out. This had caught him utterly flat-footed, because in most sections of London, people were far too busy with their own business to pay attention to anything anyone else had to say. But when he and Charley Bates had taken it upon themselves to pick the pocket of Mr. Brownlow, the results had been nothing less than disastrous. Mr. Brownlow had shouted, "Stop, thief!" in full voice, and in many other parts of London, such bellows would go unattended. Not in Mutton Hill, though, where the cry had immediately been taken up by absolutely everyone in the area. The Artful and Master Bates had managed to vanish into nearby doorways and elude pursuit, but young Oliver had been borne down by an accusatory crowd and moments later dragged off to the domain of the police magistrate, one Mr. Fang. It had been Dodger's introduction to Mr. Fang, witnessing Oliver's quick and unfair trial, and he had made a mental note that he would be wise to stay away from the area.

That, however, was no longer an option. He needed to confront Mr. Fang. Ideally, he had to kill Mr. Fang. He had no idea how he was going to go about that, but he knew it had to be done. It was Drina's only chance.

Their coach had brought them to Mutton Hill, and Dodger and Bram disembarked from it. Bram looked around curiously. "Quite a busy market. Surprising that it's so occupied, considering the hour." The hour was at that point closing on nine o'clock. The Artful was aware of their deadline, and his mind was racing with how to cope with it. "So what do we do now?" asked Bram.

"We steal something," said Dodger. "We steal something, we get caught, and we get dragged in front of Mr. Fang."

"And then?"

"You still have your cross?"

"Naturally."

"All right," said Dodger. "Here's the plan then. When we're brought before Mr. Fang, you will bring out the cross. If he's like any other non-Jewish vampyre, he will shrink back from it. We use his screaming and hating the cross to get the other police officers to realize what he is. They help us kill him, and the problem is solved."

Bram was silent.

"What?" Dodger asked impatiently when he saw that Bram did not seem enamored of the scheme.

"We're counting on the help of the police? Is that wise? I mean, won't they just see us as thieves and street urchins and not be especially inclined to give us aid?"

"I don't care what they sees us as," said Dodger. "All I care is what *I* sees us as. And *I* sees us as Drina's last hope. So let's get on it and do it right."

"All right," said Bram with the tone of a verbal shrug. "So where do we start then?"

"We start with getting caught, as I said. And the easiest way to get caught is to nick a copper."

"What do you mean?"

"I mean exactly what I said. We find a police officer, try to take something from him, and get caught doing it. Just need to find . . . ah—there's a likely subject."

The object of Artful's interest was the most rotund police officer that Bram had ever seen. He was standing by a corner, idly tapping his club against his leg, looking around and trying to see someone who might be interested in causing some problems. As fate—or perhaps Dodger's simply wise positioning—would have it, he was looking in more or less every direction except at the individual who was in fact planning on engaging in some mischief.

The Artful slowly crept up on him, gesturing for Bram to join him in his advance. Bram dutifully did so, although he was still clearly looking a bit unsure about the entire endeavor. Very, very carefully Dodger came up behind the police officer. The man's purse was visible, bulging in his pocket. Artful slipped his hand into the pocket, and as he did so, made a point of bumping up against the man so that the thrust would be felt.

Instantly, the police officer reacted exactly as Dodger expected him to. He whipped around, grabbing Dodger by his wrist, and demanded, "What's all this!" Or at least that is what he began to say. The words, however, caught in his throat as he took one look at Dodger. His eyes widened in shock, and he let out a thunderous, infuriated roar. *"You!"* he practically bellowed.

Dodger had no idea whence came the recognition or why the police officer was reacting in such a manner. "Here now," said Dodger. "What's all—?"

He did not manage to get out another word. The police officer's stick flew almost as if it were alive and struck Dodger on the side of the head. It caught Dodger completely off guard. He had seen his fellows arrested any number of times. He himself had been brought down low on one occasion that he despised thinking about. Never, in any instance, had there been this sort of brutality and outright fury. He could not comprehend it. Then again, considering his mind was whirling, it's entirely possible that reciting the alphabet might have presented a serious challenge to him at that moment.

Passersby were stunned as they saw the policeman batter the stunned Dodger to his knees. It was astonishing. The purse fell from his hand, forgotten, and his walking stick fell from the other. All he could think about was trying to backpedal from the infuriated police officer.

"Did ye think I'd ever forget ye?" demanded the police officer. "Years may have passed, but your face ain't changed that much."

"What're you . . .?" Dodger started to say, but suddenly he realized whom he was facing. The officer had been wearing a different uniform back in the day, but it was unquestionably the same man: the jailer from whom Dodger had managed to escape back when he was supposed to be shipped to the far-off country of Australia.

"Do you have any idea what you did t'my career?" demanded the police officer. He continued to swing the club. This time he didn't get quite so clear a shot at Artful because the lad brought his arms up and managed to shield his head from direct contact. Nevertheless, the blows landed on his upper arms, shaking the flesh, jarring the bones. Dodger prayed that one or more of those bones wouldn't be shattered from the impact. "Six months! Six months I spent in a cell 'cause of you! Fired from the best job I ever had! Stuck as a bloody street officer, that's what I am! Because of you! You!" The blows continued to rain down.

Fearing for Dodger's life, Bram did the only thing he could think of. He charged forward and leaped off his feet. The police officer's back was to him, and Bram landed squarely on it. His small fists started pounding on the officer's shoulders and the back of his head.

"What now!?" demanded the befuddled officer. None of the blows were of sufficient strength to hurt, but they certainly served as a distraction. He reached around with his overlarge arms and finally managed to pry the angry Bram off his back. "And who are you now! A friend of Dawkins's!"

"That's right," said Bram. "A friend of the bravest, truest young man I've ever met."

The Artful was on the ground, still moaning softly from the beating he had sustained and not quite sure if he had heard correctly. Nevertheless, he managed to whisper, "Thanks, Bram. Much 'preciated."

The officer did not waste time; instead, he slammed Bram to the ground with as much force as he could muster. A bystander picked up the fallen purse and handed it to the police officer, who managed to utter a brusque thank-you before turning his attention back to the lads. He shoved his baton into his belt and grabbed up the thrown-down Bram by the back of his neck. "You will be dealt with in time. As for Dawkins, he'll be dealt with now."

Dodger still hadn't moved from where the police officer had dropped him. Partly, that was because, naturally, he wanted to be apprehended. But it was also partly from inability. The beating he had sustained had been so severe that at the moment he was incapable of getting to his feet. He managed to feel his face. The right half was starting to swell, and he felt a warm, salty taste in his mouth that he spat out. A red puddle spread on the sidewalk in front of his face. Then he was being hauled to his feet. At first, his knees gave way, and he would have fallen had not the police officer been holding him upright. He had lifted Dodger upward and was actually holding him a few inches in the air. "No struggling now!" he snarled.

"No struggling," Dodger managed to say. He coughed up a bit more blood, but was relieved to see that that appeared to be the end of it.

We would love to tell you that the police officer brought them to the police station with no more discourse, but that was most definitely not the case. Instead, the officer continued to excoriate Dodger for the entire angry walk, telling him that with any luck there would be no extradition this time, but instead a direct walk straight to the noose. Australia would doubtless be the destination for Dodger's accomplice—that much was sure. And perhaps finally, after all this time, the police officer—whose name was Hudgens, we should mention, because we have been remiss in not telling you that until this moment—would be able to reacquire the job from which he had been summarily dismissed.

The Artful paid little to no attention to the police officer's speech. He had his own priorities, such as retaining consciousness. The last thing he wanted to do was pass out and find himself awakening in a jail cell, having bypassed his confrontation with Mr. Fang and been sent straight to whatever unfortunate fate was awaiting him.

Minutes later, they were hauled into Mutton Hill Station. When Oliver Twist had been brought there, he had been ushered into a cell and kept there to await his confrontation with Mr. Fang, but that was not the case with Dodger and Bram. Instead, they were dragged across a small courtyard and under a narrowly arched door into the police headquarters. Dodger was grateful for this; the prospect of being tossed into a cell had been the one thing he'd worried about. He had not been certain about how much time they would be locked up for; if it extended into hours or even the next day, their deadline would be past, and Drina would be lost to them, presuming she wasn't already. He had a brief mental image of Drina sinking her fangs into the throat of some helpless victim and shuddered inwardly. "Resist, Drina," he whispered to no one at all, hoping that the sentiment could somehow cross the fog-covered rooftops of London and reach her ears.

The police officer ushered the boys past a small desk where a senior officer was seated. "Have a couple of miscreants we want served up right now!" declared Hudgens. "Don't dare turn your back on them! They're tricky, these two are!"

The Artful was by this point managing to walk on his own. "Yes, we're very tricky," he said. "You want to bring us before Mr. Fang right now, right this very moment."

"He's not here," said the police officer.

The words sent Dodger and Bram into a near panic. It was everything Dodger could do to keep that fear from surging upward. "Where . . . where is he?"

"None of your business."

Bram was clearly not taking that as a response. "Where," he repeated slowly, "is he." He did not give the intonation of a question. Rather, he was clearly expecting an answer.

Somehow to Dodger's surprise, the older officer hesitated a moment and then replied, "All right, if you must know: He's off to Buckingham Palace. Our own Mr. Fang has been invited to a late sup with the royal family. How's that for a magistrate, eh?"

"It's wonderful," said Dodger. "Couldn't be happier for him."

The older officer didn't seem the slightest bit impressed by Dodger's nonexistent joy for Mr. Fang's dinner plans. "Take him through there," he nodded to Hudgens. "Magistrate Grind will be with them posthaste."

The Artful said nothing but merely exchanged worried looks with Bram. Bram didn't have to respond; he knew the problem. None of this was going according to plan. A slight twitch in the boy's otherwise impassive face seemed to clearly say, "I told you so" to the Artful in a way Bram's mouth did not.

Hudgens hauled the two boys forward into the small magistrate chamber. Magistrate Grind was seated there. The Artful was unfamiliar with him; he was a middle-aged man with a sallow face and a clearly dyspeptic disposition. "And who are these lads?" he said. His voice was clipped and proper.

"This," said Hudgens, "is Mr. Jack Dawkins. The courts had already disposed of him to Australia, but he was able to escape imprisonment. But I finally managed to find him . . . and with his hand in me pocket, of all places!"

"A cutpurse, eh?" scowled Mr. Grind. "Well, I think we know what to do with his sort. And what of this one?"

"An aide of his," said Hudgens, indicating Dodger. "He assaulted me!"

Grind's scowl deepened even further. "He assaulted you?" His incredulity garnered some amused laughter from the couple of other officers who were in the room. "He looks as if he weighs almost nothing. How in God's name did he assault you?"

"He . . . ." Hudgens's voice trailed off at first, and then he rallied. "He climbed upon me. He's very sneaky."

"Yes, I'm sure," said Mr. Grind sarcastically.

Bram suddenly produced his cross from beneath his shirt. Without saying a word, he stepped out of the accused box into which they had been shoved and advanced on Mr. Grind. Dim light reflected off the cross.

Mr. Grind stared at it blankly. "What do you think you're doing, lad?"

"Testing you," said Bram.

He drew closer, and now Officer Hudgens had come in from behind him and clamped a hand on his shoulder. He stopped Bram several paces shy of Mr. Grind, who continued not to react to the cross, beyond utter puzzlement that it was being waved at him. "And have I passed the test?" asked Mr. Grind, clearly quite curious as to what Bram was up to.

Slowly, Bram lowered the cross. "You're not a vampyre. Or if you are, you've certainly got more control than any I've ever seen."

"Any you've ever seen?" Mr. Grind said, and raised an eyebrow. He clearly found this to be an amusing statement. "And who are you to have seen mythical creatures, eh?"

"My name is Abraham van Helsing. And I've seen more than you can possibly believe exist."

"I don't recognize your accent, boy. Where do you come from?"

"I'm Dutch."

"You sound more German than Dutch."

"My mother is German. I'm told I got the accent from her. But I am Dutch."

"Well, I don't know how matters transpire in Dutchland," said Mr. Grind, "but here in England, we don't have vampyres—mythical, realistic, or any other kind."

"That is how much you know," said Bram. "I know all about them, including how to handle them."

"Really. I'd like to see that," said an amused Mr. Grind.

By this point, Hudgens had had enough. He pulled Bram by the shoulder and said, "Come, boy. Back in your place."

Bram snapped his right arm forward. A stake slid out from his sleeve and into his palm. He whirled, dropped to his knees, and slammed the stake directly into Hudgens's foot.

Hudgens let out an ear-piercing screech.

"Run!" shouted Bram. "Go now!"

Bram stood, spun, and jabbed the stake at the first police officer that came near. He wasn't aiming for the officer's chest; if he had been, the officer would have been dead. As it was, the point sank into the right side of the man's chest, between his second and third ribs. The officer let out a scream and clutched at his chest as blood seeped out between his fingers.

Hudgens was jumping up and down, holding the foot and howling a series of profanities. Mr. Grind had slid back in his chair in alarm and was bellowing at the top of his lungs for help.

Help was quick in coming. From a far door, half a dozen police officers burst in, not having the slightest idea what was happening, but knowing from all that screaming that something certainly was.

Bram stood in the midst of the room. He still had the stake in his hand; it was tinted red with blood. Hudgens had stopped hopping, choosing instead to fall to the ground and clutch forlornly at his boot. The police officer that Bram had stabbed was leaning against the wall, putting pressure on the bleeding that was already slowing. Meanwhile, Bram was continuing his attack, having extracted a knife from a hidden pocket in his coat. He was waving it threateningly in his left hand. He lunged left, right, left. The officers kept moving forward and then falling back, clearly unsure of how to deal with the berserk young man.

Finally, they converged upon him together. He might have been formidable for his age in one-to-one battle, but not even a formidable adult would readily be able to deal with six full-grown adults charging as one. They came together then, and although Bram tried to drive them back with his weapons, he was unsuccessful. The stake glanced off the arm of the nearest officer, who then slapped it away out of Bram's grasp.

Disarming him of the knife only took another moment, and Bram was borne to the ground by the collective weight of the police officers. Bram went down, all the officers atop him. He tried to crawl out from under them—and nearly made it, but one of them grabbed him by the ankle and held firm. Seconds later, Bram was yanked upward to his feet.

His face seemed utterly calm. There was nothing about his personality to indicate that he had been the center of any sort of battle at all.

Mr. Grind pointed a quavering finger at the lad. "Take this boy away! Lock him in a cell! Leave him for Mr. Fang to deal with! But I'll tell you this, lad: Best resign yourself to switching to an Australian accent, because I'll warrant that that's where you're going to find yourself winding up! And as for your associate . . ." His voice trailed off. "Where's the other lad? Where's Dawkins?"

Jack Dawkins, the Artful Dodger, was gone. While Bram had been fighting the officers, his imprecations of "Run!" had not been lost upon the individual toward whom they were aimed. So it was that although Bram was firmly in the hands of the police, Dodger was still free, and Drina still had the chance to avoid her terrible doom.

It was just not a particularly great chance.

❧ ✳ ❧

The Artful Dodger fled into the street. As the evening hour had progressed, the last remnants of buyers had gone home, and the shops had closed up. Now it was relatively deserted passageways that Dodger traversed. While he did so, his heart was beating rapidly, and his mind was racing fiercely.

Mr. Fang had gone to Buckingham Palace? He was supping with the royal family? The Artful didn't have the faintest idea how that had happened . . . .

No, he did. Upon further thought, he knew exactly how it had happened. This had Mr. Fang's villainy all over it. It was actually brilliant. Now it was more clear to Dodger than ever before: Fang had definitely been the one who had transformed Drina. And his next move was to return her to the home from which she had fled. He would present himself as her savior, and the royal family, having no way of knowing about the actions he had taken against her, would welcome him with open arms.

And then what?

And then *anything*.

Between the gratitude of the royals and his obvious ability to control Drina, he would be able to accomplish whatever he wished. He could set himself up in some sort of powerful advisory capacity to the royal family. They might even bestow a title upon him. Provide him with property, servants, whatever he desired. It was a remarkable opportunity for him to form a base of power and perhaps extend his control of the government— who knew how far? Plus he had control over Drina, and she would become the queen some day (far more power, we should take the time to note, than he wielded over Fagin, because Fagin was the very first vampyre that he had turned, and he had not been quite as skilled in the art of mental domination during that transition). Still, how much power could one man, or one creature, be permitted to have?

And now Dodger was alone. Bram had sacrificed himself to provide a distraction so that Dodger could elude the clutches of the police officers. It had been a brilliant move—certainly far more clever than anything that Dodger himself had come up with.

He should have realized that Mr. Fang might not be there; indeed, *would* not. His desires had moved on to manipulating his masterful new acquisition, the future queen of all England. Happenings at the police station were no longer of any interest to him. He had far greater things to concern himself about.

Only Jack Dawkins could stop him.

He just didn't have the slightest idea how to do it.

He only knew he had to get away from the area, and quickly. By now, the police would realize that the Artful Dodger had made his getaway and would likely be spreading out to try to find him before he could vacate the area. Which was precisely what he was trying to do.

The coach was right ahead, waiting for him as obediently as he could have hoped. Quinn was seated atop it, cloaked in shadow. Dodger ran to it as quickly as he could and scrambled into the interior. "Get out of here, Quinn. Now!"

"But what about Bram?" Quinn called down.

"He's fine," Dodger lied, and he flopped back into the seat as the coach rolled forward. He lay there, slumped and exhausted and never feeling more defeated than he did right then. He wanted to ask someone's advice as to what to do, but there was no one.

No one except . . . .

"Quinn," called Dodger, "as soon as we're away from this area, pull over and come down here! I need to talk with you about something."

"What?" Quinn couldn't hear him over the horse's hoofbeats.

The Artful started to repeat himself, and suddenly the carriage swayed wildly off course. It veered left and then right, and Dodger was thrown side to side. "What the bloody hell?" he called out.

Quinn did not respond. The silence alone should have tipped Dodger off to the fact that something was terribly wrong, but he was too busy dealing with being tossed about to have an interest in anything other than a cessation of being thrown around.

Quinn must have pulled on the reins, because the horse suddenly skidded to a stop. The Artful was thrown forward this time and bounced off the far end of the carriage. For a second time, he shouted, *"What the bloody hell?"* because Quinn hadn't provided him an answer the first time.

As the carriage had come to a halt, although hardly a smooth one, Dodger threw open the door and jumped out of it. "Quinn!" he shouted.

Quinn didn't hear him. Quinn didn't hear anything because his lifeless body was thrown from the top of the coach. Dodger gasped and leaped back as the body thudded onto the street next to him.

A man whom Dodger did not know descended from the seat. He was remarkably tall and wore a black greatcoat that swirled around him. He seemed to exude fog, as if he were partly made of it.

"Who are you?" Dodger managed to whisper.

The man bowed slightly and mockingly. "They call me Harry—Sanguine Harry—do those who have a feel for the occasional pun. And you are the Artful Dodger, yes?"

Slowly Dodger nodded. All he wanted to do was flee, but he was paralyzed. He was actually sending mental commands to his legs to work, but they remained straight and stuck to the area.

"You made quite the mistake, Dodger. You went to Mr. Fang's place of business. Did you think we did not anticipate that you might do such a thing? Did you think we were not watching it and waiting and preparing for it? Now Bram is safely in police hands, and they should attend to him. You, however, are far too free. You need to be taken care of, and I'm afraid that I've been designated to do so."

Slowly, he advanced on Dodger. His voice was low and seductive. "Here's a suggestion, Mr. Dawkins. Don't move. Don't resist. I will make certain that your death is quick."

The Artful did the only thing he could think of to do. He threw his foot forward in a kick, aiming for Sanguine Harry's crotch, in hopes of doubling him over in pain. The blow landed solidly, but Harry simply stared at him in mild amusement. "I'm dead, boy—down there, perhaps more so. You can't hurt a dead man."

He reached for Dodger, who dropped to the ground and scampered under the coach.

"Oh, for crying out loud," Sanguine Harry said with a snarl. "What do you think you're doing? Hahhh!" That last shout was aimed at the horse as Harry smacked the animal in its flank to get it to roll forward. The horse, already skittish, readily accommodated and moved forward, hauling the carriage with it.

Artful was no longer there. Having rolled out the other side of the carriage, he was now sprinting down the closest street as quickly as his legs would carry him.

Sanguine Harry stood there for a long moment, shaking his head in disappointment and frustration. "You're dragging this out, boy," he said and set off after Dodger.

We would love to tell you that it was a prolonged and daring race through the streets of London. That Dodger used his knowledge of the back streets to give Harry an incredibly difficult time, and even to lose him once or twice in the shadows of the night. Unfortunately, that was most definitely not the case. The Artful managed to get not more than a hundred or so feet, and then something grabbed him by the back of the shirt and pulled him up short. He tried to pull free, but he was utterly unable to do so.

Harry spun him around to face him. The Artful desperately wished he too were carrying a stake, that he had been even half as well armed as Bram had been. But he had nothing, no weapons, and now there was a hungry vampyre upon him. *I've lost. I'm so sorry, Drina. I've lost.*

Sanguine Harry smiled grimly into Dodger's face. "You gave it a good run, lad. You truly did. Tell you what: You'd make a worthwhile student. How about if I don't kill you? How about I turn you into one of me?"

"One of you? A vampyre, you mean?"

"O' course that's what I mean. Granted, it'd run contrary to orders. But I doubt that Mr. Fang would offer too strenuous an objection once the deed was done. Better to ask forgiveness than permission, I always say." He nudged Dodger. It was almost a friendly gesture. "Come on, lad. You'll wind up just like your precious Victoria. You'd probably enjoy it."

"I probably would."

"All right!" Sanguine Harry for the first time actually seemed cheered by the prospect. "So first, I drain you. And then I open a vein and you drink from me. Ya ready?"

"Sure," said Dodger, trying to grin.

Sanguine Harry brought his face down toward Dodger's throat, and that was when the Artful Dodger slammed his head forward as hard as he could. It crashed into Harry's face, and the vampyre let out a loud yell of pain. He staggered, clutching at his face, and he momentarily lost his hold on Dodger. The Artful pulled away from him, his shirt tearing slightly as he did so, and he started to run. Unfortunately, he only managed to get five feet this time and then Sanguine Harry was upon him. Harry was clearly taking no more chances as he bore Dodger to the ground, face down. The Artful slammed into the walkway with such jarring force that it almost knocked a tooth loose.

From behind him, Harry snarled, "I gave you a chance, boy. I could have made you one of us. Now, though . . . now you die."

The Artful braced himself as Sanguine Harry brought his teeth down toward Dodger's throat. He tossed out a final prayer to a God that he was sure wasn't bothering to listen to him, that Bram somehow managed to get out of police custody and take over for him in rescuing Drina during the few hours they had left.

He expected to hear nothing but silence from the Lord. What he didn't expect was Sanguine Harry gasping into his ear.

He frowned and tried to look behind him but was not in a good position to see much of anything. Then Sanguine Harry gasped again and started to tremble violently. He was no longer making any effort to keep Dodger flat upon the ground, and Artful managed to twist around and shove Harry off himself. He gaped in astonishment at what he saw.

A stake was sticking out of Sanguine Harry's back. Harry's eyes had blackened over, and his head was still shaking violently.

Someone was standing behind Harry; clearly, it was the individual who had shoved the stake home. The Artful stared at him and he could not believe what he was seeing.

It was Fagin.

His mouth was twisted into a triumphant snarl. "Hello, dearie," he said, his voice an amused whisper.

Harry was actually trying to get to his feet, but Fagin gave him no opportunity. Instead, he interlaced his fingers and slammed them down in a two-fisted smash onto the part of the stake that was protruding. It drove the stake even more thoroughly into Sanguine Harry's heart, and Harry let out a scream so loud that Dodger clapped his hands over his ears.

It wasn't necessary, for as quickly as the scream had released, Harry fell forward with a disgusting splotching sound. His body began to rot away, aging what seemed a thousand years in a matter of seconds. Just that fast, his body was gone, and the threat of Sanguine Harry along with it.

A long silence followed as Dodger clambered to his feet and faced his former mentor. Then Fagin reached down and yanked the stake out of Harry's back. The remains of his body trembled ever so slightly, and then the last of the aging passed through him. He crumbled away into nothing except a pile of old clothes.

Fagin stared down at him for a moment and picked up the coat. Then he tossed it over to Dodger, who caught it more automatically than out of desire. "It'll be big on ye, but that's 'ardly a new sensation for ye, eh?"

"Why?" said Dodger. "Why did you do it? Why did you kill him?"

"Because he irritated me somethin' fierce," said Fagin. He was studying the stake as if it was something new to him. "As he did ye as well, I'd guess. Here," he said, lobbing the stake to Dodger, who caught it easily. "You'll prob'ly be needing this. You're going after Mr. Fang, I imagine."

"That's the plan."

"Best of luck to ye then."

The Artful couldn't believe it. "You just killed the thing that was trying t'kill me and now you're walking away?"

"That's right," said Fagin. "B'cause there may be no love lost twixt me and Mr. Fang, but that don't mean I'm tending to go face to face with 'im. Best leave that to ye, Dodger. And Mr. Fang *is* who ye want. He's the one what changed your little princess into one of us."

"I know."

"Oh, ye know, do ye? Best hurry to the palace then if ye have any hope of trying to stop him from making the change permanent. As for us,"—and he gestured toward Dodger and then himself—"I fancy we're even now."

"Even?"

"For my small part in the death of yer mum. Granted, I didn't do the deed meself, but I was still part of the entire business, and believe it or not, I felt bad about it for quite some time. But now I saved yer life, so t'my mind, we're square. A life for a life."

"We," said Dodger quietly, "will never be even, Fagin. Not ever. My life was destroyed 'cause of you, and I will never f'get that or f'give you."

"Well then," said Fagin, and he bowed mockingly, "then best of luck to ye anyway. And perhaps we will meet in more favorable circumstances at some point in the future."

With that, Fagin backed away into the shadows, which reached out and swallowed him, leaving Dodger alone in the street.

His mind was in a tumult. He was reeling from Hudgens's beating, as well as Harry's attack, and now Fagin saving him. He could scarcely parse a bit of it. And it was then that things clicked for Dodger: There was no time for making sense. Only time for action. Observe and react, just as he'd been doing his whole life—just as he'd failed to do when his mother was killed.

Realizing he had no other choice, Dodger returned to the carriage. Quinn's body was lying on the ground, and the horse was neighing pitifully. Unsure of what to do, Dodger decided that the first thing he needed to do was attend to Quinn. He managed to haul Quinn's body upright and slowly, laboriously, shoved the body into the carriage. He was huffing and puffing mightily and, once the feat was accomplished, he slammed the door. Quinn's dead body sat upright in the carriage, slumped over to one side.

Now what? Now what? The same frantic thought kept on racing through his head, but no immediate reply was presenting itself. Now what indeed? *Figure out the situation and then react, old chum.* He had to find a way to get into Buckingham Palace so that he could get to Drina and, even more importantly, to

Mr. Fang. If he did not manage to slay Mr. Fang, Drina would permanently be a vampyre once the clock struck midnight.

Of course, his reaction—his plan—wasn't quite as fully formed as he might have hoped. He still had to get into Buckingham. He had to get past the assortment of guards and penetrate the deepest recesses of the most heavily guarded building in the entirety of the kingdom. And counting travel time to get to Westminster, he would have barely an hour or so to figure it out.

"Then I's got an hour to do the figurin'," he said. He clambered up onto the seat that Quinn had previously been occupying. He hoped that the horse knew what to do, because Dodger only had the vaguest idea. "Yah!" he shouted because he felt obliged to shout something. The horse actually turned and looked at him in bewilderment, as if trying to figure out who this new individual was and what in the world had happened to the man who was supposed to be there. The Artful shouted, "Yah!" a second time, snapping the reins with what he hoped was pronounced authority. The horse seemed to respect this to a certain degree, and it started forward. The Artful flicked the reins one more time, and the horse actually sped up. It wasn't galloping, but at least it was moving at a brisk trot.

Now all he had to do was figure out how he was going to gain access into the palace.

Fast.

FIFTEEN

In Which We Learn the Details of
Drina's Return Home

We have thus far been remiss in describing, in any detail, Princess Alexandrina Victoria's homecoming (which is entirely our responsibility) due to the fact that there was so much transpiring with Dodger and Bram that our attention remained focused upon them, but now, because we have a few minutes to breathe while Dodger makes his way to the place where the climax of our tale is to be found, we feel constrained to flesh out for you the circumstances of Drina's return.

At first, believe it or not, she had trouble gaining access to her own home. Pity the guards, none of whom had ever actually had the opportunity to view their future monarch in any sort of proximity. So what they beheld was the unassuming, if mildly threatening, form of Mr. Fang approaching the great front gates in the company of a somewhat disheveled streetwalker. One of the guards stepped smartly forward, bringing his rifle across his upper body as a means of quietly informing the two approaching individuals that they were not to advance any farther.

"What do you think you're doing?" Mr. Fang inquired.

"I am stopping you in your path, sir," replied the guard. "What is your business here?"

"My business is with the mother of Princess Alexandrina Victoria."

"And what business could you possibly have with her?"

"I have her daughter right here."

The guard stared at him skeptically. "You have the princess with you. This . . . person?" He flicked a skeptical look at Drina.

"This person," said Mr. Fang, "is your future queen, and I strongly suggest you provide her with the respect that her office is due."

The guard actually chuckled at that. Think kindly of him, we beg you: He was in fact unaware that the princess had departed the palace. The adults in her life had done a superb job of keeping that fact as quiet as possible, and even the guardsmen had been kept from knowing. So he had no reason to think that Mr. Fang was anything other than a nutter. "This is the future queen? This is Princess Alexandrina Victoria?"

"That is correct."

"Right. And I'm the king o' Spain." He pointed at the street. "Be off with you."

Mr. Fang was not to be deterred. "I wish to speak with your commanding officer. Now, if you please."

The guard blew some air impatiently through his mouth. At this point, he was inclined to march them to the street, but the turmoil being created by Mr. Fang's insistence served to accomplish exactly what he had desired: The noise and the back and forth was overheard by the captain of the palace guard, who chose to discover just what was responsible for causing such a ruckus.

And so the captain strode forward and said brusquely, "What is it?"

Mr. Fang started to speak, but Drina put a hand on his shoulder to indicate that she would handle matters from here. She strode forward and looked into the eyes of the captain of the guards. "Roderick, is it not?" was all she said.

The captain seemed to see her for the first time, and then he gasped. "Princess!" he cried out. "What . . . I don't understand . . . I . . ." Then he managed to gain control of himself, snapped upright, and saluted her smartly while simultaneously averting his eyes so that he was not staring directly into hers. "Highness! How can we help you?"

"You can let me into my home," she said in a soft but commanding voice.

"At once, Highness. Guards!" he called out, clapping his hands briskly. The guards immediately came running. The younger guard who had challenged her when she had first arrived had gone deathly white. The only thing he could think of to do was stand perfectly still, his right hand snapped into a salute at the brim of his tall black hat. The rest of the guards in the immediate area formed a circle around Drina and Mr. Fang and escorted them to the interior confines of Buckingham Palace.

Princess Victoria, the mother of Princess Alexandrina Victoria, was there to meet her at the door. Her full name, it should be noted in the interest of being complete, was Princess Mary Louise Victoria of Saxe-Coburg-Saalfeld, but Princess Victoria was how she was more routinely referred to around the palace. Thus was her daughter frequently referred to as the Princess Alexandrina so that everyone knew whom everyone else was talking about at any given moment. It is unclear how she knew that her daughter had returned, but nevertheless there she was. Her entire body was sagging in relief the moment that her daughter was in view. *"Alexandrina!"* she cried out. "Oh my lord! Where have you been? I've been worried sick about you! Absolutely sick!" Truth to tell, it was a somewhat extraordinary and over-the-top reaction for a personage of royal blood to be indulging in—although not for a mother—and certainly no one felt it was their place to gainsay her.

Drina approached her slowly, and her mother met her halfway, throwing her arms around her and embracing her tightly.

"How could you do that?" she demanded. The princess was endeavoring to apply her sterner mother's voice rather than her concerned mother's voice, with a variance of success. "How could you sneak out of the palace in such a way?"

"No harm came from it, Mother."

"No harm! Look at you! You look as if you haven't bathed in days! And what is this dress that you're wearing? And . . ." Her attention finally seemed to focus on Drina's companion. "And who is this?"

"This is Mr. Fang," said Drina. She gestured for him to approach, which he obediently did. "He is a police magistrate. He is the one who found me out in the streets and took it upon himself to return me safely."

"Well, then!" said the princess. "It behooves me to thank him properly."

The princess was an attractive woman. Her hair was short, brown and curly; her eyes were brown; her face, round and comely. She approached Mr. Fang with an arm still draped around her daughter's shoulders, holding her tightly against her body. "Mr. . . . . Fang, is it?"

"Yes, your Highness." He bowed deeply.

"Mr. Fang, the royal family is in your debt. And in England, such debts are paid in full. Do you have a price in mind?"

He gave her an odd look and then permitted a smile. "I assure you, Highness, I seek no remuneration. The time I've had to spend with your daughter is certainly compensation enough."

"Nonsense!" said Drina, perfectly on cue. "I insist that Mr. Fang be welcomed to Buckingham as if it were his own home and join us in a late repast."

"That will not be necessary," Mr. Fang assured them. "I am not even hungry." That was a clever thing for him to say as he would, in fact, not be especially inclined to eat any food put out for him. Drina was still recent enough to her human incarnation that she was capable of ingesting human food, but Mr. Fang had long left such delicacies behind.

"I insist," Drina repeated, "and as a princess, I feel it is my right to have my wishes accommodated."

"Alexandrina," her mother said stiffly, "if the man has no desire . . . ."

To her mother's utter astonishment, Drina refused to take no for an answer. "I insist, Mother."

Princess Victoria's mouth moved for a long moment, but no words emerged. Then she forced a smile. "Of course. Whatever you wish, Alexandrina. Pintel!" The voice rang over the space of the great hall, and seconds later a servant appeared, seemingly out of nowhere. "Pintel, bring Mr. Fang to a waiting room. Then inform the kitchen we would appreciate a light repast be set up. See to it, would you? Oh, and inform Sir Conroy of the current situation."

"Yes, Highness," said Pintel, bowing deeply. He turned to Mr. Fang and gestured for him to follow, which Mr. Fang did. Princess Victoria then took her daughter's arm in her own and walked quickly to the huge, main stairs. They walked up the stairs, without a word, until they finally arrived at Drina's bedroom. The princess closed the door behind her and her daughter.

"Mother," Drina started to say.

She did not get past the first syllable. The princess's hand flew and struck Alexandrina across her right cheek. Drina staggered, and Victoria struck her a second time. This time the blow was so vicious that it literally knocked Drina off her feet. She fell to the ground, landing heavily, cracking her elbow badly.

"How dare you!" her mother said with uncontained fury. "How dare you slip out of the palace! How dare you go off on your own! Do you have any idea who you are? Do you know what sort of responsibilities you have to both yourself and your kingdom? If your father were alive, he would likely kill you with his own hands!"

Drina lay where she was for a long moment. In her head, her response to the princess's actions was quite clear. In her head, she leaped to her feet, and her fangs snapped out. She vaulted across the distance of the room between them, landing on her mother's chest and slamming her to the floor. Her mother screeched and squirmed under her, begging for mercy, not quite understanding what was happening to her. Then Drina sank her fangs into her mother's throat, and Princess Victoria screamed and thrashed violently. She did everything she could to extricate herself from her daughter's attentions, but it did no good. All that happened was that her thrusts and shoves became weaker and weaker, and within moments ceased altogether. At that point, Drina lifted her head and let out a triumphant shriek, as if she were loudly welcoming her entire life to come.

All of this, as we said, passed through her mind. She did not, however, do it. Instead, she remained where she was, rubbing her jaw but otherwise not saying anything. She simply stared levelly at her mother, without speaking.

Her mother was breathing heavily from the strain of slapping her daughter so viciously. Finally, her temper began to settle. Then tears started to dribble from her eyes. Drina was appalled at the sentimental display. She'd almost have preferred that her mother continue to batter her, because perhaps that would finally have provoked her into physical retaliation.

Instead, her mother sighed heavily, wiping the tears away. "I am so sorry, Alexandrina. I should not have done that. I was angry, yes, but that is no excuse for taking such an action against you. Can you forgive me?"

Drina was not the least bit interested in forgiving her. Drina wanted to drain her dry. It would take no time at all.

But she knew she could not—*must* not. That was not Mr. Fang's plan. His plan was very specific, and her mother needed to live, at least for a while, for the plan to reach fruition. There were too many people in Drina's life who could stand in opposition to Mr. Fang, and at least for the time being Princess Victoria was going to be necessary to accomplish that.

And so, lying through her fanged teeth, Drina simply nodded and said, "Yes. Yes, of course I forgive you."

Her mother went to her and extended a hand. Drina took it and allowed her mother to haul her to her feet. Her mother looked her up and down and shook her head. "Where did you get this ensemble?" she asked.

"From a woman. She was trying to help. My own clothes were soiled."

"Well, let's get you bathed and attended to. And then we shall join your Mr. Fang for a meal, and all will be accounted for."

"That would be superb," said Drina, and she forced a smile.

⊰ ✳ ⊱

Mr. Fang was rather impressed by the room in which he had been asked to wait. It was filled with paintings of heroic, armored individuals. He found it a bit amusing to see Britons so valiantly represented in the midst of combat.

The furniture was likewise quite luxurious. Mr. Fang dropped into one particularly ornate chair and simply sat there, unmoving and unbreathing, although it would have taken a particularly sharp eye to make note of that second fact.

There was a noise at the double doors that provided entrance into the room. Immediately, Mr. Fang was on his feet, taking the time to straighten his coat in anticipation of the princess's entrance. It was not, however, a princess who entered—either princess. Instead, it was a tall, stately, dignified gentleman. His black hair, streaked with a few shades of gray, was brushed back, and he sported rather large, and yet understated, muttonchops. He looked down his nose at Mr. Fang in a way that Mr. Fang found rather off-putting. But he tolerated it because killing the man did not seem a reasonable option.

The man walked stiffly with an elegant walking stick. He didn't require it for actual locomotion; it was simply for show.

"May I help you?" Mr. Fang said with measured politeness.

"I," said the gentleman, "am Sir John Conroy."

"Ah." Mr. Fang nodded. "Yes, of course. I believe I've heard of you. You have some influence within the royal household."

"More than just influence, good sir," said Sir Conroy. "The duchess and I have a good deal of influence over the day-to-day schooling of young Alexandrina."

"The duchess? Oh, the princess. Yes, yes," said Mr. Fang. "I've heard that. I have, in fact, heard a great deal."

"Have you?"

"Why, yes. I heard that you created the entire educational system under which the princess has been schooled."

"Absolutely correct," said Sir Conroy. He tugged at his jacket yet again. It was some sort of nervous habit; that much was clear to Mr. Fang. "It has benefited her tremendously."

"Clearly so. Benefited her so thoroughly that she fled the palace in order to escape it."

Conroy's face did not fall. He had far too much self-control to display such an open reaction. Instead, he permitted the smallest of smiles. "Sadly, it is impossible to predict every reaction that a teenage girl may experience or undergo. We will deal with her actions appropriately."

"*You* will deal with them? You had no idea where she was or who she was with," Mr. Fang informed him. "If we were still waiting for you to take action, no action would have been taken. That is simple truth, Sir Conroy. You know it as well as I."

Sir Conroy's tone dropped into one of pure frost, and his façade cracked just a touch. "I do not believe I need to be lectured by you, Mr. Fang."

"You certainly need to be lectured by somebody, and I do not see why it cannot be me."

Conroy took a deep breath and then let it out very slowly. "Mr. Fang . . . obviously, we owe you a debt. That debt shall be repaid. I was thinking perhaps five hundred pounds sterling should settle the matter nicely. Certainly a generous sum."

"To be sure," agreed Mr. Fang. "Most generous indeed. And to be blunt, sir, it almost seems that you are seeing this as some sort of opportunity to buy me off. Or am I misinterpreting your intentions?"

There was a good deal that Sir Conroy could have said at that moment. All manner of protestations came to mind, but quickly he realized that it would likely come to naught. Instead, his small smile became even more diminutive. "Mr. Fang," he said, pronouncing his words very carefully, "what do you believe is going to happen here this evening?"

"I believe that I will be supping with the princesses quite shortly. And then I believe that Princess Alexandrina Victoria is going to make me a permanent member of her staff. Her chief advisor, as it were."

"And what in the world would lead you to that conclusion?"

"The words of Princess Alexandrina herself. She seemed quite taken with me when I rescued her from the threats of the street. Threats that she was only in because she was fleeing your imprisoning teaching methods. Or did I not make that sufficiently clear?"

"More than," said Sir Conroy stiffly. "And now, sir, I am going to have to ask you to leave such promises behind, and depart the palace immediately."

"Against the wishes of the princess?"

"The princess is not entitled to have wishes."

"I believe that she is. And I further believe that, sooner or later . . . sooner, by my reckoning . . . she is going to be the queen of England. Once that happens, in how high accord do you think she is going to hold someone who dismisses her desires so casually?"

Conroy paused for half a heartbeat and then called loudly, "Guards!"

The doors sprang open, and two guards strode in. They took five steps forward, came to a halt, and thudded their gun butts to indicate that they were at attention and ready to receive commands.

"See this fellow out," said Sir Conroy.

It was at that point that Mr. Fang decided stronger measures needed to be taken. Fortunately enough, Sir Conroy was looking him directly in the eyes. Perhaps he felt that his severe gaze would be sufficient to persuade Mr. Fang that it was time to depart. Luckily for Mr. Fang, the direct stare into his eyes was all that he required to accomplish what he needed to.

He sent his mind into the thoughts of Sir Conroy and enveloped them quite easily. It was not difficult at all because Sir Conroy was so confident in himself that the thought of being hypnotized by someone, much less an unassuming police magistrate such as Mr. Fang, never would have occurred to him—mostly because he had never thought of hypnotism in his entire life.

"That won't be necessary," said Mr. Fang. "Your guards can return to their posts."

"He's quite right," said Sir Conroy immediately, so quickly that the guards literally froze in position, bewildered as to what was happening. "Both of you can return to your posts."

The taller of the guards looked at Conroy, then at his fellow guardsman, and then back at Conroy. "Are you quite sure, Sir Conroy?" he asked.

"Yes, yes, quite sure." Conroy even sounded a bit irritated. "I'm unaccustomed to having to repeat myself."

"Yes, sir," said the guard. Without another word, he and his companion strode briskly out the door, closing it behind them.

The moment that they had departed, confusion appeared on Sir Conroy's face. He looked after the guards and then to Mr. Fang. "What . . . I don't . . . ?"

"You decided that the wishes of Princess Alexandrina should be attended to," said Mr. Fang. "As simple as that, really. Is there anything else we need to discuss?"

"I . . . suppose not," said Sir Conroy.

And for the moment, there was not.

SIXTEEN

In Which the Dodger Assails Buckingham Palace
and Unexpectedly Runs Into an Old Friend

B
uckingham Palace was well known as one of the most heavily guarded buildings in the world, so much so that no one in his right mind—and for that matter, even most people in their wrong mind—would ever have considered for so much as a heartbeat the challenge of trying to break into it, and yet that was exactly the situation into which the Artful Dodger was finding himself thrust.

And he did not have the faintest idea how to go about doing so. Breaking into an ordinary house, something that he had indeed done before, was very different from attempting to gain entrance into Buckingham Palace.

Driving the coach was not the easiest endeavor that he had undertaken, but fortunately the horse seemed to be genuinely responsive to his hand. He pounded down the road, heading toward Buckingham Palace, determined to come up with some means of gaining entrance while en route. Nothing, however, came to him during the entire journey. As a result, the closer he drew to the recognizable spires of Buckingham, the more he began to slow down. Eventually, five hundred feet from the approach, he drew the carriage to a halt. The guards were lined up, unflappable as they typically were. Not a single one of them was looking at Dodger. He had not registered on them, or if he had, they were managing to keep it to themselves.

"Think," said Dodger to himself. Nothing was coming to mind. "Any suggestions?" he called to the horse, but the animal did not seem especially inclined to contribute to the conversation. That left Dodger back on his own. He desperately wished that Bram were there to lend a hand, but unfortunately that brave lad was being held in the police station, under armed guard probably. And if Dodger had to deal with one set of armed guards, he knew it was going to be the ones in front of the palace.

Oddly, his thoughts about Bram led his thoughts to wishing that Fagin was there—on some level, at least. Certainly, the creature's vampyric ability would be of some use. With Fagin's aid, he could climb up the side of the building, enter through a window, and find Drina that way. As quickly as the notion occurred to him, however, he rejected it. Whatever happened this evening, he had no desire to share credit for its outcome with the monstrous Fagin. He would have to stand or fall on his own, even though the only ally he had left to him was Quinn's corpse in the carriage.

Then it hit him. It was not the most wonderful idea in the land, but at least it was something, and it was certainly far better than having nothing at all.

Quickly Dodger clambered down from the seat and threw open the door. Quinn was lying on his side, looking extremely rumpled and disheveled. Dodger's heart went out to him. Quinn had been a decent and brave sort, and the fact that he had died during this endeavor was almost enough to cause the Artful's own bravery to waver. With an effort, though, he shoved that bravery back into place and forced himself to think of Quinn as nothing more than a prop, in order to accomplish what he needed to do.

The Artful stripped off Quinn's distinctive riding jacket. He was wearing a white shirt underneath that looked vaguely formal. His trousers were scruffy, though, so Dodger grabbed a blanket from the seat across from him and draped it across his legs. The result was that he looked fairly nondescript. He could have been a driver, yes, but he also could have been more or less anyone. That was exactly what Dodger required.

Artful made sure that Quinn was upright, leaning slightly against the right-hand side of the coach so that he would remain in a sitting position. "Make this work," Dodger muttered to both himself and the corpse of Quinn. Then he climbed back up into the driver's seat, snapped the reins, and drove the horse forward.

The horse moved at a brisk trot toward the main gates of Buckingham. Eventually, they drew sufficiently within range that the guards reacted to his approach. One of them came forward and put up one hand to indicate that the carriage should be drawn to a halt. The Artful obeyed, as he knew he would have to, slowing the carriage down until it was even with the guard.

"What's all this, lad?" the guard asked.

The Artful's heart was slamming against his chest, but with Herculean effort he managed to keep his voice level. "Sir Fensterdale is here for his appointment with the princess."

"Sir Fensterdale?" The guard frowned slightly. "I know of no Sir Fensterdale due here."

This, of course, did not surprise Dodger. He'd fabricated the name because he did not, off the top of his head, know any lords, ladies, sirs, or otherwise—other than the princess, of course. The specifics of it did not matter, though. All that mattered was getting the conversation started and then praying that matters went amicably from there. "Of course you don't," said Dodger. "Very hush-hush. Very secretive mission indeed. At least, that's what I'm told, and it's not as if they tell me much of anything."

"Do you have any official papers?"

"Papers?" The Artful did his best to suppress a laugh. "Someone of Sir Fensterdale's rank don't need papers. He comes and goes where he pleases."

"Well, my lad, this is Buckingham Palace, and I'm afraid no one comes and goes where he pleases here. So unless you have some proper paperwork, I'm afraid you're going to have to turn this coach right around and go back where you came from."

"Are you funning me?" said Dodger with rising incredulity. "You would treat Sir Fensterdale in such a manner? You must have no regard for your continued position as a guard here."

"I'll take my chances," said the guard. He seemed more amused about Dodger's attitude than anything else.

"If that's your decision," said Dodger, "then I suggest you tell it to the sir himself."

"Not my job, lad," said the guard.

That was unfortunate. It meant Artful was going to have to work even harder to pull this off. He was, however, game for it. Why not? He had no choice.

The Artful hopped down from his chair and walked around to the door. He banged authoritatively on it and then waited for the response that he knew would not be forthcoming. "Sir Fensterdale?" he called after several seconds had passed. "We're havin' some trouble with the guards." When "Fensterdale" continued not to respond, he banged with more urgency. "Sir Fensterdale?"

Then he took a deep breath, praying that he could sell what came next. He pulled open the door, saying, "Sir Fensterdale?"

Then he counted to three and raised his voice in carefully controlled alarm. *"Sir Fensterdale!"* This was it. This is what he was going to have to do to sell his entrance. Quickly he yanked his head out from within the confines of the carriage and shouted, "Something's wrong! Something's wrong with Sir Fensterdale! He's not breathin'!"

The pure panic in his voice was sufficient to spur the guards forward. The one who had been speaking with Artful was the first one to the carriage. He pushed his head in and said, "Sir Fensterdale?" When "Sir Fensterdale" did not respond to the prompting, the guard reached over and shook his arm. He was instantly able to discern the fact that he was not dealing with a living human being. Quickly, he withdrew his head and called out in exactly what Dodger was hoping to hear—borderline panic—"Captain! We have a problem!"

The summons did not just draw the captain. It also pulled over a number of other guards who were curious to see what was going on. The Artful was backing up as quickly as he could, grabbing at guards as he went, crying out, "I . . . I think he's dead! My God, I think he's dead! What am I going to do!?" He kept pointing at the carriage as he continued to get closer, closer to the palace gates—ever closer. All the guards' attention was on the carriage, and no one was giving any serious regard toward the panicked driver.

Thirty feet to the main gates, twenty . . .

Then a firm hand clamped onto Dodger's shoulder. His head whipped around, and he saw a large guard with a thick mustache standing in his path, preventing him from moving another step. "And where do you think you're going, young man?"

The Artful had no ready response to that, and so he did the only thing he could think of: He drove his fist straight up into the guard's face. It connected solidly with the guard's chin, snapping his head back. The guard was so startled by the move that he actually lost his grip on his rifle. Instantly, Dodger grabbed it, even as inwardly he felt a fresh surge of panic. He was holding a weapon in a yard filled with men who were also armed and, more to the point, were schooled in using it, whereas he'd only attended the school of hard knocks.

So the idea of running into the palace armed seemed an amazingly bad one.

He reversed the rifle and swung it as hard as he could. The rifle butt cracked against the head of the guard, and the guard went down, his head striking the ground with a nasty sound.

The Artful spun. Amazingly, there were no other guards between him and the entrance; everyone else had been distracted by the emergency with the coach. With no time to lose, he sprinted at top speed toward the palace, and it was at that moment that the alarm was sounded for his approach.

Just as he arrived at the great doors to the palace, two more guards emerged. The Artful was no longer holding the rifle, having dropped it moments after clubbing his opponent. This was fortunate because certainly the guards, if they had seen an armed intruder approaching, would have opened fire upon him, and Dodger's adventure would have been over. Indeed, if he had been a full-grown man, they likely would have shot him just to play it safe.

Instead, they saw a teenage boy charging at them. As he approached, they both reached for him and simultaneously grabbed his overlong coat.

Which was exactly what Dodger was hoping they would do. He dropped to the ground and thus slid out of the coat. The two guards were left holding his empty coat. "Stop!" cried one of them, and he brought his rifle up, aimed true, and fired.

The Artful, in anticipation of being shot at—and true to his name—dodged to the right, and the bullet flew past him. Seconds later, he had entered the great hall of Buckingham Palace.

He wanted to pause, to stop and take in the splendor around him. A great staircase curved upward to the second floor, and servants were moving through the corridor. They stopped and gaped at Dodger, but none made a move upon him. These, after all, were people who were accustomed to being given orders, and if no one was ordering them to take the Artful Dodger in hand, then none of them was inclined to do anything except stare.

At random, the Artful picked a door to his right. He charged through it and into a large room that appeared to be some sort of library. Books stretched to the top of the ceiling; he could not recall seeing so many books in his life. If he had had sufficient facility insofar as reading was concerned, he might well have stopped and grabbed some books to take with him. But he had neither the time nor the inclination and so ran into the next room. This was some manner of stately room. He had no idea what it would be used for, but it certainly had enough courtly decorations.

He heard guards shouting from behind him:

"Find him!"

"Find the intruder!"

"Find the boy!"

Their voices echoed off the walls around him. He was not inclined to figure out from which direction the voices were coming; he just kept running, with no set plan, and simply hoped that perhaps he would happen to run into the princess or, even better (or worse), Mr. Fang.

He caught a look at a clock as he ran through one room and his heart sank. It was twenty minutes until the hour of twelve. He was losing time but had no means of stopping it or even slowing it down. And Mr. Fang could be anywhere. For all the Artful knew, Mr. Fang had already departed the halls of Buckingham Palace, and he, Dodger, was simply engaged in a pointless chase.

He ran into yet another room. This one seemed to be some sort of dining room. Clearly, people had recently eaten in it; there were dishes upon the table. If that was the case, then it meant that the servants were in the process of clearing it, which made this the last room in which Dodger wanted to be.

He started to run for the door at the far side, and suddenly he heard the voice of a young man calling, "I'm on it! I'll get the rest!" This was exactly the third-to-last thing Dodger wanted to hear—the second-to-last thing being "I got him!" and the last thing being the clock chiming midnight— because the boy would surely sound the alert now that the staff doubtless knew of the intruder's presence. He started to turn back in order to retrace his steps, but in the distance he heard the sounds of feet stomping in his direction. The guards were in hot pursuit.

He backed up, looking right and left desperately. There was a door to his right that seemed to be some sort of closet. He threw it open, and sure enough, it led to a place for the storage of linens and such things as would be used to decorate a table. He clambered in and closed the door behind himself just as the door through which he had heard the lad speaking was opened. He heard the boy gasp; he'd been spotted. And there was nothing he could do about it.

He heard steps crossing quickly to the closet door. The Artful tried to curl up, to find somewhere within the closet that he could find coverage, but nothing presented itself. Seconds later, the door flew open, the light from the room pouring in and fully illuminating it. The shadowed form of a young man was standing there. If Dodger had been thinking faster, he might well have leaped to the attack, but his mind was shutting down over the enormity of his task and his certain inability to accomplish it.

Suddenly, Dodger heard the far door crashing open. He knew that the boy would immediately shout that he had found the intruder hiding within the closet, and the new arrivals in the room, doubtless the guards, would immediately imprison him.

The Artful had failed, totally and utterly. Mr. Fang would live on and exert his influence, and Princess Alexandrina Victoria would be a monster of a monarch. Never had such a wave of frustration and despair swept over someone as it did now upon the Artful Dodger.

"You! Boy! What's in the closet?" called a voice sharply.

Here he is, sir! The boy you're seeking! Come take him away! The surely soon-to-be-uttered words spun through Dodger's mind.

To Dodger's utter shock, the boy said—calm as anyone could please—"Nothing but table linens, sir. Naught t'worry about."

He released the door and allowed it to slam shut.

The Artful Dodger was stunned. What in the world had just happened? Why had the boy not immediately turned him over to the forces of the royal family? This made no sense at all.

He heard some conversation between the lad and the guardsman. He couldn't make out what was being said exactly; as near as he could determine, the guard was providing a description of Dodger and telling the lad to be on the lookout for him. The lad, in return, said that he would take care to have his eyes peeled. This continued to be senseless to Dodger. The boy was covering for him. Why in the world would he do that?

The Artful heard the far door close; clearly, the guard had gone out upon his business. Then footsteps approached the closet. For a moment, Dodger thought that maybe somehow the boy simply had not, in fact, seen him. But he surely would now and promptly sound the alarm. Certainly, Dodger had gained only a few seconds respite.

Seconds indeed; the door was pulled open yet again, and the boy stood there, staring right at Dodger. Yet no alarm did he cry.

"Dodger?" he said.

Artful froze. He couldn't quite believe it. Slowly, he sat up, then stood, and from this angle was able to look straight into the face of his savior.

Now: As we have mentioned, unlikely coincidence was hardly unprecedented in the life of Dodger and his friends. We simply have to say that this is yet another instance of the happenstances that seem to pervade the lives of the Artful and those in his acquaintance.

There stood Master Bates.

"Charley?" said the astounded Dodger. "Charley Bates?"

"Th' same. But what the 'ell are ye doin' here!"

"What am *I* doin' here? What are *ye* doin' here?"

"I work here," said Charley Bates. "So it's natural that I'd be, ye know, workin' here."

The Artful slowly emerged from the closet. "How?"

"I had me ways," said Charley with a shrug. "Made some well-placed friends who took pity on a boy of the streets. Washed me up, got me out. One thing led to another, and here's where I wound up, on the serving staff."

There was so much he wanted to ask Charley Bates in terms of how he had come to work at the palace. But the minutes were dwindling down. He did take the time, however, to throw his arms briefly around his old mate from his Fagin days, just to reestablish contact. "I can scarce believe it," he whispered, practically in Charley's ear. "You showin' up here, now. Runnin' guard for me against the guards."

"Well, old times," said Charley with a shrug. He stepped back and looked Dodger up and down. "But what are ye doin' here? Ye still haven't told me."

The Artful licked his lips nervously. He didn't see any other way around it save to leap straight into it. "Has a man come here? His name is Mr. Fang."

"Mr. Fang? The police magistrate?" Charley made a face of clear disgust. "Sure 'n he did. He sat right over there," he said, pointing at a nearby chair. "Didn't eat much of anythin'."

"Or perhaps nothing at all?"

Charley frowned, considering it. "Ya may be right, now that I think on it. Put a fork to some stuff, nibbled maybe, but never actually seemed t'swallow nothin'. Wonder why."

"Because"—and there was no other way for Dodger to say it—"he's a vampyre."

"He is?"

The Artful nodded and then braced himself for an outpouring of skepticism and disbelief. Charley Bates was as grounded a young man as Dodger had ever seen, and not for one moment did he expect him to believe a word of it.

To his astonishment, instead Charley nodded. "Awright. That 'splains a bit, actually."

"It does?"

"'Course it does. We have some of the best food in the world here at the palace. What man in his right mind would pass it up lest he wouldn't eat it because he don't eat nothing 'cept fresh blood."

"And . . ." The Artful was having deep trouble accepting the acceptance. "And you believe me?"

"'Course I b'lieve ya, Dodger! My whole life, ya never lied t'me. Not once. And b'sides, if ya were gonna lie 'bout somethin', I got a feeling that it wouldn't be somethin' like that. So what do ya need from me?"

It was then Dodger asked the question, the answer to which he was dreading the most. "Is he still here?"

"Mr. Fang?"

"Yah."

"Best of my knowledge, yeah. They went to the drawing room for a nightcap t'talk business. Him, Sir Conroy, and the princess and her mum. The mum wasn't keen on it none, but the others talked her into it."

"Then you've got to get me there! Quickly! We only have maybe ten minutes." He looked nervously at the clock hung on the wall nearby that was counting down toward midnight.

"Awright." Charley's mind was racing. "Awright. Just stay right here a minute."

Without another word, he closed the door in Dodger's face. Naturally, Artful found this disconcerting, but he didn't see any way around it. Providence had dropped him into Charley's lap, and now Dodger had no choice but to allow fate to pull him in whatever direction it desired. In his head, a minute passed, then two, then ten, and it was too late; it was past midnight, and Drina was forever lost to both him and the kingdom.

Then the door flew open what seemed a half hour later, and Dodger saw, to his shock, that only a minute had passed. Charley was standing there with clothing draped over his arms, and he whispered, "Quickly. Change into this." He handed the clothes to Dodger and also gave him a dampened washcloth. "And this too. Wipe down your face. It's filthy. Just do the best ya can." He mostly closed the door but allowed it to remain slightly open so that a sliver of light would be there for Dodger's use.

The Artful quickly changed. Moments later, he was attired in clothing similar to Charley Bates's. He finished scrubbing down his face and glanced in a nearby mirror. There were a few smudges of dirt still on his face, and he suspected that they were ingrained by this point in his life. He would have to live with it. At least he was cleaned up enough, he hoped, to avoid detection by the guards of Buckingham Palace.

"All right," said Dodger. "Now what?"

"Now we go to the sitting room. Or at least one of the sitting rooms."

"How many are there?"

"Ten, last I checked."

The Artful was stunned. "How much sitting does the royal family need to do?"

"We have over seven hundred rooms in this place, Dodger. Just count yerself lucky ya ran into me or ye'd never find her."

The Artful couldn't deny that. So he simply nodded and fell into step behind Charley Bates.

Charley was not empty-handed. While Dodger had been changing, Charley had hastily assembled a tea service. He was carrying it with both hands, and his hands were shaking slightly, betraying his nervousness. The Artful appreciated Charley's gumption, considering the circumstances.

They made their way quickly through the corridors. The Artful was desperately thinking about how he was going to manage to get close enough to Mr. Fang to accomplish what he needed to do. He had the stake up the sleeve of his white jacket, and he was holding it tightly.

"Here now!"

The voice was sharp, and Artful recognized it immediately. It was one of the guards who had been pursuing him. Charley turned to face him, passing off the tea service to Dodger as he did so. The Artful kept his back to their pursuer.

"Where are you off to?" said the guard.

"Sittin' room," Charley said immediately. "Royal family wants some tea."

"At this time of night?" the guard said skeptically.

Charley shrugged. "I didn't see it as my place t'argue with 'em. Do you want to take it up with 'em?"

The guard actually chuckled at that. "I'll pass, thanks. Say, you haven't seen a scruffy street boy running around through here, have you?"

"Yes," said Charley, a response that froze Dodger in his spot. Before Dodger could muster himself to bolt, Charley continued,

"I'm reasonably sure I saw some lad runnin' in that d'rection. Seemed a little odd t'me, actually."

"Good work!" said the guard. Without hesitation, he sped off in the direction that Charley had indicated. Charley then promptly kept walking, and Dodger followed him.

"Dodger, this better be a fair cop," Charley muttered, "because otherwise this may've just cost me my job, or worse."

"It's more than fair," Dodger assured him.

They headed up a long, winding staircase. Every footstep, every passing second loomed large for Dodger. He suspected that somewhere a clock would strike the midnight toll, and he dreaded the thought of Mr. Fang still being alive when that happened. But at that point, he could do nothing, because he was still carrying the tea tray. Charley had scurried on ahead, presumably to clear the way and make certain that no other guards would impede them.

Around a corner, and then another and another, and Dodger was certain that midnight was closer and closer. Then, from just ahead he heard a voice speaking, a loud, proper female voice, and she did not sound happy. Not happy at all. It was coming from a room two doors down to the right, the doors shuttered against any intruders. Artful looked at Charley questioningly, and Charley simply nodded. This was where they were going, all right. This was the location of Mr. Fang.

The Artful was suddenly aware of his Adam's apple for some reason. It seemed large in his throat. He had no idea why this was, and it's not especially relevant to the narrative, but he felt it, and so we make note of it.

Charley took several steps in front of Dodger and rapped briskly on the door. "Tea, your Highness," he called out and opened the door. Without waiting for an invitation to be offered—a scandalous breach of etiquette in and of itself—Dodger strode in, looking down studiously at the tea and making eye contact with no one.

"We did not request tea," said a woman that Dodger intuited, correctly, was Princess Victoria. To her immediate right was a distinguished looking gentleman, and to her left . . . .

His blood froze. It was Mr. Fang. Mr. Fang was not paying him the slightest bit of attention. Instead, he was entirely focused on the princess, who seemed rather put out about something.

Drina was not with the group of adults. Instead, she was off to the side, standing at a window and staring out blankly at the full moon that hung in the sky. It was impossible to determine what was in her mind, and Dodger shoved it away as being unimportant.

The room was rather homey, considering the caliber of the individuals seated within. Dodger made particular notice of not only a roaring fireplace nearby but a clock that was situated upon the hearth. It was two minutes to midnight.

Two minutes. My God!

"Oh, very well," said Princess Victoria, and she gestured preemptively toward Dodger. "Put the tea on the table and just go. We can attend to it ourselves." Without giving him any further thought, she turned back to the focus of her attention, Mr. Fang. "To be blunt, Mr. Fang, I do not care in the least what my daughter's desires are. Although we are naturally grateful for your returning her, I simply do not understand her wish to maintain you as some sort of permanent council."

"With respect, Highness, it is not for you to understand," Mr. Fang said with arch respect. "Alexandrina is the future queen of England. It is simply for you to attend to her wishes."

"Mr. Fang is quite right, my dear," said the officious looking gentleman.

Princess Victoria stared at him with clear bewilderment and also a hint of betrayal. "Sir Conroy, I find it hard to believe that you, of all people, would accede to this request."

"Mr. Fang is quite right, my dear."

The princess frowned. "You just said that."

"It bears repeating," he said without hesitation.

The Artful lowered the tea service slowly onto the short table that was between the three seated adults. His hand trembled slightly as he bent forward and prepared to make his move.

It was at that moment that the stake slipped out of his sleeve and fell to the floor.

SEVENTEEN

In Which the Final Battle is Held

T he Artful did not intend for that to happen, of course; remember that he had been careful to keep the stake secured within the sleeve of his jacket, but between bending forward and having to hold onto the tea set as well, he was unable to hold onto the stake as securely as he had been, and consequently he was unable to retain his grip, and the stake tumbled out of his sleeve and clattered noisily to the floor.

Charley Bates audibly gulped. The Artful froze where he was, having just put the tea service down upon the table. Princess Victoria stared down at it, not understanding what she was looking at. Drina glanced over, taking her eyes from the moon. Sir Conroy did not react at all; he simply continued to stare forward.

Mr. Fang, however, looked down at the stake and then his eyes snapped upward and took in Dodger. He had never actually seen him before; he had simply heard about him from the lips of his servants. Now, though, face to face with him, he knew exactly whom he was staring at.

"The Artful!" bellowed Mr. Fang.

The Artful did not for a moment wonder how in the world Mr. Fang knew who he was. Instead, as quickly as he could, he lunged forward for the stake.

Mr. Fang was faster. He stretched out a foot and kicked the stake just before Dodger could get his hand on it. It skittered across the floor, out of Dodger's reach, rolling under a couch and back through the other side.

Then Mr. Fang lunged for Dodger himself. The Artful twisted away, grabbed the teapot, and threw it at Mr. Fang. This was no inexpensive metal teapot: It was a Staffordshire teapot made out of fine china. Consequently, it cracked solidly against Mr. Fang's head and shattered into a hundred pieces. Hot water spilled everywhere and Mr. Fang let out an agonized and infuriated howl.

Princess Victoria also howled, but instead of inarticulate pain, she cried out, *"Guards!"* And the guards most definitely would have been forthcoming, save for the fact that the sitting room only had one entrance into it, and Charley Bates had just locked the door. His arms to either side, he braced himself against the door and shouted for Dodger to hurry up and do what needed to be done.

Sir Conroy continued to stare straight ahead. He made no motions, took no action. It was as if he were awaiting instructions, which he most certainly was.

The Artful scrambled toward the couch and leaped over it. The stake was lying on the floor. He grabbed for it, his hands encircling it.

A foot stamped down on his hand, preventing him from getting a grip on it. He looked up. Drina was standing there, her lips pulled back in a snarl of hatred and her fangs visible.

Princess Victoria saw it. She was a few feet away, and every drop of blood drained from her face. "What in God's name—?" she gasped out.

The Artful had no choice. He lunged forward, slamming into Drina. She hadn't been expecting the move and tumbled backward. She hit the ground heavily, and Dodger grabbed up the stake and turned.

Mr. Fang was standing right there, right behind him. He grabbed Dodger's wrist and immobilized it. The Artful grunted, and Mr. Fang shook his hand violently, causing him to drop the stake. Mr. Fang caught it and then in one smooth motion tossed the stake across the room.

"No!" cried out Dodger, but it was too late. Mr. Fang's aim had been perfect. The stake landed in the fireplace. The flames immediately began to consume it.

Mr. Fang snarled into Dodger's face. "Did you really think you would get away with it?"

The Artful answered by slamming his forehead forward into Mr. Fang's face. He hit Mr. Fang's nose so hard that it audibly snapped.

Mr. Fang let out an agonized groan, and Dodger yanked back, hard. His shirt tore and he pulled free of Mr. Fang's grasp. Infuriated, Mr. Fang leaped at him, but for once it was Dodger that was too quick. He vaulted to one side, and Mr. Fang sailed past him.

"What is happening? What is going on?" screamed Princess Victoria.

From the door, Charley Bates shouted, "Your guest is a vampyre, your Highness!" The door was now banging behind him, thanks to the guards who were repeatedly slamming into it.

"A what?" Clearly, she wasn't certain she had heard him properly. "A what?" she repeated.

If Charley answered, the Artful didn't hear the response. Instead, he ran toward the fireplace. The stake was burning viciously. He tried to reach for it, tried to pull it from the fire, but he was unable to get his fingers near it. And now Mr. Fang was coming toward him. The police magistrate was so furious that he was incapable of speech. An inarticulate string of syllables tumbled from his lips; that was all he was able to manage.

The clock clicked toward midnight. In the distance, probably from a grandfather clock, Dodger heard a steady, sonorous pounding of a bell begin to clang.

His head whipped around as he looked desperately for something, anything, to use as a weapon.

Then he spotted Sir Conroy's walking stick. More to the point, he recognized it instantly for what it was. He had seen one identical to it before, and he prayed that he was not mistaken.

He lunged for Sir Conroy under Mr. Fang's outstretched arms. Somersaulting across the floor, he came up within a foot of Conroy and yanked the walking stick from his hand. Conroy simply sat there, still staring ahead.

The Artful Dodger pulled on the stick and for half a heartbeat, it held together, and his spirit was crushed because he thought he had guessed wrong. But then the walking stick split apart, and he was holding a bladed saber in his hand, just as Mr. Fang got to him, his hands outstretched, his fangs exposed.

The Artful whirled in one smooth motion.

Understand that Dodger had never in his life engaged in swordplay of any sort. But that did not deter him from swinging the sword as quickly and viciously as he could. Fortunately for him, it was not a foil or something that was intended for stabbing. Nevertheless, had Dodger been fighting a normal human individual, he might have managed to slice the skin but not much more than that.

That was not the case here. He was battling an animated corpse that was bone dry of any sort of liquid.

As a result, the sword cut through the air and Mr. Fang's neck so fast that it was as if there were nothing there to impede it. Mr. Fang gurgled in protest, and his eyes widened in complete surprise. A thin line of black goo appeared across his throat. He clutched at his throat, gasped, tried to say something, but was unable to verbalize.

The bells continued to sound. Six, seven . . .

The Artful whipped the sword back as quickly as he could. The blade sliced through again, and this time it was a harder cut because it was driving through more skin and gristle. The black liquid gushed as if oil had been struck, and then Mr. Fang's head toppled backward. It fell off his shoulders and tumbled to the ground, and the Artful was certain that he actually heard the monster say something as the head rolled away.

The body was actually still standing, and it was staggering toward Dodger, its arms flailing around. The Artful stepped to the side and stuck out his foot, and the body collapsed to the floor where it twitched for a few moments before finally laying still.

That was when Drina let out a high-pitched, ululating scream.

She stumbled as her own head snapped back, and inhuman gurgling noises poured from her lips. It was if she too had felt the blade's sweeping blows, though no visible wounds were apparent. Nevertheless, she staggered, her feet twitching, and then she fell to the floor.

The Artful started toward her, and that was when he suddenly became aware of the rhythmic pounding at the door, right before it burst open. Charley Bates was sent flying as half a dozen royal guards, rifles at the ready, burst through. The Artful's path to the princess was cut off as guards stepped between and brought their rifles to bear. "Don't move!" they shouted almost in unison, which was all the encouragement Dodger needed to remain right where he was. Charley Bates was on the floor and was staying there, with his arms raised and a very nervous expression on his face.

The princess was continuing to cry out, and she was grabbing at her mouth as she did so. The guards had no idea what they should do. They looked at each other questioningly; no one wanted to get anywhere near the shrieking member of the royal family.

In the distance, more clearly now that the door had been shattered, Dodger heard the final clanging of the clock as midnight struck. And as the final chime of the bell sounded, Princess Alexandria Victoria suddenly sat bolt upright, her eyes looking set to burst from her face. She was gasping loudly, and she reached up toward her teeth. She ran her fingers across them and Dodger was able to see, even from his angle, that there was no sign of any fangs.

"My God," she whispered. "Oh, my dear God."

"What's all this?" Sir Conroy had bounded up from the couch and was staring at the disturbance within the sitting room with a complete lack of understanding. "What are you men doing in here? What are *you* doing here?" he demanded when his eyes fell upon Dodger. Then he added with a confused look, "What am *I* doing here? I don't remember coming up here. I don't . . . good heavens!"

That latter reaction was to the headless body that was lying several feet away. To the shock of almost everyone in the room—save Dodger, of course—the thick black liquid was continuing to seep out of the body. It could not remotely be mistaken for blood by anyone, and not only that: As it leaked out, the body began to deflate much like a balloon being robbed of air. A faint hissing was audible as the body shrank in a manner that did not remotely approach anything that transpired for human beings.

No one said anything as the body shriveled. All in the room were aware that they were staring at something unworldly; they just did not know for sure what they *were* looking at. One of the guards looked questioningly at Dodger, and Dodger simply said, "Vampyre."

"Oh, well that explains it," said one of the guards and was promptly punched in the shoulder by his superior.

Princess Alexandrina Victoria had now managed to get to her feet and was staggering toward her mother. She collapsed into the older woman's arms and then did the only thing that seemed appropriate under the circumstances: She passed out.

"Get her to her bedchambers," Sir Conroy immediately barked to the guards. Then he noticed Dodger standing there. "As for this one and his friend," he said, indicating Charley Bates, "take him to the Tower immediately!"

"Wait . . . what!" said Dodger. "But I just—!"

They were not the least bit interested in listening to him, and moments later the Artful Dodger and Master Charley Bates were chained up and being escorted to the Tower of London.

EIGHTEEN

In Which All is Made as Right as Could Possibly Be, Considering the Circumstances

Bram Van Helsing sat in his cell and kept running the recent events through his mind, trying to determine what he might have done differently to have matters turn out in such a way that he could continue to contribute positively to things, and unfortunately for him, nothing was coming readily to his mind.

The Artful's plan had always been borderline insane anyway, but the truth was that Bram had not been able to come up with anything better. So he hardly felt in a position to be critical of Dodger.

He walked the perimeter of his cage for what seemed the hundredth time, running his hands across the bars as he passed.

Then he heard something. It was distant, from down the hallway, but it was very distinctive: It was barking. Not only was it barking, but it was extremely familiar to him.

"Father?" he called as loudly as he could, which as it happened was not loudly at all, for it had been some hours since he had had anything to drink, and his throat was hoarse. *"Father?"* he tried again.

"Abraham?" His father's familiar voice floated down the corridor toward him.

"Here! I'm here!"

Moments later Isaac Van Helsing was in front of him, holding the leash of his dog firmly. His father gasped upon seeing his son, as if not trusting himself to be filled with joy until he actually beheld the lad with his own eyes. "You're here! You're here!"

Bram nodded. "And you are, too."

A police officer was accompanying Isaac Van Helsing, and the doctor turned to the officer and said, "This is my son. Release him immediately."

"We ain't releasin' anyone until Mr. Fang says so," the police officer replied brusquely.

"Mr. Fang is a villain of the highest order," said Isaac.

"Mr. Fang is a police magistrate and I will thank you to watch your tone and words." The threat was implicit: If Isaac didn't take care of what he said, he might wind up sharing the cell with his son.

Isaac was trembling with barely suppressed rage, but he managed to rein it in. Instead, he kept his response to a curt nod and then said, "I wish to speak with my son. I hope that will not serve as a hardship to you."

The officer actually appeared to be considering it, and then he simply nodded. He strode away down the corridor, leaving the Van Helsings to themselves.

"How did you find me?" Bram said immediately.

His father was rummaging in his pocket. "I never stopped looking for you. I have been checking at various police stations ever since you disappeared. To be blunt, I was checking to see if your body turned up. Honestly, I did not expect that you would be able to escape your captors."

"It wasn't a hardship," said Bram. "It's been rather exciting as it so happens. What are you doing?"

His father produced a slender metal rod from within his right coat pocket. "Getting you out. Stand back."

Bram did as he was instructed. The elder Van Helsing slid the metal into the lock and made several quick turns. Almost immediately, the lock snapped open and Isaac pulled wide the jail door. Bram could not suppress his surprise. He knew his father was a gifted lock pick, but even for him, this was fast work.

Quickly joining his father, Bram looked at him expectantly. "Now what?"

"Now we leave."

Isaac Van Helsing started walking. Bram fell into step next to him. The dog's head swiveled back and forth as if it were taking in all their surroundings and appraising them from a strategic point of view.

Moments later, they encountered the police officer who had escorted Isaac to the cell. He was heading right toward them, and his jaw dropped when he saw that Bram had been freed from his cell.

It should be noted that London policemen did not carry firearms of any sort. Had they done so, matters might have turned out quite differently. Instead, they carried whistles and sticks, and the policeman's stick was now in his hand. That did not deter Isaac in the slightest. He strode forward quickly, catching the police officer's wrist before he could wield his club in any sort of offensive fashion. One quick twist from Isaac, and the police officer dropped the club from his numb hand. Isaac then slammed his elbow around, catching the police officer in the side of the head. The officer gasped as he went down, and Isaac drove a fast kick upward that caught him square in the face. The police officer fell backward onto the floor.

Isaac stepped right over him, Bram following—neither really having broken stride. A few instants later, they ran into another policeman, and Isaac immediately pointed behind himself and said, in a perfect imitation of a British accent, "Your man appears to have had some sort of attack and passed out. You may want to attend to him."

"Yes sir! Thank you, sir!" said the police officer immediately. He didn't have the faintest idea who Isaac was, but his attitude and certainty appeared to mark him as some sort of senior officer. So instead of attempting to arrest Isaac Van Helsing, the police officer tossed off a fast salute and ran to help his fallen fellow.

The Van Helsings then walked straight out of the precinct. Whenever anyone happened to step into their path, a fast bark of their dog would clear the obstruction from their way. Moments later, they were in the street and departing the area as fast as they could.

The sun was just coming up over the horizon. Immediately, Bram said, "Father, we have to do something! Princess Alexandrina Victoria has been made into a vampyre by Mr. Fang!"

Isaac turned and looked at his son, his eyes wide. "Are you certain?"

"Yes."

"All right, then. We have no choice."

There was a coach waiting for them. Isaac ushered his son into the cab's interior, then the dog, and then the man himself. Within a few minutes, the cab was rushing forward.

Bram sat back in his seat, letting out a deep breath. His mind had felt so scattered while he was being held in a cell. Now, though, he was reunited with his father, and he had apprised him of the immediate situation. There was no doubt in his mind that his father would know exactly what to do.

For the first time in what seemed ages, Bram actually was able to relax. He had not seemingly slept in days, but now, finally, his exhaustion would not be denied, and Bram sank into slumber.

"Bram."

He awakened all at once rather than slowly. It was how he always awoke; one never knew if a vampyre was about to attack, and he had simply developed the habit of waking up immediately just in case the situation called for it.

He was confused, however, for the carriage had stopped moving, and his father and the dog were already out. "Finally, you awaken," said Isaac. "I couldn't rouse you when we stopped briefly at the inn to gather our belongings. How nice to know you have finally rejoined the land of the living."

"The inn . . .?" Bram didn't understand at first. Was there something that his father had left in their personal belongings that would enable them to deal with the challenge that was before them? He wondered what it could possibly be.

Then he saw where they were, and he stared in confusion. They were at the docks, and a large boat was situated there. People were boarding it, cheerful tourists or determined travelers. He heard a variety of accents as people spoke animatedly.

The sun was now high in the sky. The noon hour had to be approaching.

"Father, what is this? Where are we going—?"

"Home. We take this vessel to Spain and connect there to—"

"But I don't understand!" said Bram, his voice rising. For the first time in a long time, he was actually starting to sound his age. "Father, we have to help Drina! And Dodger! I haven't even told you about him!"

"It doesn't matter."

"It does!"

"No, it does not," Isaac Van Helsing said firmly. "You are telling me that Mr. Fang has taken over the royal family. If that is the case, then we have no choice save to flee the country as quickly as possible. This is much too big for a pair of vampyre hunters, Abraham. Mr. Fang is now much too powerful. I would be an utterly reckless father if I subjected you to the amount of danger that we would be faced with, and in the end it would not matter. We have already lost. The country is lost. Frankly, we should be grateful that it is not our country."

"But . . . but we cannot just leave matters as they are . . . ."

"Yes, we can," said Isaac Van Helsing. "And you will come with me now, and we will never speak of this again."

"But Father—!"

Isaac silenced him by raising a single finger. "This is not easy for me, Abraham. By departing this country, I am allowing Mr. Fang and his cohorts to win. It goes against the fiber of my being. If that is what I have to do in order to guarantee your health, however, then that is what I am going to do."

"I still think you are wrong."

"You are welcome to your opinion, as long as you are wise enough to keep it to yourself."

They disembarked from the carriage. Bram seemed disinclined to pick up his bag, and his father had no interest in prolonging matters. So he picked up Bram's bag and started toward the ship, the dog trotting obediently behind.

Bram had never felt more frustrated, more alone. He looked around the docks, trying to decide whether perhaps he should just run off and seek to aid the Artful. Even as the thought crossed his mind, however, he knew it was futile. He had no idea where the Dodger was, or what he was up to, or even if he was still in London.

But he knew what he had to do.

Before the hansom cab that he had vacated had pulled away, he quickly approached it and banged on the door. "Excuse me," he called. The driver looked down at him questioningly. "Do you know the way to Baker Street?"

"Of course."

"Good. Take me there, please."

He clambered into the cab before the driver could say anything else. The driver shrugged and snapped the reins.

By the time Isaac Van Helsing turned around, he was astounded to see that his son was gone.

⊰ ✳ ⊱

The Artful Dodger and Charley Bates sat in the Tower of London and wondered if they were ever going to see the light of day.

The cell itself was rather spare: a square room that didn't seem to be more than ten feet wide in any direction. A chamber pot sat uninvitingly in a corner, and straw was strewn on the floor, presumably in case the chamber pot wasn't sufficient to accommodate the needs of the person in the cell. A small window with three bars was situated in the wall above them.

The Artful was not remotely convinced that he would be entitled to any sort of trial, no matter how the laws of England were written. Due process under the law was more of a privilege for those that could afford it, and Dodger knew that he was not amongst that privileged few. There was every chance that he could remain locked up in the Tower for the rest of his life. He had, after all, murdered a man, in full view of the royal family, after illegally breaking into Buckingham Palace. Trespass and murder. It would not matter to any judge in the world that he had gained entrance to the palace because he was desperate to save Princess Alexandrina Victoria. Nor would it matter that the man he had slain had clearly not been a human being, at least insofar as anyone could determine by what had transpired with his body. No, what mattered was that the dead man had been a personal guest of the royal family, and you simply could not break into the home of the royals and slay someone with whom they were speaking.

"Don' t' cha worry," Charley Bates spoke up. "We'll get out of here right enough."

"You might get out of here," said Dodger. "After all, your major crime was holding the guards back. So you might see daylight in ten, maybe twenty years. Me . . . either I'm going to die here or die out there. Latter, most like." He nodded toward the small window in the wall. "They're prob'ly buildin' a noose to dangle me from right now."

"Oh, I doubt that. They already have plenty of nooses, so they don't have to build no . . . ." His voice trailed off and he looked apologetically at Dodger. "Sorry. Weren't thinkin' none."

"Don't'cha worry, Charley. I think more than enough for the both of us."

The Artful had lost track of how long they remained within the cell. No food was brought to them, and his stomach was fairly howling at him for sustenance, but he was hardly in a position to accommodate it. All he knew was that there was daylight out. Then he heard the sounds of footsteps approaching the door in steady rhythm. It wasn't just that someone was approaching; the sound seemed to be marching. For some reason, Dodger found this to be vaguely disconcerting.

The footsteps were moving together in perfect synchronization, and that said to Dodger that it was palace guards. He had no proof that they were heading for his cell, but he suspected that was the case. "On your feet, Charley," he said. "Think we're about t'have company."

Charley scrambled to his feet, and sure enough, there was the sound of a key in the lock of the door. Moments later it swung open, and a coterie of palace guards was standing there. The Artful briefly considered trying to run past, in hopes that he would be able to escape, but he quickly dismissed the idea. The guards were standing much too close together. It was almost as if they were expecting him to make the attempt.

"Come with us," said the lead guard.

"Where to?" asked Dodger. "A court? Or Australia? Or straight to the hangman?"

"Come with us," repeated the guard.

The Artful let out a deep sigh. He didn't know what was about to happen to him, but he very much suspected he wasn't going to like it. As the guards let Charley and Dodger out of the cell, however, at least he was able to take refuge in an irrefutable fact: No matter what they did to him, he had accomplished his goal. He had managed to save the life of the future queen of England. No matter what she did in her life, she would owe her existence to him, and he could take some pride in that. He just prayed that she did something worthwhile with the second chance that he had provided her.

The Artful and Charley were escorted down to a rolling cell, a sort of jail cell on wheels with a horse attached to it. Once the lads were locked in, the horse started moving, guided by the horseman. The guards were now all mounted on horseback and rode alongside. Clearly, they were taking no chance that Dodger might find some means of escaping.

The noose it was, then. He wondered if there would be a crowd of people watching. Perhaps even Fagin would be there, hiding in the shadows, safe from the sun's rays.

No. There was little chance of that. His hanging would not attract a crowd because, at the end of the day, he was just some random youngster who had run afoul of the law, and who would give a damn about him?

The cart continued to travel for a time. They rolled past groups of people who stared in curiosity as it passed but who didn't care so much that it distracted them from going about their business. The Artful wished he had some business to go about—other than that of dying, that is.

And then, to Dodger's surprise, the cart began to slow. And then it stopped in front of an anonymous townhouse. The Artful stared at it uncomprehendingly. The townhouse was unfamiliar to him. It was certainly not a location for a courthouse. It was in a rather nice neighborhood, but beyond that Dodger had no idea of where they had been brought. He looked at Charley questioningly, but Master Bates simply shrugged. He was as clueless as Dodger.

A guard opened up the back of the cart and said sternly, "Come with us. Don't try to run, or you will be shot immediately."

Despite his earlier inclination, the Artful had no intention of running. Granted, he had the impulse to try and sprint out of there, but also he was overwhelmingly curious as to where they had been brought. So he simply nodded to acknowledge that the instruction had been received and eased himself out of the rolling cell. Charley came out behind him, and together the boys were led into the townhouse.

It was even nicer once they were inside. The Artful nodded approvingly; there were pristine paintings and fine china as decorations in the small but well-furnished rooms.

They were taken to the right, rather than up the stairs, and brought into a small sitting room.

Sir Conroy was standing there, straight, tall, and proud.

Seated next to him was Drina. Sunlight was beaming through a nearby window and straight on her, but she was displaying no ill effects. That alone caused Dodger to let out an inward sigh of relief.

"Master Bates," said Sir Conroy stiffly. "Master . . . Dawkins, I understand your name to be?"

"Yes, sir," said Dodger.

"My further understanding is that you have met the princess before. Nevertheless, I feel constrained to officially introduce you to Princess Alexandrina Victoria."

The Artful nodded and then realized that something more profound was in order, and so he bowed deeply. When he stood upright once more, he blinked in surprise. Sir Conroy was holding Dodger's top hat in his hands. He also had a coat draped over his arm.

"These are yours?"

The Artful nodded and, realizing that the gentleman was proffering them to him, stepped forward quickly and took them off his hands. Then he stood and waited, although he was unsure what he was waiting for.

"The princess's mother would be here," continued Sir Conroy, "but she is . . . not well, at the moment. Recent events were rather stressful for her. She may be part of the royal family, but she remains ultimately a woman."

"I wouldn't dismiss her on that basis," said Dodger. "I've become rather impressed with what women can do once they sets their minds to it."

Sir Conroy did not seem similarly impressed, but he clearly decided to let it slide. "So . . . Master Bates. Do you wish to return to your employ at the palace?"

Charley looked astounded. He had clearly not wrapped himself around what was happening, but he wasn't about to let an opportunity slip away from him. "Yes, sir," he said immediately. "I love it there."

"Very well." He gestured toward the Buckingham Palace guard who was standing by the door. "This officer will escort you there immediately. Good day to you."

The message was clear: His time in this small, puzzling room was done. His crimes, such as they were, had been excused. He took a moment to look briefly at Dodger, who shrugged in response, and then bowed quickly toward Dodger. The Artful bowed back and just like that, Charley Bates was gone.

"Now, sir, as for you—" Conroy began to say.

And then to Conroy's obvious surprise, Drina interrupted. "Sir Conroy, I would like to handle this. You may leave."

Conroy smiled patronizingly. "Princess, I have honored your request to be here, but I cannot—"

"I am not asking you to honor my request. I am giving you an order and am expecting you to obey it."

"Princess, I—"

"Now. Before I call a guard in here and have him enforce my will."

Sir Conroy clearly had no idea how to respond to that. So he took the proper way out by bowing deeply and heading for the door. Moments later, the Artful Dodger was alone in the room with Princess Alexandrina Victoria.

To Dodger's utter shock, the princess rose from her chair walked to Dodger, and bowed deeply before him. "Thank you," she said, her voice choked with emotion. "Thank you for saving me from my own folly."

"I saved you from a vampyre is all," said Dodger. "It weren't no folly to want to get out on your own for a bit. If I was in yer situation, I'd probably want t'do the same thing. In fact, I think you should do it more. With a proper escort, of course. Go around and visit different parts of England. In a few years, you'll be runnin' it, after all. Think it might help you t'be familiar with it."

"Yes," she said, smiling. "And I am looking forward to you coming with me on those trips."

"Comin' with?"

"I would like you to be a permanent advisor to me, Dodger. Come live at Buckingham Palace. Become a true gentleman of the court. Never want for anything, ever again."

"Is that an order?"

She blinked in confusion. "Do I need to make it such? I would assume that you would jump at the opportunity. Are you not interested?"

The Artful, as much to his own surprise as hers, looked away from her. "I . . . can't see myself livin' as a gen'leman, if you want t'know the truth. I mean, in my own mind, I am. I am as much a gen'leman as anyone could be. But I know that that's . . . ." His voice trailed off and then he said, "I'd rather be a gen'leman in me own mind than in title or reality. Because if it's real, then that means

I might become too much like that which I despise. I mean, the thought of turnin' into Sir Conroy . . ." He shivered slightly at the notion.

"Are you quite certain?"

" 'Fraid so, Drina . . . sorry. Highness."

"Very well. What about a cash reward?"

"Oh, that I'd have no problem with."

Drina laughed slightly at that. She reached into a large bag that was situated on the floor nearby and extracted a small but bulging purse from within. "Here you go," she said.

The Artful immediately took it from her, restraining himself from actually grabbing it out of her hands. He felt the heft of it and was extremely satisfied.

"Be aware, though," continued Drina, "that there may be times in the future where I have need of your services. May I feel free to call upon you at those times?"

"Of course," he said. "You are still my future queen, after all. Whatever ya need me for, I will be there. Oh! And please contact the police at Mutton Hill and make certain that Bram is reunited with his father."

"I will make sure that it is done," said Drina, unaware of what had transpired with Bram and his father.

"Oh, and the carriage that I arrived in, with the dead man . . . it belongs to a Mr. Brownlow. I don't know his first name, but he has an adopted son named Oliver. And he asked me to send his regards. So I've done that. Could you see that it's returned to him?"

"Absolutely."

For a moment, Dodger wanted to give her a fast embrace, but just as quickly he discarded the idea. With all that had happened, she was still the princess, and there were certain things that a young street robber such as the Artful Dodger simply did not do. So instead, he simply bowed to her again, extending his hand.

To his surprise, she took it firmly, drew her to him, and kissed him on the cheek. "Your Highness, that's . . ."

And then she kissed him on the mouth. Passionately. Deliberately.

For a moment, part of him froze because, of course, he was aware of whom he was kissing. And then the thought flew from his head, and he was simply kissing a young woman who was clearly interested in . . . .

In what?

He pulled back from her and stepped back a few paces to reconfigure his thoughts. "Highness . . ."

"Drina," she said. "Please call me Drina."

"Drina, then. What do you . . . I mean, I don't . . ."

"Come with me," she said with greater urgency. "I know you don't want to. I heard all that you said. But I'm offering you so much . . . a life that you could only have dreamt of."

"A life as what?" He was tempted to laugh but managed to suppress it. "Your advisor? Your . . ."—he gestured helplessly—"whatever?"

"Whatever," she said. "I'm going to be the queen, Dodger. And you can be my whatever you want."

"Drina, I can't . . ."

"Then I can," she said. She pointed behind them, and he saw there was another door out of the room. "We can go out that way. It's unguarded."

"And go where?"

"Wherever. Wherever we want. I have plenty of money. We have enough to get us wherever we wish to go. We can have adventures together, you and me."

"And what about England?"

"They'll be fine without me. My mother can rule. She can . . ."

He took her firmly by the shoulders and whispered to her, "Drina . . . what's going on?"

To his surprise, she looked downward as if ashamed to be staring into his eyes. "I care about you . . . Jack. I care about you a good deal."

"And ya care about your realm as well. You know it, and I know it. And some day our adventures will wear thin, and you'll feel the need t'go back, and ya know what else? You'll wind up blamin' me for draggin' you away from it all."

"I'd never!"

"Ya might."

"I know I wouldn't."

"But'cha might. And I don't want to take the chance."

Her face hardened. "This is so easy for you, isn't it. Just tossing me aside. Just . . . ."

"*Easy?*" He was unable to keep the incredulity from his voice. "Ya think this is easy? Ya think I don't want to . . . to run off with you? To hide from the world with you? I . . . ." His voice choked and he looked away from her. "I've loved two women in me life b'fore you came along. And then there's you, and what I feel for you . . . I felt it for them, and they're both gone. It ain't you, Drina. It's me. Whoever I love, I lose. Bad. And I almost lost you, too, and I can't ever take the chance again. I can't go through it." He turned to her and angrily wiped the tears from his face. "I beg you not to make me. Please. I never asked you for nothin'. I'm askin' you for this."

For a long moment, Drina sat there and stared at him. Then she held him tightly, giving him one final squeeze, and she whispered in his ear, "If you ever change your mind, you know where to find me."

"I do."

She stepped back, and the Artful watched as she assumed her regal bearing, cloaking it around her like a shroud.

"Off with you then, Jack Dawkins."

"Yes'm," he managed to mutter and quickly hastened out of the room.

He strode into the street, bowed to the guards who were still there, and then walked away. The streets of London seemed to summon him. Still, he found himself considering the invitation that she had extended him and wondered—for what would not be the last time in his life—whether he was right, or in the right mind, to pass it up. Then he decided to stop thinking about it, for Dodger had already made up his mind, and that was that, more or less.

"'Scuse me, sir? Help us, sir?"

The Artful stopped in his tracks. He was passing an alleyway, and sitting there was a young boy, no more than ten years old, and a young girl who was several years younger. They were shabbily dressed and shivering from the cold and crisp London air. They had a small box in front of them that had a couple of crumpled pound notes strewn in it.

The Artful said nothing for a time. Then: "Where are your parents?"

"'Nother street, sir. They're beggin' too, sir."

The Artful let out a long sigh. Then he reached into his pocket and held the weighted purse. He jiggled it slightly, then opened it and extracted a few gold coins from it.

Then he dropped the rest of the purse into the box.

The children's faces registered their astonishment. "Have a good meal," said Dodger, knowing that the money within the purse would be more than enough for quite a few good meals to come.

He turned on his heel and walked away, dropping the few coins he had extracted into his pocket.

"My, my."

He looked up in surprise. Wiggins was standing a few feet away. He seemed impressed. "Givin' money away. What's happened to you?"

Dodger shrugged. "I was never much for travelin' with much in me pockets anyway."

Wiggins nodded and then said, "Here's somethin', then. Message for you."

"For me?" Dodger took the folded paper. "From who?"

"That lad you were with."

"Bram?!"

"That's him. He found me on Baker Street, gave me this note t'give to you should I find you. Which, obviously, I did."

Dodger ripped it open, stared at it blankly, and frowned. The cursive handwriting was flowing and impossible for him to decipher.

Immediately figuring out the problem, Wiggins took the letter back from Dodger.

Dodger . . . by the time you read this, I will be back on a boat with my father heading home. I'm sorry I wasn't able to do more to help, but despite what my father thinks, I believe you found a way to beat the vampyres and save England. I firmly believe the fate of England could not be in braver hands. Yours sincerely, Abraham Van Helsing.

Wiggins looked at Dodger questioningly. "Should I read it again?"

"No, no, that's . . . fine. Thank ye, Wiggins." He stuck out a hand, and Wiggins shook it firmly.

"No. Thank you, Dodger." He paused and then said, "Ya know . . . there's a place for you on the Irregulars, if you're interested."

"I'll think about it," said the Dodger, and tipped his hat.

Wiggins went on his way, then, and Dodger on his.

The Artful ran the events of recent days through his head. Mr. Fang was dead. Check. Bram would be attended to. Check. Mr. Brownlow's carriage would be returned. Check.

The only item on his mental slate remaining unchecked was Fagin, and it disturbed Dodger greatly. There was no denying that Fagin had done him a great service by saving his life.

However, there was far too much anger in the lad toward Fagin than would permit him to forgive his old mentor. And so he vowed at that moment that he would never rest until he had managed to drag Fagin from the shadows and expose him to the scathing light of day.

Unfortunately, as strong as the vow was in his heart, actually enforcing that vow would have to wait for a great many years. By the time the Artful Dodger would once again come face to face with Fagin, Princess Alexandrina Victoria would have long been Queen Victoria.

The Artful Dodger would have grown from a young street thug to a man in his fifties.

And Fagin, otherwise known as Spring-Heeled Jack, would have changed his name yet again, to Jack the Ripper.

THE END

ACKNOWLEDGMENTS

This book would obviously not be possible without the works of the esteemed Mr. Dickens. This book had its genesis in the fact that I happened to be reading *Oliver Twist* one day for no particular reason, and I began noticing some oddities in the personage of Fagin. That prompted me to realize that Fagin was likely a vampyre, and the story just sort of flowed from there.

I wish to thank Andy Zack for selling this novel and editor David Pomerico and the fine folks at Amazon Books for presenting it to you. Thanks also to cover artist Douglas Smith whose outstanding work has graced such novels as the *Wicked* books.

Finally, my greatest thanks go to my wife, Kathleen, without whom I literally would not be able to function.

ABOUT THE AUTHOR

Peter David, writer of stuff, is a *New York Times* best-selling author of over one hundred novels. These include *Fearless, Tigerheart*, various novels published under the imprint of www.crazy8press.com, and many Star Trek novels for Pocket Books. He has also written over a thousand comics, including *The Incredible Hulk, Fallen Angel, X-Factor*, and *Stephen King's Dark Tower*. He co-created the TV series *Space Cases* with Bill Mumy for Nickelodeon. Peter lives in Long Island with his wife, Kathleen, and has four daughters: Shana, Gwen, Ariel, and Caroline.